TEMPTING PRINCE CHARMING

Ever After - Book 2

LAUREN SMITH

This book is a work of fiction. Names, characters, places, and incidents are the product of the author's imagination or are used fictitiously. Any resemblance to actual events, locales, or persons, living or dead, is coincidental.

Cover Art by Croco Designs

ISBN: 978-1-952063-10-7 (e-book edition)
ISBN: 978-1-952063-11-4 (print edition)

live like
there is no
Midnight

ONCE UPON A TIME...

THERE LIVED A YOUNG WOMAN WHO FEARED
THE MAGIC OF LOVE WOULDN'T LAST PAST
THE STROKE OF MIDNIGHT...

1

Thad Worthington hastily shoved his stack of work papers off his lap and onto the seat beside him. "Stop the car!"

His private driver hit the brakes and the Rolls-Royce Phantom stopped along the curb.

"Sir?" His driver's eyes flicked to Thad in the rearview mirror.

"Just a moment," Thad said, his gaze drawn to the sight outside his window.

They were on a quiet neighborhood street in Chicago, off Thad's usual beaten path—by choice, of course—and yet he hadn't ever remembered seeing this impressive brownstone residence before. The gloom of a wintry, rain-soaked evening had settled on the city, yet this home glowed with warmth and light.

He tilted his head, studying the home with undeniable curiosity. The first floor had been converted into a coffee shop. *The Chi-Bean* was painted in pale blue letters on the front door.

Something inside Thad shifted, like the deep rumbling of tectonic plates beneath the earth's surface. He had to go inside.

"Simon, I feel like a cup of coffee. I'll text you when I'm ready for you to pick me up."

"Of course, sir." Simon pulled to the curb and Thad moved his papers into his briefcase. All thoughts of his various real estate deals were, at this moment, tossed firmly to the side. The glowing illumination of that brownstone and its coffee shop made him a moth to it's warm, welcoming flame.

He stepped out of the car and a thick, misting rain immediately coated his bespoke suit and coat. He raked a hand through his hair and strode toward the entrance, pausing as he read a sign taped to the inside of the door.

"Open Mic Night—Thursdays 8pm to 10pm. All singers welcome. Guitar provided."

His heart gave a little jolt. Could he do it? Could he sing in public? It was something he'd only ever done in the privacy of his penthouse. Singing opened something inside him, something that spread its wings and took flight whenever he strummed his guitar and let the words of a song pour from his lips.

It was cathartic, like dropping beneath the surface of

the stillest lake. And at the same time, his heart came alive like it had been struck by lightning.

He wasn't afraid of anything in the boardrooms where he made his multimillion-dollar deals, but singing... that cut him open, left him exposed, vulnerable.

He wanted to feel that tonight, surrender to it, and the quiet euphoria it left behind.

He curled his fingers around the door handle and pulled.

A wave of warm air hit him as he stepped inside. He took in his surroundings carefully, noting the architecture and the quality of the building itself. He'd always believed a building was more than just four walls, that it could resonate as something people could feel to the point where it became part of them. He knew it sounded foolish, but he did believe it.

This place was full of love, from the cozy tables, to the fireplace with an actual fire going, and the stacks of board games nearby. Seats held a mix of college kids, late night dates, and anyone who wanted a place to escape the rain for a bit.

With a charming smile, he strode to the counter where two women were manning the Chi-Bean's counter. One was a young college girl, a blonde with big green eyes. She stared at him like a kid who'd just walked into the largest candy store she'd ever seen. Thad was used to that response. Plenty of women tripped over themselves when he was around. It wasn't about his features alone, plenty of men were handsome. And it wasn't about his tailored suits, which anyone could buy. But if you combined those elements and added in his confidence, poise, and respect, people acted like a movie star had entered the room. He tried not to abuse his power... when possible, but it didn't stop him from using his charm on the women he met.

The other woman only glanced at him, more interested in her work, but he was instantly struck by the cascade of her black hair that almost looked violet in the room's lighting. The first girl jabbed her out of the way so she could take Thad's order.

"What can I get you?"

Thad studied the menu carefully before making a choice. "A large lemon ginger tea, please."

He glanced toward the fireplace, noticing the empty stool and microphone on a stand. A lone guitar was propped up next to them. It was close to eight. Any minute now, singers would be lining up to pour their hearts out over the mic...and he planned to be one of them.

"OH MY GOD, CHRIS HEMSWORTH JUST WALKED IN."

Veronica Hannigan jerked up under the cupboard as she put away creamer bottles in a small fridge, slamming her head against the bottom of the wood counter.

"*Ow...*" she hissed, then retreated from the cupboard and glanced at her employee Zelda, who was manning the coffee counter.

"What did you say?" she asked.

"*Chris Hemsworth* just walked into your shop." Zelda muttered from the corner of her mouth before she changed her voice to greet a customer. "What can I get you?"

Veronica shoved the last bottle of creamer inside the fridge and got to her feet. The Chi-Bean was on the first floor of the five thousand square-foot brownstone she lived in. Her whole world and everything she cared about were underneath this roof. It had been her childhood home; she couldn't imagine living anywhere else, which was one of the reasons she'd spent her life's savings to open up the coffee shop.

Finished with her customer, Zelda nudged Veronica with her elbow. "Over there."

Just inside the door stood a man who was at least six foot four with dark gold hair and hazel green eyes. Veronica's mouth dropped open. He *did* look like Chris Hemsworth, one of her favorite actors, but he clearly wasn't that man.

The man wore a fine suit, though most of it was covered by a wool knee-length grey coat which only added to his mystique. He looked around the shop, taking in the bakery counters, the tables, and the stack of board games near the lit fireplace that kept out the October chill.

The man's gaze touched upon her and Zelda briefly before moving on. It was like he was trying to read the history of the building itself as he examined the cozy shop's interior. Veronica had worked hard to make the Chi-Bean warm and inviting. This business was all she had, and she was damn proud of it.

The man finally came toward the counter and Zelda artfully nudged Veronica out of the way. Veronica had to roll her eyes at the younger girl's antics sometimes. Hot men were Zelda's territory. That was the rule. Not that Veronica cared to argue. She had plenty to do running the shop, so tending the customers was rare for her. .

"What can I get you?" Zelda asked the man.

Veronica discreetly moved behind one of their espresso machines so she could watch Mr. Tall and Too Gorgeous place his order. The way a person took their coffee told her a lot about them. If she had to guess, this guy was a straight coffee guy: no decaf, black, and probably nothing else.

He studied the menu carefully, unbothered by the customers lining up behind him. It was nearly eight o'clock, one of her busier times because it happened to be open mic night, where singers could play for the small crowd already gathered.

"A large lemon ginger tea, please." said the Chris

Hemsworth look-alike. His voice was deep, a perfect baritone and almost melodic. Was that even a thing for a man's voice? If it was, he had it in spades.

"No problem!" Zelda swiped his credit card before handing it back. "You should stick around. Our open mic night starts in a few minutes."

"Anyone can sing, right?" he asked.

"Anyone who wants to, right boss?" Zelda shot a look at Veronica, who had to step away from her espresso shield to meet the demands of his soft but intense look.

"Yes, that's right. Anyone can play. You just sign up over there by the stool."

As he turned to leave, the man's lips curved in a playful smile that made her heart flutter. The sensation was so unexpected she actually forgot to breathe. When she finally remembered, she gasped.

"You okay?" Zelda whispered.

Veronica pressed her palms on the counter. "Yeah..."

But she wasn't. It had been six years since she felt like this. Six years since she'd last felt that zing of attraction. She wasn't used to it, even more so because it was for a man she would likely never see again.

"Zelda, get the open mic night started. I'll handle the counter."

Zelda practically bounced with energy as she rushed around the counter toward the fireplace where the stool sat empty next to a well-loved guitar.

She grinned at the audience as she picked up the

mic. "Welcome to our weekly open mic night." Her green eyes twinkled as she fully embraced the spotlight. "Who's ready to become the next internet signing sensation? Just kidding, but seriously, if anyone gets famous after singing here, you better mention the Chi-Bean!" The audience laughed and she laid out the rules for the night.

Veronica was only too happy to hide behind her counter and listen to whatever music came from the patrons tonight. Music had saved her, offering a light in a world that had dimmed so much she feared it would never be bright again. And whenever she filled the space she worked in with those melodies, it reminded her of how much she'd survived and how lucky she was.

Over the next half hour, she listened with a smile and refilled orders from returning customers.

"Hey boss, we need more venti cups," Zelda called out as she rang up another order.

"I'll get them." Veronica opened the door to the storeroom and dug through a large cardboard box until she found a sheath of the right sized cups.

The coffee shop grew quiet as the performers changed, then a deep voice came over the microphone.

"I'm Thad, and I'm going to sing 'You Are the Reason' by Calum Scott." There was a moment of silence before a soothing, yet haunting, guitar melody began to play and the man started to sing.

Veronica froze. Her skin tingled with goosebumps as

she listened to his words. He sang of his heart beating and losing sleep over the woman of his dreams. It was a song sung to lull a woman into a sweet hazy spell of heartache and a breathless joy all at once. Pain filled his voice as he sang about being broken and needing to fix it, if only he could turn back the clock.

But it was the line about making sure the light defeated the dark and how he would spend every hour making sure the woman he loved was safe that broke Veronica. The song dug into her soul, dragging her back four years to that night her life changed forever...

The flashing blue and white lights outside her window. Opening the door to a pair of officers and rain-drenched slickers. They exchanged a glance and removed their caps as they stepped onto her porch. She didn't remember the exact words they said. It all became noise to her.

"Very sorry... There was an accident... The storm..."

She remembered the way her porch light lit up the rain just behind the officers, and she remembered *the small fluttering kicks in her womb as her unborn child seemed to understand what the police were telling her.*

"We're so sorry..."More noise.

That was the day the darkness consumed her world. Only Lyra's birth a month later brought the light back, but the shadows still lingered at the edges of her heart. How could a stranger's haunting voice and song do this to her?

Veronica struggled to breathe while the words

washed over her like the ocean battering a wild, rocky shore. It was somehow less painful to embrace the tidal wave of emotions rather than try to hold them off.

She wasn't sure at what point she started crying, but she felt the tears roll down her cheeks, dripping off her chin and wetting the baby blue apron she wore. She sniffed and scrambled around the storeroom until she found a box of tissues and wiped her face. The man's voice died away, and the last bit of the guitar's notes hummed in the air. There was a heavy silence for a moment before the coffee shop erupted into applause.

"Thank you," the man murmured. He sounded almost embarrassed.

Veronica stayed where she was in the storeroom until the next song began. After an extra moment, she emerged and handed Zelda the sheath of cups.

"Hey, Ronnie, are you okay?" Zelda asked she got a better look at her face.

"Yeah, I'm fine." They both knew it was a lie, but Zelda was nice enough not to pry.

Veronica glanced around the room at the customers. "Who sang that Calum Scott song?"

Zelda grinned. "The Chris Hemsworth look-alike. His voice was everything, wasn't it?" she sighed dreamily.

"Yeah." Veronica looked for him, but the mysterious stranger was gone. Yet his words and the sound of his voice lingered in her mind long after she and Zelda closed down the shop.

She saw her employee safely out, then climbed the stairs to the residential floors of the brownstone and unlocked her apartment door.

"Mommy!" a little voice trilled. Veronica groaned as she caught the four-year-old bundle of energy as she barreled into her arms. If it wasn't for Lyra, Veronica wouldn't have been able to rebuild her life into what it was now.

"You should be in bed, honey." She frowned at Lyra. Her blonde curls bounced, and her soft blue eyes were full of mischief. In those moments, Lyra looked so much like her father, especially her blond hair.

"Sorry, Mrs. Hannigan," the babysitter said as she stepped into the hall. Katie was her next-door neighbor's daughter who helped Veronica watch over Lyra on evenings when Veronica had only Zelda working downstairs. Veronica had two other part-time employees during the week, but on nights like this, Katie was a godsend in the form of a sixteen-year-old girl.

"It's fine, Katie. I know she's a handful sometimes."

Katie laughed as Lyra spun around in her Princess Elsa costume. Lyra was at that fun age when she never wanted to wear anything else except for the Elsa dress if she could help it.

"Here you go." Veronica handed Katie two twenty dollar bills and Katie gave Lyra a quick hug before she left for the night.

"Alright, kiddo. Bedtime for real. It's after ten, and mommy has to be up at five."

Lyra followed her into the bedroom and leaped onto the white wood twin bed while Veronica pulled some PJs out of the dresser.

"Elsa PJs?" Veronica offered, waving the jammies in front of her daughter. "That way mommy can wash your dress so it's all clean for tomorrow?"

Lyra studied her intently, the way all young children did when they were debating whether or not to trust their parent during such negotiations.

"Okay." Lyra let Veronica change her into her PJs, then climbed under the sheets.

Veronica kissed her head.

"Get some sleep." She tickled Lyra's arms and the girl giggled but quickly started to calm. Her eyelids grew heavy while she watched Veronica pick up the costume from the floor.

"Alexa, play the lullaby mix," Veronica asked the smart speaker in Lyra's room. Almost immediately, the device began to play soothing sweet music.

As Veronica stepped outside her daughter's door, she heard Lyra speak to the device.

"Alexa, can you bring me a daddy?"

"I'M SORRY, I CANNOT ORDER A DADDY," THE DEVICE replied.

Veronica sucked in a breath as pain squeezed her chest. Ever since Lyra had learned that you could order things from the device, she tried over and over to ask it for a father.

That was the one thing Veronica couldn't give her, no matter how much she wanted to. Her heart was permanently broken.

Veronica walked into the laundry room feeling numb. She put the tiny Elsa costume into the washing machine with the rest of her load before she turned it on. Then she went into her own bedroom and collapsed on her bed, exhausted.

Across from her was a dresser with a collection of photos in frames. The one in the middle held her attention. It showed a man with a hand on the woman's rounded belly, his lips pressed in a kiss against the sun dress covered shape of an unborn child. *Lyra.*

"I miss you, Parker," she whispered. "I miss you so much."

But no matter how much it hurt, she couldn't hide the photos of him. Sometimes the pain of what she lost was the only thing that kept her grounded. Someday maybe it wouldn't hurt so much, but right now she had to be strong for Lyra.

Veronica changed into a loose t-shirt and boxers and climbed into bed with a heavy sigh. She reached for the bedside lamp and killed the light.

❄

THAD STROLLED INTO THE LOBBY OF THE GOLD CIRCLE hotel. It was full of life, glittering with 1920s art deco design and accompanied by an energetic night scene. A crowd of people left one of the remodeled ballrooms where their exclusive concert had been playing tonight. He slipped through the crowd, moving against the tide of people as he had every night since he and his father had reopened the old hotel in downtown Chicago.

Once inside the elevators, he swiped his keycard for access to the penthouse suite. The doors opened to a three thousand square-foot apartment. He tossed his keys, wallet, and keycard on the gray granite kitchen countertop before he removed his coat. Normally, the empty rooms of his home bothered him, but the feeling was worse tonight.

His mind was still buzzing from his moment in the spotlight. He could still feel the electricity that crawled along his senses as he sang, and soon, his thoughts turned toward the little, elegant brownstone house itself. If he had to guess, it was worth around three million, with a lease on the first floor for the coffee shop and a lease on the residential property upstairs.

Thad closed his eyes and leaned back against the kitchen counter, picturing the brownstone's first-floor interior. It was *just* the sort of thing he was looking for.

While he loved living in the Gold Circle hotel, he wanted a space away from downtown so he could make this suite his perfect bachelor pad. It would always be ready for a night of seduction, and he wouldn't have to worry that a woman would get too attached when she knew it was just a crash pad for the night. The last thing he wanted was to give the women he dated the wrong impression; he had no plans to settle down anytime soon.

He'd been featured in last month's *GQ* and ever since, he couldn't set foot outside the hotel during the day without getting mobbed by at least a handful of women. Instead, he resorted to going out mostly at night, making him feel like a damned vampire. He was glad the real estate offices of Worthington Enterprises were only a block away, otherwise he would have had a hell of a time getting to work.

He and his driver, Simon, had a carefully planned routine. In the mornings, Simon would text Thad that he was outside, and Thad would go down and get straight into the car. Any delays meant a chance to be recognized from the billboards all over town with his face on them. His butler, Winston, also helped him handle anything else he might need, including sneaking in and out of the hotel.

Thad found his cellphone and dialed his personal assistant, Brandon. The kid was twenty-two, smart as a whip, a hard worker, and on call 24/7.

"Hey, Mr. Worthington!" he answered enthusiastically despite the late hour.

"Brandon, I'm going to text you an address. When you get into the office tomorrow, find out who owns it and what its current value is."

"Sure thing," Brandon replied.

"Thanks." Thad hung up and crossed the kitchen into his large living room. His guitar sat in a stand by the fireplace. He picked it up and sat down on the couch, the weight of the instrument giving him an immediate sense of peace. He brushed his fingertips over the strings and listened to the vibrations ripple through the quiet apartment. After a moment, he started to play the "The Sound of Silence." He let the words move through him as though they had a soul of their own.

Tonight he'd conquered his only fear: singing in public. Something about letting people hear his voice, knowing they could judge him for it, had always terrified him. Thad wasn't used to fear. He lived with confidence. Money, power, and connections, combined with good looks, had given him just about every advantage in the world.

But tonight, he'd put himself on the line in a way he'd never done before. It had felt so good and seemed to leave him in a different sort of headspace. For the first time in a long time, he'd felt connected to something, not separated from it.

It had to be the brownstone; that house had some

sort of energy that called to him. He could feel himself becoming fixated.

He continued to sing and play, letting his usually smooth voice turn almost ragged with desperation near the end.

As the last notes faded into silence, he thought again of that cozy little building and how he was going to own it, no matter what it cost him.

2

Thad pushed through the misted glass doors and entered the main lobby of their company. He was instantly greeted by his assistant. "Mr. Worthington, you're early!"

Thad gave his usual reply. "I'm always early."

The offices of Worthington Enterprises were sleek and modern, with a touch of antique gilding, a faded memory of the roaring twenties. Its design was tempered by the modern age and was a style Thad very much loved.

He'd gone through a period in college where he'd been obsessed with *The Great Gatsby* by F. Scott Fitzgerald. Perhaps it was a bit of hubris, to be obsessed with a mysterious billionaire literary figure, but Gatsby had been his idol.

It wasn't because of what people usually thought

when they read the book. Gatsby was a tragic figure, not a hero, and what drew Thad to him was knowing the man had lived his whole life with one vision: winning the heart of a woman he could never truly have. He'd built up a glittering, powerful empire, only to have it crumble just as he foolishly believed he held the woman of his dreams in his arms forever.

There was something to the irony of getting what a person truly wanted, only to lose everything else. In a way, he identified with it. He shoved thoughts of Gatsby aside and focused on his assistant.

"What did you find out about that brownstone?" he asked. Brandon stuck by his side, matching his pace as they walked toward his office.

"I've got the owner's name, phone number, and the current market value with the specs on the house." He handed Thad the information, neatly printed on expensive card stock with the company letterhead. Thad brushed his thumb over the name Annette Becker.

"My father in yet?"

"He is. Your mother will be by for lunch with the both of you later."

"Thanks, Brandon. I sent you some reports early this morning. Review and we'll discuss them in an hour. I want to hear your thoughts."

"You got it," the young man replied eagerly. He was the son of a friend of Thad's father. Despite how nepotism usually worked out in the workplace—that is to say, badly—Thad had been pleasantly surprised by Brandon's intelligence and work ethic. Most Ivy League kids were smart but putting in the necessary effort left most of them clueless. Thad supposed most people would think the same of him, but they would be wrong. He'd gone to Princeton on an academic scholarship and later approached his father, who'd been an investment banker at the time, to open Worthington Enterprises with him four years ago. With Thad's aggressive confidence and his father's reserved analytical approach to balance each other out, they made a great team.

Thad didn't go see his father just yet. First, he went to his own office and pulled his cell out. He dialed the number for Annette Becker and watched the Chicago skyline as he listened to the phone ring.

"Hello?" a woman answered.

"Ms. Becker?"

"*Mrs.* Becker," she corrected, and he realized he was speaking to someone a little older, perhaps his parents' age. "Who is this?"

"Mrs. Becker, my name is Thad Worthington. I understand you own a brownstone on North Astor Street? The one with the coffee shop on the first floor?"

"It's actually in a trust over which I'm the sole trustee with discretion to sell. Has my tenant done something? If that—" the woman cut herself off. "I'm sorry, what did you say was the reason you called?"

"I am interested in making an offer on it, if you

wouldn't mind showing me the rest of the property at a time that's convenient for you?"

"I might," Mrs. Becker said slowly. "My asking price is three and half million."

He checked the details that Brandon had written down. "Zillow has it listed for $2,895,000." The report said it had three bedrooms and two bathrooms upstairs with a business property on the first floor for a total of 5100 square feet. Half of that was likely downstairs and had been modified with the construction of the coffee shop, but he could easily put money in to have it restored to a normal residence when he moved in.

"Yes, well, the home has sentimental value. It belonged to my late husband."

"My sincerest condolences." He said at once, even though the woman didn't sound at all that upset. "If you aren't interested in selling, I completely understand." He gave the customary pause, letting her think it over.

"I can make time to show it to you on Sunday. I will make sure the renters are out when you arrive."

"Wonderful." Thad gave Mrs. Becker his cell number. "Just text me a time for Sunday."

"I will," she assured him in a much sweeter voice than she'd initially used. She was definitely willing to sell and the thought made him smile. Today was Friday, so he would only have to wait a few days to check out the brownstone's upper floors.

With his personal project out of the way for now, it

was time to visit his father. Whereas most men in his father's position would have a corner office, or at least have a large window, Timothy Worthington did not. Thad's father preferred an office in the center of the floor, where he could be close to his employees and feel approachable. It represented the sort of man Timothy was: a good, kind man who'd been glad to leave the exhausting hours of investment banking behind. Thad's mother had also been thrilled by the career change.

Thad knocked on his father's half open door.

"Come in."

Thad pushed his way inside and grinned at the sight of his father examining a model of a new hotel structure. It was one Thad didn't recognize.

"New project?"

His father gave a delighted smile. "Yes, it's the model for a series of two-story beach houses along the Gold Coast, though I'm tempted to rebuild some of the old mansions that were torn down. What do you think would be better?"

"You know what my vote would be." Thad would rather have a glorious mansion turned into a modern hotel than have dozens of small beach homes litter the coast.

"Restored mansions it is." His father set the beach house model aside and leaned back in his chair. "Our afternoon meeting got pushed back to tomorrow. You're free if you have anything you need to do around the city."

That was good news. Thad wanted to see the brownstone again in daylight. He'd learned early on that a person had to see a space in both the light and the dark before they could truly judge its worth.

"I'm thinking of buying a place on North Astor Street..." He wasn't sure why he needed to tell his father, other than to see if he approved. That was rare; he usually didn't seek approval from his parents. Thad was close to both of them, but he'd always been confident enough to do what he wished on his own. But something about this property felt different. It was a personal investment as opposed to a business interest.

"One of those lovely houses?" His father stroked his chin. "Are you thinking of moving out of the penthouse?"

"Sort of. I still want to keep that space for entertaining."

Timothy chuckled, understanding what Thad meant, albeit in a vague way. "Well, you never needed my opinion before, but I'd say go after it. Those places were built to last."

"Thanks."

When Thad returned to his office, he sat back in his chair and steepled his fingers. The walls were covered with black and white photos of various real estate projects. He liked the sharp contrast the photos provided. His gaze drifted past the frames and far into the distance as his thoughts left work behind.

All he could think about was that house, and how he'd felt last night as he sang with his whole heart and soul under its roof.

"HE'S BACK!" ZELDA ANNOUNCED WITH AN EXCITED whisper.

Veronica was busy cleaning out one of the smoothie blenders in the sink. It had broken...again. The damn thing had been a piece of crap from the moment it had arrived. "Who?"

"Chris Hemsworth!"

"Zelda!" She spun around to tell Zelda to hush but froze as she saw that *he* was standing at the counter. Zelda was in a daze, as though the man's ridiculously good looks were somehow more hypnotic in daylight.

Veronica gently nudged Zelda away from the cash machine to talk to the attractive stranger.

"What can I get you?"

"Black coffee, light cream."

"Sure thing." Veronica accepted his credit card and couldn't help but notice the name. *Thad Worthington.* He had one of those heavy black credit cards she knew had no monetary limit. The thought made her dizzy and his name sounded super rich, like the hot jerk a girl would crush on at an elite boarding school in some cheesy coming-of-age rom-com.

Veronica glanced up and found him smiling at her in a way that brought back the same fluttering in her stomach from the other night.

"I don't suppose I can have my card back?" he asked, still smiling.

"Oh, God. I'm so sorry." She handed it back quickly. "I don't usually get so—" she trailed off before she admitted she'd been gawking at him.

"It's okay. I get that a lot, ever since the article."

"What article?"

"The one in... Never mind." Thad's eyes, a soft hazel green that burned like ginger fire, focused on her intently. "You really don't recognize me?"

"I...should I?" Veronica felt like she was the butt of a joke the universe was telling and she was missing the punchline. "Wait, are you in a band?"

"No, it's... It's not important," Thad recovered quickly. "Thank you." He glanced down at her chest and she flushed at such undisguised appraisal. Then she realized he was just looking for a name tag. She'd forgotten hers in the back of the shop.

"Veronica... I'm Veronica." She could have smacked herself. This guy didn't care what her name was.

"I'm Thad. Nice to meet you." He extended his hand and Veronica took it. His grip was strong but not threatening. He gave it a gentle shake.

"It's nice to meet you, too," she said, feeling incredibly shy beneath the gentle but no less intense gaze of this gorgeous man.

When he released her hand, the world around her came crashing back. Zelda running the espresso machine, the buzz and chatter of customers. For a moment, this man had erased the background completely. Only Parker had ever done that to her before.

Thad gave her one last look before he chose a table facing the street and sat down.

"Wow..." Zelda said the word, managing to give it three syllables. "Put your eyes back in your head, boss."

Veronica tried, but damned if she wasn't distracted for the next half hour glancing at the man who sat quietly reading the newspaper. Veronica had let Zelda deliver the coffee to him and despite her sweet flirtations, Zelda returned to the counter with a defeated frown.

"He has to have some superhot girlfriend, right? Probably dates models or something," Zelda muttered as she scrubbed almost too vigorously at the imaginary stains on the countertop.

"A guy like that?" Veronica chuckled. "He *definitely* has a girlfriend, maybe even a dozen. He looks like a player."

Veronica forced her focus away from Thad, and it was a short while later when she glanced back, that her heart sank. Another attractive man had joined Thad at the table, carrying a baby carrier. The man reached down, pulled the baby out and handed the child to Thad, who accepted with a sheepish grin and bounced the baby on his knee, making the child squeal.

"Oh damn, he's gay. I *knew* he was too freaking gorgeous to be straight," Zelda said. She sighed. "They make a beautiful couple, though, don't they?"

"Yeah, you're right. They look good together." Veronica turned her back and buried any of the silly daydreams she'd started to form about Thad in the sweet nebulous clouds of her mind.

THAD HANDED BACK HIS BEST FRIEND'S ONE-YEAR-OLD daughter, Hayley, despite the fact that she wanted to play more. "So, how's things?"

Jared Redmond was a top-flight real estate attorney who'd recently married a woman who worked at the Chicago Art Institute as a junior director. They both kept long hours, but somehow had managed to do the whole "raise a kid thing," something which still impressed Thad.

Jared sighed and leaned back in his chair, a picture of ease. "Things are great. Felicity sends her love, by the way."

"Fatherhood looks good on you." Thad couldn't resist

teasing Jared about that. Hayley had been an unexpected but welcome surprise to the couple.

"Yeah, it does." Jared's eyes softened as he shot a peek into the baby carrier at his feet. "So, why are we here? We usually do drinks at Hackney's," Jared asked.

"I wanted your opinion." Thad nodded subtly at the brownstone around them.

Jared didn't pick up on his hint. "On?"

"This place." Thad pointed a finger upstairs. "It's got a residence upstairs."

"Yeah? Have you seen it yet?"

"No. I will this weekend, though." He grinned. "I love the feel of this place."

Jared seemed to notice the change in Thad as he spoke of the brownstone. "So you're thinking of living here? What about the penthouse?"

"I'll keep it open for fun, but it would be nice to have a place that's out of the way."

His friend smiled. "You want a *real* home."

He hadn't thought of it like that but that was indeed what this was going to be. A *real* home. He could leave his wild party days and endless women for the penthouse.

"Let me get this straight. You, Thad, the man who only gives a girl one date, is thinking of settling down?"

"No," Thad laughed. "I just want to keep that part of my life separate. When I own this place, I want it to be my private sanctuary."

"You mean No Girls Allowed."

"Not quite so Calvin and Hobbes, but yeah."

Jared shook his head. "You and your damn models. You know none of those women are real, right? Real women are sweet and sexy by being themselves, not acting like a man's boyhood fantasy. You should try dating a *real* woman if you want a *real* home."

Thad played with his empty coffee cup. "You *stole* the real woman I wanted. You also knocked her up and married her."

Jared's laughter died. "Don't forget I got there *first*. I staked my claim on Felicity before you ever met her."

Thad watched his best friend turn all caveman over his wife. Felicity had been the first woman to tempt Thad into changing his ways, but it had been clear from the moment they met that she was never going to be his, and he'd done the honorable thing and helped get her and Jared back together.

Thad wasn't even sure if he would ever fall in love the way Jared had. He'd thought he'd been in love once, but he'd been wrong. Ever since then, he'd kept his emotional distance.

"You know what? You need a real date for a change. Not with the usual girls you date. You need someone who isn't pretending to be someone else." Jared looked around the coffee shop. "You need to date someone... like her." He gave a subtle jerk of his head toward the Chi-Bean's counter.

Thad followed his gaze to the woman currently smacking a possibly broken smoothie machine with a furious yet adorable snarl on her face. She had the most stunning black hair pulled into a ponytail that he remembered from the first night he was here. He'd introduced himself to her earlier when he'd realized she hadn't recognized him from the GQ magazine interview. It had been refreshing for a woman not to know who he was. She'd still given him that adorable "deer-in-the-headlights" look like other women did though.

"You know that she's not a challenge, right?" Thad said. Seducing a girl like that would be all too easy.

"Oh, but *that's* not the challenge. The challenge is you *can't* sleep with her until fifteen dates in."

The gauntlet thrown, Thad stared at his best friend. "You think I can't make it fifteen dates without sex?"

"I *know* you can't." Jared's smug smile made Thad lean in to growl in response.

"Want to bet on it?"

"What's the point? You'd only lose." Jared shot back.

"Fine, if I win..." Thad grinned eagerly. "You have to name your next little tyke after me."

"And if I win, you name your next new hotel 'Jared's Place.'"

Thad snorted. He could make it fifteen dates just hanging out with a woman.

"Deal." He thrust his hand out and Jared shook it.

Thad glanced over at the young woman in question.

She'd abandoned the smoothie machine and was now on the phone, still angry. She looked kind of cute when she was pissed. His eyes moved over her body, noting how the baby blue apron hugged her curves.

"Batter up," Jared chuckled and sat back to watch Thad go to work.

Thad headed for the counter, catching snippets of the woman's conversation.

"The warranty's still good. Yes, that's why I'm calling. I need a replacement. It's been giving me trouble since the day I bought it. It's a lemon, okay?" She paused, then closed her eyes and sighed. "Yes, that's my address. Please expedite the shipping if you can. Thank you." She hung up and turned to face him only to gasp and go red.

"Oh gosh! I'm so sorry. Can I get you something?"

"Veronica, right?" He was fairly certain that was what she told him half an hour ago.

"Yeah..." Veronica's eyes were that lovely storm blue and held a hint of gray. She was very pretty, and he was going to enjoy proving Jared wrong. He had self-control. He could make it fifteen dates with this girl. She couldn't be more than twenty-three or twenty-four. He'd be careful not to break her heart. She looked so damn innocent, not like some of the women he'd dated. Those girls he'd been with always tried to look older than they were, sophisticated and sexy...but Jared was right about them. It was all a performance, completely unreal. It hadn't bothered him, though, until today.

God, he'd become jaded, hadn't he? Maybe it would be nice to be with a real woman for a while, someone whose beauty was natural, who wore clothes not designed to seduce, and whose unguarded smiles were its own reward.

"Sir?" Veronica broke through his thoughts.

He smiled at her but didn't lay it on too thick. *Go slow,* he reminded himself. "This is going to sound crazy, but can I have your number?"

"For the Chi-Bean? Sure it's—" she started to pick up one of the coffee house business cards on a little stand. Thad reached out and gently caught her wrist.

"No, *your* number." He never let his eyes leave hers. He was beginning to become obsessed with that shade of blue. What would those eyes look like when she was gazing at him in full arousal, her body writhing beneath him as he covered her with kisses? Thad slammed the door shut on that mental image before he got too carried away.

"*My* number?" Veronica stared at him. Her gaze darted toward the table with Jared and then back to him.

"Yeah, I'd take you out for coffee, but you seem to have that covered here. How about drinks instead?" Thad gave a charming chuckle that made her flush an even deeper red.

Veronica continued to stare at him. Suddenly the other employee, the cute college kid who'd tried to flirt with him earlier materialized next to Veronica.

"Here's her number." She nodded toward Jared as she handed Thad a slip of paper with a number on it. "We both thought you were taken."

"Thanks. I'm definitely not taken. That's a friend of mine." He glanced at Jared who was watching him intently, a smile twitching at the corners of his lips.

"I'm Zelda," the girl said and nudged Veronica out of her state of shock.

"Look sir, I'm sorry. I really don't think—"

"Don't," Thad smiled. "*Think* that is. This is just a drink, a chance to get to know each other when you're not on the clock. It'll be fun. How about tonight?"

"I..." Veronica's expressions were so easy to read. She was trying to find a way out of this. That was interesting...

"We close at ten tonight, but she can meet you here at eight," Zelda said.

At this, Veronica shot her a glare. "I'm sorry, but I can't. I need to be home at nine, *remember*?"

Zelda shrugged. "Talk to Katie. She can cover for you for one extra hour, right?" Zelda's face had hardened to stone, but there was nothing mean about the expression. More like she was determined to win the argument.

"It's *one* hour," Zelda continued.

"I won't keep you past that. Scout's honor." Thad winked at her.

"Okay," she agreed slowly. "But I really have to be back by nine."

"Excellent." He typed her details into his phone and sent her a text with his name.

"I'll be here at eight to pick you up, Veronica." He turned and went back to his table, excited but also curious about the woman's hesitation. Was his game off?

Back at his table, Jared was grinning even more smugly than before.

"Real women aren't so easy, are they? Even starstruck, she still had to be pushed into it. You might make it fifteen dates after all. I think I made this too easy for you."

Thad clenched his jaw. He definitely hadn't expected so much resistance from the girl and while a challenge was fun, he didn't want Jared to think he had a chance of winning.

"I can't wait for you to tell Felicity her next kid is going to be named Thaddeus or Thadosia."

"Thadosia?" His friend laughed, startling a few of the customers drinking their foaming lattes.

"Shut up before you scare your kid." Thad grumbled as they got up and left the Chi-Bean.

"You are *so* off your game. I have to call Angelo. He *has* to hear this." Jared pulled out a cell phone to call Angelo, Thad's other best friend.

Today was going to be a long day. But tonight... Tonight he was taking Veronica, a cute coffee barista out for drinks. A nice, normal girl on a nice, normal date. How hard could it be?

3

"Zelda, I'm going to kill you." Veronica snapped the moment Thad and his gorgeous plantonic friend walked out the door.

Zelda turned wide and guileless brown eyes on her. "What? Me?" she asked before dissolving into giggles.

"You know I don't want to go out with him." Well, that was a bald faced lie. There was something about Thad—a lot of somethings, honestly—that made her skin tingle. That hadn't happened in a long time. She really didn't need this, not today when everything was going wrong.

Their blender had broken and she'd yelled at the customer service rep when they'd tried to avoid honoring her warranty. Veronica began stacking cups aggressively. Now she was going to spend the next several hours freaking out over a date she never asked for and worrying about whether Katie would agree to watch Lyra a little longer this evening.

"How long has it been since you dated?" Zelda was more serious now, and that didn't make Veronica feel any better.

She paused before she answered, her mind already replaying the succession of failed attempts to get back out there. "Two years."

Two years and half a lifetime ago. She'd tried a couple of online dating apps, but the men there had inspired nothing in her but dread when she'd actually met with them. She'd even thrown up in the bathroom of one of the restaurants after her date was over because she'd panicked when the man asked to see her again.

But the truth was, there'd been nothing wrong with the guy; she'd merely freaked out at the thought of committing to a relationship again. She wasn't ready yet. Hell, she might *never* be ready.

Veronica could hear Parker's voice in her head. *"You know what I love about you, babe? You love with your whole heart."*

She did, and that was her curse.

But this Thad guy...well, he didn't seem to be a guy who would be around long term. He was clearly a one night kind of guy. It wasn't like he would want to marry her and start a life with her. What did she have to lose? Maybe she could just enjoy herself. That little realization sparked a flair of excitement deep in her belly.

Fun. She deserved a bit of that, didn't she?

"Just have drinks with Chris Hemsworth and bask in the beauty of that manly scenery. I know I would."

"You have to stop calling him that." Veronica tried not to laugh. "Or else I might accidentally call him that too."

"Just think." Zelda twirled her counter wiping cloth playfully. "He could speak to you in an Aussie accent, or maybe he could dress up in a Thor costume... Talk about some seriously hot role-playing."

Zelda ducked as Veronica chucked a dishrag at her. "His name is Thad."

"Thad? That sounds sexy." Zelda was still giggling.

"I think it's short for Thaddeus," Veronica mused. A rare name, for sure, but it fit the handsome, mysterious man.

"Now it sounds almost Roman — oh! Dress him up in a gladiator costume and—"

The next dishrag smacked Zelda right in the face.

The coffee shop door opened, and Katie came in with Lyra, who was bouncing with excitement. Her preschool was five days a week from nine to four and Katie's high school was only a block away, which made it easy for the teenager to walk Lyra home. Plus, it saved Veronica from trying to make time away from the shop to pick her up.

"Mommy!" Lyra marched up to her. Her backpack, which was almost as big as her, bounced against her tiny body, reminding Veronica how small her baby was, even though she'd grown so much in the last year.

"Hey, honey. How was school?"

She struggled to open her bag. "Cool! We had drawing lessons." Katie rushed to get her away from the counter before her backpack exploded, as it tended to do the moment Lyra got home every day.

"Let's go get a table, Lyra. We can show some of your drawings to your mom there."

"Thank you." Veronica told Katie. "Zelda, can you manage the counter for a minute?"

"Sure thing."

Veronica removed her apron and joined Katie and Lyra at an empty table to see her daughter's most recent artistic masterpieces from daycare. Most of them were very crude stick figures. They had circles for hands and tiny lines for fingers, which made Veronica smile. She tried to keep track of the basic developmental milestones, but overall she was a pretty relaxed parent. Probably because working so hard at the coffee shop meant she didn't have the energy to become a tiger mom.

"What did you draw?"

Lyra pointed a tiny finger at the scene. "Me, you, and the beach."

She pointed a figure beside her in the drawing. "And who is this?"

"That's my daddy."

A lump formed in her throat. "That's Parker?"

She'd had the talk with Lyra last year about where Parker was, but children processed death so differently than adults. She wasn't sure if Lyra understood it.

"No, this is my second daddy. My first one's in heaven, remember?" Lyra's nose wrinkled as she looked at Veronica.

"Your second daddy?" Her stomach plummeted at the thought. Then, completely unbidden, her thoughts strayed to Thad and how crazy it was she'd agreed—under duress—to go out with a man who had a definite effect on her.

"Uh huh," Lyra said with the distracted confidence of a child who was certain it would happen.

Katie's eyes met Veronica's. The girl was only sixteen, but she was mature for her age. She could tell how sensitive the whole subject was. Veronica tried to smile at the teen without making the girl pity her any more than she already did. She jerked her head, motioning for Katie to join her a little away from the table.

"Katie, can I ask you for a favor?"

"What's up, Mrs. Hannigan?" Katie's voice dropped, her head inclined toward Veronica, concern clear in her eyes.

"I...have a date tonight."

"What? Oh my God, that's wonderful!" Katie was hugging her before Veronica had even finished. "Sorry!"

Katie released her. "So what time? Do you need me to watch Lyra?"

"Could you? I promise I'll only be gone for an hour, from eight to nine pm."

"No problem. Lyra is good about reading her stories or watching a movie if I need to do homework. We'll be fine."

"Thank you so much, seriously."

The teenager blushed. "It's no trouble. I'm really happy for you, Mrs. Hannigan."

"It's just one date," Veronica murmured, blushing.

"Yeah, for now, but if this guy is smart, he'll want you forever." Katie said this with such certainty that Veronica almost believed her. Katie was a young, hopeless romantic, much like she'd been at her age.

"I'll take her upstairs and get her settled in, Mrs. Hannigan." Her daughter waved at her as they went through the door marked *Private*, which led up to the residential part of the brownstone.

By seven-thirty that night, Veronica was digging through her closet in a panic. She had nothing to wear for a date. What was even appropriate for dates these days anyway?

"You need some help?" Katie asked.

Veronica gasped and turned to see her on the doorjamb just a few inches away, a hopeful smile lighting up her young face.

"Oh God, yes. I have no idea what to wear."

"Do you know where he's taking you?" Katie bent to pick up several discarded pieces of clothing from the floor before she joined Veronica in the closet.

"Drinks? That's all he said."

"Drinks, huh? That could go either way. How was he dressed?"

"In a nice suit." Veronica watched the teenager with bemusement, wondering how the girl knew anything about dating.

"So we can likely count out a seedy dive bar where they serve hot wings. He'll probably take you somewhere decent, but not too fancy, if he didn't warn you ahead of time. How about this?" Katie plucked a few items off the hangers and tossed them to Veronica. Skinny jeans, a bright pink, loose-fitting, silk blouse with a somewhat low neckline, and a pair of leopard print ballet flats.

"Leave your hair down and try this on." Katie handed her a long golden necklace that had a locket on it.

Veronica eyed the old necklace. It was one she'd had forever. The necklace was nothing fancy, but it had been a gift from her mother a year before she died. "Really?"

"Yeah. Lockets are super sexy. They imply you've got a secret. Guys love that stuff."

"Oh they do, do they?" Veronica teased. They were only eight years apart, but it felt more like decades sometimes.

"Trust me." Katie chuckled and left the room.

Veronica changed into the clothes and stared at her

reflection in the full-length mirror. She looked...not bad, really. At least it didn't scream "exhausted, single, working mom" or "overworked coffee shop owner." She looked normal, *nice*. Not nice enough to date a man like Thad, but she wasn't worried. This was just a date. Worst case scenario, they'd have a nice conversation and that would be the end of it. Best case scenario, she might have a bit of fun.

"He's downstairs!" Katie squealed.

Veronica emerged from her bedroom. "Who's downstairs?" Lyra asked. The four-year-old was swinging her tiny feet on the couch as she watched *The Little Mermaid* for the hundredth time.

"Just a friend, sweetie. Stay with Katie, okay? I'll be back in an hour."

Lyra gave her a questioning look, but Veronica grabbed her purse and rushed out the door.

"You didn't tell me how hot he was," Katie whispered as they stepped into the stairwell. "You know he looks like—"

"Chris Hemsworth, I know." Veronica still couldn't believe it. Parker had been handsome as well, but so much had changed in the last four years. Veronica didn't feel young anymore. She felt ancient. A part of her wondered how long it would take Thad to see that tonight and, how quickly he would find an excuse to end the date when he did.

Thad was just outside the Chi-bean, his phone pressed to his ear. He paced as he talked and didn't seem to hear her leave the shop. She had a moment to take in the man she was going out with tonight. He was dressed to perfection. No longer in a suit, he wore dark trousers and a sweater that clung to his body. His hair was styled in such a way that it looked messy, but artfully so, and long enough to run her hands through, if she got to that point.

She listened to his business tone as he spoke, more serious, lacking the flirtatious charm he'd shown her that afternoon, yet she liked this voice too. It was strong... decisive. His voice shouldn't have made her flush all over, but it did.

"Did you see the Orlando proposal I sent?" Thad said. "I'm going down in a few weeks to check it out myself... Yeah..." He laughed softly at something the other person said. "Right. I've got to go. I'll follow up with you tomorrow morning."

He ended the call and pulled back the cuff of his sweater, checking the time. He still hadn't noticed her just out of his line of vision. She was almost ten minutes late and he clearly knew it.

"Hey Thad, sorry I'm late," she said.

When Thad turned, his face lit up with excitement and relief. "I was worried you might not show up."

"I was so nervous I almost didn't," she blurted out, and instantly regretted it.

Thad grinned, a slightly boyish look to his face. He cocked an arm out to her. "Shall we?"

She shyly tucked her arm in his. "Where are we going?"

"Vol. 39. Have you ever been?"

"No, where is it?"

"Inside the Kimpton Gray Hotel."

Veronica was too nervous to ask much more as he led her to a private car and guided her inside.

"This is my driver, Simon." Thad gestured to the man in the front seat, who looked like he was in his late thirties.

"Hello, Ms. Hannigan," Simon greeted.

"It's nice to meet you, Simon." Veronica tried not to think about the fact that Thad was rich enough to have a private car and driver.

They both sat in the back seat, close, but not touching. He slipped his phone in his pocket and asked her about her day, about the situation with the blender, and about what a typical day at the shop was like.

Veronica found she was able to laugh a little at the chaos of her day as she explained it. He listened to all of it, even the damn blender, and his eyes never left her. There really was nothing sexier than a man who gave a woman his full attention like he was doing. It excited her, but also made her nervous. She was used to blending in and going unnoticed by men, not being their sole focus.

"Here we are, sir." Simon stopped the car. Thad thanked him and helped Veronica out, offering her a hand. That, too, she liked: the respect Thad offered.

The hotel wasn't cheap or fake glitzy. The décor was gray flannel upholstered furniture and soft, lightly floral wallpaper that gave everything undertones of an old English country estate. It definitely felt different than most hotels.

"What kind of people usually stay here?" she asked as they stepped into an elevator in the lobby. He offered her his arm and she wound hers through. It felt strange to cling to him, but he felt safe. Sexy as hell and irresistible, sure, but still strangely *safe*.

"Mostly lawyers and financiers who appreciate a good cocktail but don't want to be bothered with crowds."

"You've been here a lot?"

"A fair amount. I'm in real estate. Developing hotels and resorts is my passion. I love this hotel in particular. All the rooms have sleek platform beds and pendant lamps which feel midcentury modern, but they also have these wonderful dark, wooden armoires that have bright, bold interiors, giving them an exotic feel beneath their buttoned-up first appearance."

Veronica could actually picture one of those rooms as he talked, modern with just a hint of wild. She liked the idea a lot and she liked it even more that Thad had noticed such details and could share them so easily with her.

"And what about the bar?" she asked.

He grinned as the elevator doors opened. "You'll see."

The Vol. 39 bar looked like a law office from the 1940s that had been given a romantic makeover. Leather tufted sofas were a decadent addition to the space, and the walls were lined with black painted wooden bookshelves filled with red, gold, tan and black striped texts. Bottom lights along the front of the shelves lit up the glowing spines, making the bookshelves, alone, art. It was classy, sexy and, thankfully, not threatening. Veronica had been afraid he would take her to an intense nightclub scene she wasn't ready for.

"This okay with you?" Thad studied her, his eyes missing nothing.

She smiled shyly back. "Yeah. I just wasn't sure what to expect."

"Here we can have a quiet drink and talk about things without it being too much of anything," he said.

Thad led her to a pair of couches with a black coffee table between them. Small circular candles were lit, warming the room with a golden hue.

"I'll get us some drinks." He paused. "Would you like an old fashioned? That's their specialty here. It's served with a 30-year-old Armagnac and a barrel-aged demerara sugar."

"I've never had one. I'd love to try it." Veronica set her purse down after Thad left and studied the books on the shelf—they seemed to be legal texts—before turning her attention to the art on the walls opposite the shelves. Beautiful black and white silhouettes of faces in profile decorated the blank spaces. Special lamps hung above each piece to illuminate and add drama.

"It's nice, isn't it?" Thad said from behind her.

She took the glass he handed her and finally sat down. Surprisingly, he didn't sit on the couch next to her like she expected him to. Instead, he sat on the couch opposite. She sipped her cocktail and was relieved to see it wasn't too strong. She hadn't had much alcohol since Lyra was born and her tolerance was low.

"So, you're in real estate?" she asked.

He took a sip of his drink and nodded. "And you, have you always been into espresso machines?" There was a teasing tone to his words, but it wasn't like he was trying to make her feel bad about being a coffee shop owner.

"No, I graduated college early and started working at the Chi-Bean right after. I like the precision involved in making things right, but also the innovation that comes with trying to make a taste and style that's all your own. I even have a game where I guess what people drink before they order. I'm usually right."

Thad flashed her a wicked smile that made her stomach quiver. "What about me? Did you guess right?"

"Not even close. I'd originally thought black coffee, nothing added. But then you ordered tea that first time and coffee with a touch of cream the second time. You were definitely a surprise." She'd liked that he hadn't been so predictable, but unpredictable could also be a bad thing.

"I saw the open mic poster outside on Thursday and I knew that if I was brave enough to sing, a soothing tea would be better for my throat. But I'm normally black coffee with just a bit of cream. Life's too short to drink bitter coffee in my opinion." He took another sip of his old fashioned. "And what's your drink of choice?"

"A frozen cherry smoothie with coconut milk."

"With coffee in it?" He looked amused and disturbed at the same time.

"What? No," she laughed. "I actually don't like the taste of coffee, just the smell."

Thad was silent a second and then he laughed. "You work at a coffee shop and you don't like the taste of coffee?"

"I know. Isn't that silly?" She giggled, knowing how ridiculous it sounded.

"No, it's not silly," Thad said more seriously. "You can love something and yet not do it yourself. I like to sing, but not in public. At least, not until Thursday."

"I heard you." Veronica's face flushed at the memory of how his singing had devastated her. "You were incredible. You ever consider a career?"

"Not really. It would somehow cheapen it for me. I know it doesn't with others, but I don't know, singing's personal to me." Thad's eyes softened as he suddenly chuckled. "I don't think I've ever told anyone that before." He took another sip of his drink. "So," he changed the subject. "You've lived in Chicago your whole life?"

"Born and bred. You?"

"I grew up in Connecticut, but my father sent me to a fancy prep school in Maryland when I turned sixteen."

"Was that awful? Like in the movies?"

"Parts of it. I missed home, but my dad was right. It gave me confidence and it's there I met two of my best friends, though we weren't friends at first. The three of us fought all the time. We had to share a big dorm room with three beds. There was no real privacy. Only Angelo was used to it because he came from a big Italian family."

"Angelo?" Veronica found herself trying to imagine Thad's life and the people in it. She had been a rich kid once, before her mother died and her father married his second wife. She quickly buried the sudden flash of ugly thoughts in her mind. She was on a date with a gorgeous guy; she was not going to let her evil stepmother ruin this moment.

"Angelo is a chef here in Chicago. And Jared..." He smirked. "The one you thought was my domestic partner, is a lawyer here in town."

Veronica covered her mouth embarrassment. "I am really sorry about that."

Thad laughed. "It's fine, really. I can't help but tease you; you're gorgeous when you blush."

That only made her blush harder.

"You aren't used to that are you?"

"Used to what?"

"Compliments. You must not date a lot."

Veronica didn't want to go into that but didn't want to lie either. "Not recently..."

"Why is that?"

"I... haven't really dated much in the last four years."

"Four years?" His eyes widened slightly.

She absently touched her bare ring finger on her left hand. "I was married... My husband died a little over four years ago."

The old, stylized clock on the wall ticked by loud enough to make her ears ring. She closed her eyes, breathing slowly to stay calm. That was it. She blew it. Any second now, he would make a polite excuse to end the evening early and take her home. Before tonight, being left alone would have been fine. But now, a part of her she'd thought was long dead struggled in the dark as it searched for the waning light of hope this man had started to shine her way.

"You don't...have to stay." She stuttered on the words as he got up from the couch. She looked up at him and expected to see pity there. Instead, she saw that same gentle intensity as he moved toward her couch and sat down beside her.

"You really *are* amazing," he said to her. "You've stunned me with your bravery." He reached up and brushed her dark hair back from her face and tucked it behind her ear. The touch sent ripples of sweet fire across her skin. "It can't be easy. Starting over. And really, that's what you've done, isn't it? Start over."

"I guess it is."

"So, what now?" he asked.

"What do you mean?"

"Well, I get the feeling your're expecting me to disappoint you right about now. Get a fake phone call or have some kind of emergency so I can bail on you."

"You don't want to do that?" The words quivered on her tongue but the way he was talking to her, he made her fears about him doing just that sound silly.

"I guess what I'm asking is, how ready are you for this? Me? I'm all in. I'd like to see you again, but I don't want you to be uncomfortable with me. It's your choice. What do you want to do?"

She shook her head and laughed a little at herself. "I was so nervous... I don't even remember how to do this whole dating thing. I got married at eighteen and that feels like a hundred years ago." She was rambling now, completely mortified, but he only smiled at her. There was nothing seductive in it, just gentleness undoing her resistance and putting her at ease. "But I haven't hated tonight...I daresay I may have even enjoyed it."

"You're doing well. You have nothing to be ashamed

of. If anything, I envy you to have known love. Not everyone has. Hell, some people even fear it." His gaze turned distant for a moment, then he took a drink and his eyes brightened. "I have an idea. Stay here." He rose from the couch.

"What? Where are you going?"

He smiled at her, sensing the concern in her voice. "Don't worry. I'm coming back," he promised as though he could sense her fear of him walking away now after she'd just bared part of her soul.

Veronica stayed on the comfortable leather couch, her heart racing as she hoped—no, *prayed*—he would actually come back.

4

Thad stopped at the Vol. 39 bartop and caught one of the bartender's attention.

"Hey, Maya," he greeted the beautiful, dark-skinned woman behind the bar. Maya was a true mixologist expert and a good friend. Thad had asked her to make two old fashioned drinks with the lightest of alcohol. He didn't want Veronica to feel uncomfortable. Maya had given him a questioning look, since he normally only came here with Jared and Angelo, but she hadn't pried.

Now her cinnamon brown eyes sparkled. "Thad... Don't tell me you need refills already? Or has your date run off on you?"

"She's still here. Could I have two bottles of water and the chat pack?"

Maya rolled her eyes as she got him the bottles and then retrieved a small plastic card shaped case.

"You're going to have a real conversation with a woman, Mr. Gentleman of the Year?"

He flashed Maya his most dangerously charming smile. "I'm going to try." She waved the dishrag at him, shooing him off.

Veronica visibly relaxed as Thad returned to the private lounge and sat back down beside her.

He handed her a bottle. "I thought you might want some water." After setting down his own water, he opened the chat pack.

She leaned toward him, curious. "What's that?" He caught a waft of her scent, a light floral blend, possibly just her shampoo. Whatever it was, he liked it. Not too heavy or expensive.

He cleared his throat. "This is a chat pack. There are a hundred questions in here we can ask each other. We can have fun while we get to know one another." He'd never used a chat pack on a date before, but he liked to come here, get passably drunk with his friends sometimes and ask each other questions. It could get really entertaining once you were buzzed.

"Okay, that could be fun." Veronica relaxed even more. "So, how does it work?"

Thad opened the pack and pulled out the first card. He leaned back and stretched an arm lazily behind her shoulders. Not touching her, but close.

He read the first question. "If you could have any object or place in the world completely to yourself for one day, what would you choose and why?"

Veronica bit her bottom lip. Such an innocent thing, but Thad had to force back all the carnal thoughts her movement had provided about those sweet lips of hers.

"The Louvre basement," she finally said.

"Intriguing... Why the basement?"

Veronica gave a cunning little smile that heated his blood. "Because the best stuff is always *hidden*. You know they have to have all the most interesting, mysterious pieces tucked away in the basement and it's rumored to be huge down there, like several levels." She finished her old fashioned cocktail. "What about you?"

"That's easy, I'd choose an object rather than a place." He swirled his almost empty glass. "I am 95% sure that the US military has been working on an Iron Man suit."

"By Iron Man suit you mean..."

"Like the superhero," he clarified.

Her nose wrinkled adorably. "Why would you want that?"

"To fly," he said simply. "To be that free but have control... It would be incredible."

"Yeah," she agreed. "I guess it would. To be able to just fly away from everything. Like a modern day Icarus. Only..." she grew quiet. "My turn?" she said suddenly.

Thad wondered what she dreamed of flying away

from, and why she stopped herself short with her thoughts about it. But now was not the time to ask. He wanted her to trust him, to be herself. The harder questions could come later.

He passed her the chat pack. She plucked out the next card out and read it.

"You've been given the chance to travel into the future to see how the world will change over the next fifty years. What change are you most interested in?"

"That's easy... Flying cars. No wait, space travel, like a colony ship or a colony on Mars," he amended. "That was too easy. You?"

"Medicine," she said more quietly. "Trauma medicine in particular." The spark in her eyes had dimmed. She was thinking of her husband.

"You mind if I ask how he died?" Thad asked. His desire to know wasn't from some morbid fascination; he wanted to better understand her and how this night was affecting her. He was also worried about saying the wrong thing without meaning to. This whole date started as a fun bet with Jared, but now that he'd gotten her talking, he was truly enjoying himself. This was definitely not like his usual dates. They would have skipped the water and gone straight to a hotel room. And yes, he wanted Veronica flat on a bed beneath him, but he also wanted other things, like to know what went on behind those eyes of hers when they turned a stormy blue.

She drew in a shaky breath. "It was a car accident.

He was coming home on his motorcycle and it was raining. A car hydroplaned and hit him." The haunted look on her face cut him deeper than he expected.

"I'm sorry. I shouldn't have asked."

"No, it's not that. I just... I tend to overthink things when it comes to sharing that part of my life, if that make sense."

"Overanalyzing every little nuance searching for hidden meaning? Yeah, I get it."

"I'm really making this night fun, aren't I?" Her question held a note of bitter, self-directed sarcasm.

Thad caught her chin when she tried to look away. "Hey, relax. You are making this night *real.* I asked *you* out, remember? I want to know you, even the sad parts."

It wasn't just a line. He actually meant it, which shocked him. Even as her pain hurt him, her genuine soul held him captivated. If Jared never made that bet at the Chi-Bean, Veronica would have been just another person in the crowd. A flare of self-loathing Thad had never experienced before suddenly reared its ugly head. He really could be a self-absorbed asshole.

"Let's do another one. Pick a fun one." She smiled and blinked her long dark lashes, trying to hide the hint of sorrow that glimmered there.

Thad brushed his thumb over her bottom lip and held his breath as her beautiful eyes darkened, but he didn't do what he normally would. No stolen kisses this time. He turned back to the chat pack and picked up a new card.

"Okay, last one. Thinking back to all the great TV series finales that you have seen over the years, which do you believe had the best final episode?"

"Oh gosh, you go first," she said.

"Hmmm... TV series finales. I think I'd say the TV movie that finished the show *Timeless*, that time-traveling adventure show."

"Oh, I loved that show." Veronica was smiling again. "The finale was excellent. Everyone got their happy ending."

"What about you?"

She sipped her water bottle and shifted closer to him. It was just an inch, but it made Thad want to cuddle her close.

"I guess I pick *Buffy the Vampire Slayer*. Have you ever watched that?"

"I've seen a few seasons," he admitted. "How does it end?"

"So, you remember Buffy was the chosen slayer, the one woman in all the world with the power to deflect evil. But there can only be one slayer, so when Buffy dies, a new girl would inherit her powers."

"Right..." He vaguely remembered that.

"So at the very end, Buffy and the gang find a way to release her powers to every girl, even the ones not yet born but are destined to be the next slayers.

Suddenly they all have their powers. There is the most amazing montage where you see girls of all ages being turned into bad ass versions of themselves. They conquer their fears, stand up for themselves and others, and become the heroes they were meant to be. It's a beautiful message for all women about confidence and self-empowerment." A fresh blush tinged her cheeks. "Guess that sounds a little silly when I say it out loud."

"Not at all," he said quite seriously. "Female empowerment is the opposite of silly."

"You think so?"

"I was raised by one of the best heart surgeons in the country. The things she's done, the accomplishments, not to mention the lives she saved..."

"Your mom?"

He nodded.

"What about your father?"

"A former investment banker. He works in real estate with me now."

"You work with your father? That must be fun..." She smiled a little. "Or maybe tough."

"Mostly fun," Thad smiled fondly. "He's not nearly as fierce as I am."

"You're fierce?" Veronica was watching him with an amused expression.

"Oh yes," he waggled his eyebrows. "I'm a beast in the boardroom. You should hear me roar!" He mimed the swiping of a clawed paw at her and she laughed. The sound, so sweet and honest, hit him behind the knees.

She gave a playful smirk. "The beast of the board-room, huh? So what do you do during the average board-room safari, Mr. Beast?"

"Mostly negotiate tough deals on properties I want to buy. My father is the man who comes prepared with all the research, but he doesn't like the negotiation stage. That's where I come in. We work well as a team."

"That sounds nice." Veronica's gaze drifted to the art around the room. Then she suddenly gasped as she saw the clock.

Thad inwardly cursed. "We have to go, don't we?"

"Yes," She sounded hesitant and disappointed. "I'm sorry..."

"Or... We could stay longer. You won't turn into a pumpkin after midnight, will you?"

"No," she laughed again. "But sometimes it feels like I might. I really have to go home."

"Okay, no problem. Let me return the chat pack to the bar and I'll get Simon to pick us up." He collected the cards and returned the set to Maya.

"Well? Did it work magic?" Maya asked.

"Actually, it did." He'd gotten Veronica to open up in a way that felt like more of a victory than any of his other dates had.

"Glad to hear it. Have a good night, Romeo." Maya

blew him a kiss and he winked at her before he joined Veronica by the elevators.

"So, was tonight okay? Be honest." He put his hand on the small of her back as they stepped into the elevator. It might have been premature, but the need to touch her in some small way was overwhelming.

"It was great... Better than I expected." Her face reddened at the admission.

"And what did you expect exactly?" He reluctantly let go of her back, knowing it would be too much too soon if he continued to touch her.

"You'll probably laugh."

"Maybe, but not at you."

"You struck me as a clubbing kind of guy. But not the dance floor type. More like, all private VIP lounge with big bass music, champagne, and limos."

This time he was the one who blushed. He rubbed the back of his neck and glanced away, but she noticed.

"Oh my God. You *are* that guy, aren't you?"

"Yeah, usually. But not this time."

"So why not take me to a club for drinks?"

"You know how loud those places are? Hard to have a real conversation there. Besides, you're different." He kicked himself because of the way she reacted to that. "I mean that as a good thing." She still didn't look convinced.

The elevator door opened, and they passed through the lobby. A bellhop waved down Simon, who was ready to take them home. They were both quiet as his car stopped in front of the Chi-Bean. He wanted to say a dozen things to her, but he felt awkward as hell after she'd pegged him for being the kind of guy to take a date to a VIP club room. He'd wanted a different experience, and he'd gotten it, but he wasn't sure he'd actually given her a fun night or if she was just ready to get home and put the whole experience behind her. Veronica was excellent at sending mixed signals.

"Are you okay to get home from here?" Thad asked.

"Yeah. I need to close up with Zelda." She got out of the car and Thad instructed his driver to wait for him. He got out and followed her to the coffee shop.

"Assuming I didn't somehow scare you off, can I take you out again?" Thad wanted to touch her again, to pull her into his arms and kiss away the tiny lines of worry creasing her brow. She pulled at something inside of him that wanted to protect her, to care for her. He'd always been a gentleman for women, always respectful and protective, but Veronica was different. She seemed to exist on another level for him in a way no any other woman he'd dated ever had.

She played with the set of keys she'd retrieved from her purse and bit her bottom lip. "You really want to see me again?"

"Yes. Very much so." Her puzzlement bothered him. She didn't think he would want to?

"Why?"

Thad heard a plethora of questions in that single word.

This time he couldn't resist. He cupped her chin and their gazes locked. "Because you're real, and I need some reality in my life." He leaned in, closing the distance between them and he pressed his lips to her forehead before he stepped away. She released a small exhale that he felt deep within him as if he'd released the same breath.

She lifted her gaze to his, and those blue eyes of hers burned through him so sweetly. "Okay."

He smiled. "Great. How about after open mic night next Thursday?"

"I think I can do that."

"It's a date. Have a great night, Veronica." He couldn't resist caressing her name on his tongue. He liked it far too much. She reminded him of Veronica from the Archie comics, a gorgeous figure with long glossy black hair, except without Veronica's brazen attitude. She was sweet and shy, way more of a Betty if he had to compare her to comic characters. What would she be like when he got her out of her shell? She would kill him, that's what. Kill him with her sweetness.

"Good night, Thad." She bit her lip again, but this time he saw it was to hide a smile as she slipped inside the coffee shop. He watched her a second longer before he slipped his hands into his coat pockets and walked back to his car.

❄

"OKAY, SPILL IT. TELL ME EVERYTHING THAT happened!" Zelda squealed. She practically pounced on Veronica when she stepped behind the counter.

"We had drinks at Vol. 39 bar at the Kimpton hotel." Veronica said, texting Katie to let her know she was back and would be upstairs shortly.

"Oh! I've heard about that bar. Classy and swanky." Zelda nodded and continued to follow her around as she finished tidying up the chairs around the tables. "So, what else happened?"

"We just had drinks and talked."

Zelda's smile wilted. "That's it?"

"That's it. I'm a very boring person," Veronica said, half-joking.

"No, you're not. A single mom who runs her business in the city? You're incredible."

"You're sweet to say that."

Zelda frowned. "Come on. You're only twenty-four, Veronica. That's only four years older than me and you're a real adult. I feel like I haven't done anything compared to you."

"You have. It's called college, Zelda. You're doing exactly what you should."

"Tell that to my student loans. A business degree wasn't as lucrative as I was led to believe." Zelda's eyes narrowed. "And he kissed you... I totally saw that."

Veronica wiped the counter where a pile of sugar cubes had spilled.

"It was just a little one and not even on the lips."

"Did you want him to plant one on you all *Gone with the Wind* style, sweeping you away in his arms?" Zelda asked, her eyes going all dreamy.

"Maybe. I don't know." Veronica wasn't ready for that. But she couldn't deny she'd wanted more. When he'd leaned in, her world had blurred at the edges, and for the first time in four years, she'd wanted to be kissed by someone other than Parker. She'd had so many dreams over the years about her husband, but with time they'd faded, and her carnal hungers had faded with them. She'd let the role of mother and businesswoman take over. Those responsibilities had given her a reason to keep going. But her desires and sexuality? Those had shut down and she didn't think they would ever come back, until tonight.

Thad had managed to reach the most feminine part of her. Veronica had wanted so many things in the moment his lips touched her forehead, but he'd sensed she wasn't ready. Yet that short caress had given her a promise of things to come.

"It's okay to want things, you know." Zelda reached out and stopped Veronica's hand from scrubbing the counter.

"I know. I'm just not used to wanting things."

"Are you going to see him again?"

"Yes, after next week's open mic night."

"Do you think he will come and sing again? You should ask him to. His voice just *slayed* me." Zelda clutched her hands to her chest and batted her lashes wildly until Veronica laughed.

"I can ask. He's some hotshot real estate guy, so he probably doesn't have a ton of time though."

"Just text him," Zelda said.

"Won't that make me look desperate."

"Definitely not. It just shows you're interested in him and you love his voice."

"Fine," Veronica shook her head with a wry chuckle and texted Thad.

Veronica: Hey, are you going to come sing an open mic night?

A moment later he responded. **Thad: you want me to?**

Veronica: You've got a great voice. It really seemed to make the crowd go crazy last time.

Thad: You got it. I'll sing for you.

"What did he say?" Zelda peered over her shoulder and read the text exchange. Her eyes widened. "Oh, damn. That's hot."

"What is?" Veronica asked.

"*I'll sing for you*," Zelda whispered in a deep voice as though she were Thad. "He's totally into you."

"You are reading into this *way* too much."

"I'm not. You'll see." Zelda grinned before she noticed a customer who needed her attention.

Veronica let Zelda close up for the night and headed upstairs to relieve Katie of her babysitting.

"So, how did it go, Mrs. Hannigan?" Katie asked, clearly trying to restrain her eagerness.

"Good. It was really nice."

"Nice as in...?"

"Nice in a good way. He's coming by for open mic night next week. Do you think you could watch Lyra again for an hour?" Veronica set her purse down on the kitchen table and got out some money to pay Katie.

Katie beamed. "Sure! By the way, you really should Google your date."

"What? Why?"

Katie giggled and collected her backpack and purse. "Just do it."

Google Thad? She wondered what Katie had found, but Veronica had to check on Lyra first. As suspected, she found her daughter asleep, so she changed into her pajamas and climbed into her own bed. Just as she pulled up the browser on her phone, it vibrated with a call.

Evil Stepmom showed up on the caller ID. *Annette.*

Dread spiked through Veronica's body as she answered.

"Hello?"

"Veronica, I need you and Lyra to be out of the

apartment and the coffee shop on Sunday from one to five PM."

"Why?" Sundays were her one day off when the shop was closed, and she liked to catch up on laundry and cleaning.

"Someone is interested in buying the building. They want to come by to have a look."

"Buy the house?" The words were like poison upon her lips.

"Yes."

"But you can't sell it. Dad left it to me when he died."

Her stepmother's tone turned acidic. "No, he didn't. He put it in your trust and after he died, I became the sole trustee with full discretionary power. I can sell all of your nonmonetary assets if I wish."

The money from any sale would go right back into the trust, of course, but that trust wasn't going to terminate until Veronica was thirty, a condition her stepmother had convinced her father was necessary since Veronica had been so irresponsible as to run off and get married at eighteen. Any money disbursed from the trust each month was very small, since, like Annette said, she had all the power.

"Annette, please." She tried not to get hysterical. "I put three years of my life into the Chi-Bean. I can't just pick up and move and still have a viable business. And this place is my *home*. It's Lyra's home too."

"Your father was too soft, letting you use the house to live in and to make that stupid coffee shop. He didn't even charge you rent."

"Because he knew I was building up my business and he was trying to support me. What do you think he would want?"

Annette snorted. "He was always too easy on you. You got away with everything. When you ran off and got married after high school, he finally saw what a mess you'd made of your life. Putting me in control before he died was the smartest thing he ever did. I keep you from squandering *his* money away."

Pain knifed Veronica's chest. She'd run away with Parker because she couldn't stand to live another minute in a house with a woman who despised her and the father who was blind to his wife's cruelty. That huge chunk of money her father left her wasn't really accessible either. Annette was supposed to pay her a decent amount of money to live on every month. But Annette, with her sole discretion, had the power to pay only a tiny amount because Veronica had the Chi-Bean income to live on. The income wasn't much, but it was enough to satisfy the trust rules.

"Annette, I'm begging you. Please don't sell the building. *Please*... Lyra and I will have to start over and—"

"That is not my problem. Be out on Sunday or you'll regret it."

Annette hung up before Veronica could say another word. The phone dropped to her lap and she stared numbly at the row of photos on the dresser.

If Annette sold this place, Veronica and Lyra would be out in the cold. Literally. She'd put all of her savings into making this place a home for her daughter. She couldn't afford a decent down payment on another place this size, not even a quarter the size. What would Lyra think if they had to leave? It would break her heart.

Veronica's vision blurred and before she knew it, she was crying. This house was her world. It was where she'd grown up and where she wanted Lyra to grow up. And it was one more thing that Annette would take away from her.

Lyra's small head peered into the doorway. "Mommy?"

"Yes, baby?" Veronica wipes at her eyes, trying to hide her tears.

"Can I sleep with you? I had a bad dream."

Veronica looked at the phone on her lap. "You and me both, baby." Lyra was usually good about sleeping in her own bed, but sometimes a child just needed to be with their mother. "Come on." Veronica threw back the covers and her daughter rushed to climb in. "What did you dream about?"

"Jellybean monsters. They were trying to eat me." Lyra's eyes were wide with fear.

"Jellybean monsters? That's easy. Why don't you eat

them!" Veronica said and tickled Lyra stomach. Within seconds her daughter was giggling and squirming on the bed.

"Do you feel better?"

"Yes." With a sleepy yawn, she burrowed beneath the blankets. Veronica watched her fall sleep, knowing sleep wouldn't come so easily for herself. What was she going to do if Annette's interested buyer made an offer on the house?

5

Thad looked up from his phone as someone opened the brownstone's front door. He stood just outside the coffee shop, which was dark inside since it was closed on Sundays. He'd been standing outside for a few minutes, leaning on the side of his car while he and Simon waited. The lack of activity in the Chi-bean had bothered him. He realized with no small amount of bemusement that he missed seeing Veronica at the counter, her hair pulled back in a ponytail as she worked the espresso machine.

"Mr. Worthington?"

A middled aged woman with blonde haired and an eager to please smile waved him toward the door.

"Mrs. Becker?" he asked.

"Yes. It's so nice to meet you." She clearly thought she hid her icy demeanor, but Thad was good at reading people. Her practiced smile failed to hide the greed in her eyes. He could tell exactly what type of woman she was—one he wanted to be careful around.

"Thank you for being flexible about the time. I wanted to make sure the tenants weren't underfoot."

They moved through the first floor to a door which Mrs. Becker unlocked, revealing a staircase that led to the floor above the Chi-Bean. "Are they on a month-to-month lease with you?"

"Yes, they had an understanding with my late husband, but I've wanted to sell this house for a while now."

"And the coffee house? What agreement do you have with the owner?" They reached the top of the stairs and Thad's heart raced with excitement. The second floor was *perfect*. A cozy living room opened to a large kitchen with clean white colors and quartz countertops that looked like they were inlaid with diamond dust.

"The same arrangement. I assume you'll close the shop and renovate back to a full residence?"

"That would be my plan." Thad noticed a tiny pair of bright blue shoes doused with glitter, half-hidden under the brown leather couch facing the TV. A family clearly lived here, but the walls were strangely devoid of photos. He would need to give them time to find a new place before he closed on the sale, but it wasn't like he was in a rush.

Mrs. Becker showed him the master bedroom and a

second bedroom which had a child's bed. Two more bedrooms were done up as guestrooms, an office with a large bay window that faced the street, a laundry room, and two bathrooms, one off the master bedroom and one off the guestrooms.

"Well, what do you think?" Mrs. Becker asked.

It was perfect but she didn't need to know that. Mrs. Becker struck him as someone who would try to screw him in a deal if she could get away with it. He slid his hands into his trouser pockets and let his gaze run around the room, examining the crown molding as he considered how to play this. A hint of something shiny on the kitchen counter caught his eye...was that more glitter? Mrs. Becker had been thorough in staging the apartment for his visit but had missed that spot.

"Not bad. Solid construction, though a less than ideal location. I'll have my office draft an offer and send it to you by the end of next week."

"Great. Let me show you out." There was a flash of triumph in her eyes, but something about it was strange. Something about her forced smile bothered him. He didn't think it had to do with him, however. She acted as though she'd scored some unseen victory. He could put it up to the fact that she was confident he would make an offer, but there was a smugness to her that put him on edge. He wondered if there was something wrong with the building, that perhaps she was trying to offload a money pit. Or the tenants were problematic.

Whatever it was, he and Jared would get to the bottom of it.

They were just leaving the Chi-Bean when Mrs. Becker flashed him an ingratiating smile. "I read your article in GQ, Mr. Worthington."

"Oh?" He was beginning to hate that article. The only woman who hadn't seemed to have read it was Veronica.

"Yes, it's an honor to meet GQ's Gentleman of the Year."

"Thank you." He wasn't sure what else he should say to that and he frankly didn't like this woman complimenting him. It reminded him of something his father used to say. *"Never let the devil shake your hand."*

He decided he would have Jared acquire a copy of the lease agreements for the coffee house and the residential floor this week. He would also schedule time for an inspection of the building from floor to basement, just to make sure nothing was amiss before he made an offer.

Mrs. Becker passed him a business card. "Here's my card. Email your offer to this email address."

"Thank you. I'll be in touch." He pocketed it and walked away. But as he waved his driver over, he had the urge to text Veronica. She'd been on his mind for the last couple of days, and despite agreeing to see him again, she hadn't texted him since. It wasn't what he expected, but Veronica had her own life, was the manager of the coffee house and it seemed like she had very little time for dating. That stopped him short for a moment. If he ended up buying the place, he'd likely close the Chi-Bean. Would Veronica be okay finding another job? She seemed to like it, but it also seemed to be stressful to manage it. He could easily help her find work at one of his many properties if she was interested. He needed to see her again.

Thad: Are you free today?

He sent off the text as Simon pulled up next to him. A mountain of work was calling his name at the office and he couldn't put it off any longer, but maybe he could see Veronica tonight for date number two. He knew was she wasn't counting but he was, and it wasn't simply to get to date fifteen anymore. There was something about Veronica that drove him forward. He needed to make her smile, needed to kiss her, to hold her in the dark and show her that life could bring her joy again.

"OKAY, SPILL IT GIRL. WHAT'S GOING ON WITH YOU?"

Veronica was staring at her phone, specifically at Thad's text, when her friend Michelle Dalton spoke up. They were sitting on a park bench while their kids played on the jungle gym. Michelle's boy Sam was chasing Lyra, roaring like he was a dinosaur.

"Nothing's going on. Why?" Veronica watched Lyra

hide behind a piece of play equipment to avoid Sam, her face beaming as she tried not to laugh.

"You are, without a doubt, the world's worst liar, Ronnie. It's all over your face. Is it the evil stepmom again?"

"Got it in one. Annette's trying to sell my home." She sighed as a wave of depression crashed into her all over again.

"Can she do that?"

"Apparently, she can. I can't afford to buy the house from her, and she has control of the trust that my father left me, that the house is part of."

"What a bitc—" Michelle cut herself off as the kids ran past them, both laughing. Sam was charging with his hands curled into claws as he acted like a Tyrannosaurus Rex.

"Be so glad you have a girl," Michelle muttered. "Boys are all monsters and mystery stains. I've watched the Jurassic Park movies so many times I can quote them all by heart. I would kill to have a little princess like Lyra."

Veronica pulled Lyra to her, hugging her. "Girls are pretty sweet." Lyra was the best kid a woman could ask for. Even on her worst days, Lyra was still wonderful.

"So, Queen Bee has her stinger out, but that doesn't explain why your face went red when you looked at your phone just now."

Veronica glanced back at her phone. She wasn't sure

what to tell Thad. She really couldn't see him today... She didn't want to bother Katie on the weekend, and she didn't want Lyra meeting Thad yet. Lyra might get her hopes up about a new dad and she would probably scare him off. Thad did not seem like the kind of guy who wanted kids. It was one more reminder that they were not well-suited.

Her phone was suddenly pulled from her hand. Michelle's eyes widened. "Well, well. Who is Thad? Please tell me you are getting some."

"Getting what?" Sam asked his mother, who was busy keeping the phone out of Veronica's reach.

"Groceries, she needs to get some. Like eggplants and peaches," Michelle explained. Her son quickly lost interest in the adult conversation and went back to chasing Lyra around the jungle gym.

Veronica finally managed to snatch the phone back. "Eggplants and peaches?"

"I was speaking in emoji. So, who is Thad?"

Veronica was about to give a vague answer but a massive digital billboard across the street from the park suddenly changed to a new picture and her jaw dropped.

"*Him...*" Michelle turned to look at the billboard and gasped.

"No effing way..." Michelle whispered and turned back to face her. "You know who that is, right?"

Veronica was still taking in the huge advertisement for *GQ* and the black-and-white photo of Thad leaning back in a chair, feet propped up on the corner of his desk. He wore a black sweater and gray trousers, the picture of a perfect man: handsome, sexy, everything a woman wanted.

"He's just a guy I met at the Chi-Bean... What is he doing there?" She felt stupid asking.

"That is *GQ*'s Gentleman of Year. It's like *People*'s Sexiest Man of the Year, only better. You have been working way too hard if you've missed that announcement, honey." Michelle's eyes widened as she seemed to realize Veronica wasn't joking. "Wait, you are *actually* going out with Thad Worthington?"

"Yeah... We just had drinks, that's all." Veronica was pretty sure drinks didn't qualify as going out, though. One date was just that, one date.

"And he's texting you... He wants to see you again."

"Yeah... But I don't... I can't... I already told him about Parker, I don't know if he could handle a second big shock when he finds out I have a kid so—"

"We can take Lyra in for dinner tonight. Steve and I were going to order pizza and binge Netflix with Sam. Lyra can join us. Come get her after your date."

"Oh, I couldn't—"

Michelle fixed her with a look. "You can and you will. If anyone deserves a date with the gentleman of the year, it's you."

Hope began to fill her. "You really wouldn't mind?"

"Not at all. Sam adores Lyra." Michelle nodded

toward the kids. Lyra was burying Sam up to his neck in sand, which was cold and wet at this time of the year, but was still grinning happily.

"See? She'll be fine. So text Mr. GQ right now."

Veronica texted Thad back, a silly grin on her face. Was she really doing this?

Veronica: I could be free tonight for a few hours.

She waited for his response, her heart pounding when the three dots appeared in the text thread.

Thad: Dinner okay? Angelo owes me a favor.

Veronica: Sure that would be great. We can meet outside the Chi-Bean, if that works for you.

Thad: It does. Pick you up at seven? Italian okay?

Veronica: Yes and yes.

Thad: See you tonight.

"Well?" Michelle asked.

Veronica bit her lip and nodded, still trying to wipe the silly grin off her face.

"Thank God. Now, if you get a chance, sleep with him. I need to know one of us is getting laid tonight," Michelle said.

"You and Steve aren't...?"

"No way. You see that little monster?" Michelle's tone was full of frustrated love. "We're lucky to get five minutes to go to the bathroom without him rocketing through the room. Sex is now merely a myth in our house."

"Michelle, let me babysit Sam next weekend on Sunday night. You can have your own date night."

Her friend raised a brow. "If you're teasing me..."

"I'm not!" Veronica laughed. "Seriously. It's the least I can do."

"Deal." Michelle grinned. "Let's get you home for your hot date."

Veronica glanced back at the billboard, which had changed back to Thad sitting in his office chair. She used to be part of that world. No, that wasn't true. She was raised in it, but never really part of it. If she had been, she would never have run off and married Parker to get away.

Annette had taken so much from her. She had wanted to like her new mother, but from the start, only poisoned apples had fallen from that tree, and Veronica knew better than to take a bite.

TWO HOURS LATER, VERONICA PUT HER HOME BACK TO rights. Annette had done a masterful job of turning their slightly chaotic home into a home that looked like it belonged in a catalog. All the family photos had been shoved into a black trash bag and pushed into a closet, which pretty much summed up Annette's view of her family.

Veronica had retrieved the sack and put the photos back one by one on the walls and the dresser. Lyra was with Michelle for the next few hours, which gave Veronica time to shower and do her hair and makeup. She couldn't do much with what she had on hand, but she looked a little better with mascara and lip gloss.

She put on a pair of jeans and a light cream sweater with a pair of her cutest gray suede boots. When she'd asked Thad about the dress code, she'd been told to just be herself. That was a huge relief. It wasn't that she didn't like to dress up now and then, but ever since she found out Thad was such a big deal, she worried about dating a guy who most likely went to black-tie affairs, which was not something she could do. Her life was not suited to private jets, trips to Paris, or galas at the Met, not anymore.

Her life was crayons, mac and cheese, glitter shoes, and princess costumes. She didn't have any regrets, not when it came to marrying Parker, striking out on her own, or having Lyra. Even if she admitted that she sometimes, *briefly*, missed that glittering world, she couldn't just drop everything and go back to it. It made her wonder if that was what Thad meant when he'd said she was real. That he'd wanted to see her because she was different, because she wasn't from his world, but dwelt in this more normal realm.

She supposed she should take offense and see that maybe he was just coming down from his proverbial Mount Olympus to hang out with a mere mortal, but at the same time...she didn't think so. The way he acted, there was a deeper interest in her than simply to kill time and amuse himself, which is what made her give him a second date.

Veronica stepped outside of the Chi-Bean ten minutes before seven and saw Thad's private car pull up. Thad got out of the back and opened the door for her.

"You look amazing," he said with his gentle smile that always surprised her. There was something magical about a gorgeous man smiling at her, but when that smile was this soft and his eyes were all bedroom-y, it was irresistible. Veronica trembled as she climbed into the car with him.

He sat close to her, his leg innocently touching hers. There was never a touch more designed to remind a woman of sex than her leg pressed against a man's. Every time she was near Thad, she expected him to whip away the mask of his gentle, seductive sexuality and show her a greedy, ambitious man beneath. But he never did.

"I'm glad you could meet me," he confessed with a bashful smile.

"Me too," she said.

Veronica knew she was developing feelings for him. As Lyra would say, she was straying dangerously into the "you *like* like him" stage. It was terrifying to admit that her heart might be opening, but she wanted to feel like a woman again, to feel beautiful and desirable. It would most likely come to an end when she worked up the courage to tell him about Lyra, but until then, she could pretend this was real and enjoy it while it lasted.

"So, where are we going?" she asked.

"You remember me telling you about my friends from prep school? Jared and Angelo?" He reached over and gently threaded his fingers through hers. That simple touch, his hand holding hers, created a slow wave of heat. It brought back memories of her and Parker, but the flash of pain she'd expected wasn't nearly as strong, nor did she compare this moment with those first few dates with Parker. This was more complicated than that. It was as though her body was finally remembering how to be a woman who was attracted to a man. It didn't matter what man. It also didn't feel like she was betraying Parker either. It felt like maybe she was finally moving on.

"Angelo runs a restaurant called the Italian Village. He's got a private room where we can talk and have the best service."

She couldn't help but smile. "I knew you were *that* guy."

Thad laughed, the rich sound rumbling through her in the best way. "I am a private room kind of guy. I won't deny it."

"With money and privilege comes certain perks, huh?"

She froze inside. What made her say that? Was she trying to sabotage this night?

Much to her relief, Thad only smiled. "In this case, I prefer to think of it as friends helping out friends, honey."

Honey. How could he make that word sound so sweet, almost wondrously, embarrassingly so…? And if Veronica was being honest, she could listen to him say that all day.

"Angelo is an Italian cook?"

"He's an Italian who cooks the best Italian dishes." Thad's praise held such loyal affection that Veronica couldn't help but love Angelo too, even though she hadn't met him yet.

She managed to relax by the time Simon dropped them off at the restaurant. She had lived in Chicago all of her life but had never been here, only knew it by reputation. They passed by the massive line that trailed out the restaurant's doors and stretched nearly half a block.

Thad wrapped his fingers around hers, leading her to the entrance of the Italian Village. A pre-server met them at the check-in desk.

"Reservation for T.W. The private room," Thad said, his hand still holding onto Veronica's.

The server smiled. "Of course! Right this way." She collected two black leather-bound menus and escorted them to the private room.

Veronica took in the walls, which were painted to resemble an Italian countryside dotted with villas. Tiny glowing lights were embedded in the wall to give the impression that the distant villas had lamps lit in their painted windows. The effect was magical. She and Thad sat down facing each other in a cozy curved booth as the server passed them their menus and told them someone would be in to take their order soon.

"Wow," Veronica said in a hushed voice, even though they were alone in the private room.

"Quite the thing, isn't it? I've been to some of the best restaurants in the world, but this place... it feels like home." Thad's smile was more open than it had been before. He didn't bother with his menu but simply sat back and watched her intently while she tried to decide what to order. But his gaze kept driving her to look at him.

"You're staring, Mr. Worthington," she said softly.

"Does it bother you?" he asked.

It did, just not in a bad way. Veronica was too embarrassed to admit it. "So, you already know what you're getting?"

He answered with a nod. "What about you?"

"There's almost too many choices," Veronica mused, her gaze leaping from one menu item to the next.

"Whatever you do, pick something Italian or Angelo will lecture me."

"Okay..." She skipped to the pasta section and

decided she would get a carbonara. When she closed her menu, the door opened and a tall, dark-haired, olive-skinned Adonis walked in.

"Thad." The words rumbled from his lips in greeting and he flashed them both a dazzling smile. Thad stood and hugged the man, slapping his back.

"And who is your enchanting date?" Angelo turned the full force of his natural charm upon Veronica, who could only stutter.

"Veronica—Hannah—Hannigan."

Angelo shared a smile with Thad before taking her hand and kissing her fingertips.

"Now you have a sweet *principessa* too" Angelo teased.

Thad's face darkened with a blush as he sat back down in the booth.

"So, what shall we drink tonight?" Angelo asked, not even bothering with a notepad.

"Veronica?" Thad looked at her expectantly.

"Whatever you're having will be fine." She'd seen the prices on the wine list and didn't want to be an expensive date. Actually, that was impossible, but at least it took the pressure off her.

"Two glasses of your best red," Thad ordered. "And I'll have the spaghetti and hotdogs."

Angelo rolled his eyes. Veronica frowned. That was on the menu?

"Thad, I swear upon my grandmother's grave, one of these days I will give you *exactly* what you ask for."

"Sorry, what's going on?" Veronica asked.

"He means spaghetti and meatballs. Of all the things I cook, he orders the same thing every time. And he calls it that every time." He confided this in a loud whisper to Veronica and she couldn't help but giggle.

"Every time?"

"Every time," Angelo confirmed with a chuckle.

"Okay, you have to explain the hotdog thing."

The two men shared an amused look and Thad sighed as if acquiescing while Angelo leaned against the side of the booth toward Veronica.

"So picture it," Angelo waved his hand in the air as if setting the scene for a film. "We're stuck one weekend in our dormitory at school and we can't leave the grounds because Thad and Jared had gotten us in trouble."

"Naturally, you blame me," Thad laughed.

"Naturally, I do," Angelo continued smoothly. "I'm the angel of the bunch, hence my name. Anyway, we needed to cook dinner and I had enough items in the common room fridge to make spaghetti and meatballs or so I thought. Turns out we just had a pack of hotdogs. This joker over her tells me to use the hotdogs."

"I wasn't serious by the way," Thad cut in.

She was biting her lip not to laugh as she sensed what was coming.

"To make a point, I cooked spaghetti and hotdog balls." Angelo grinned.

"Did it taste...edible?" Veronica asked.

Angelo shrugged and nodded at Thad. "Ask him, he ate two servings."

Thad's face was a little red and he tried to shrug off his embarrassment. "It was pretty good. I was just hungry that night after rugby practice."

"So now he always orders spaghetti and meatballs but says hotdogs just to rile me." Angelo rolled his eyes. "He won't ever try anything else when he comes here."

"It's a classic dish. I don't bother with anything else when I know what I like...and what I want." He looked directly at Veronica.

"And you?" Angelo asked, tugging her out of the spell of Thad's gaze.

"Carbonara?"

"Excellent choice." Angelo said. "I'll have the wine brought in shortly."

As he left, the sound of an accordion being played in the room next to them grew louder, then softened as the door closed.

"So that's Angelo," Veronica said, watching Thad's expression.

He grinned. "In the flesh."

"Why did his family send him to live at the boarding school?"

"He's the oldest in his family and they wanted him to

have time to be himself, to discover who he was outside of his lovable but invasive and boisterous family." Thad grinned. "He was more used to sharing his space than Jared and I were. He was quick to become the peacemaker whenever Jared and I fought."

Veronica shifted uncomfortably at the thought. She'd never had a sibling and never understood that whole dynamic.

He seemed to notice her discomfort. "It wasn't real fighting. Just stupid teenage boy stuff. Boys tend to be territorial, to establish dominance. We were basically a pack of unruly wolves at that age."

"You're lucky you never went to an all-girls school. I did for one year. It was literally the worst. Girls can be way meaner than boys at that age." Veronica wished she could forget that single final year at school, the one that Annette had convinced her father she needed to be sent to. It was one of *many* reasons she'd run away with Parker at eighteen.

"Good point,' he agreed. "Do you have any siblings?"

"No, I'm an only child."

The server interrupted them as she came in and placed their wine glasses on the table. Veronica was glad to have a drink, though she normally didn't drink often. The wine was soft and dark upon her tongue. She tasted a hint of smokiness and black cherry.

"What about your parents?" Thad seemed determined to delve into her life story. Veronica tried to relax, reminding herself that this was all part of the normal dating process. Talking about their pasts was part of the experience.

"My mom died when I was ten. My dad remarried a year later."

"That must've been difficult."

"It was." She released a heavy sigh that had been weighing upon her. "I wanted to like her, my stepmom, I mean. I tried to. My dad deserved to be happy again, but she hated me from the start." Veronica played with the black cloth napkin in her lap.

"Why did she hate you?"

"I don't know. Maybe because I look like her... my mom. It's a damn cliché, you know? Evil stepmom hates her new daughter because she looks like the dead first wife. But it's true." Veronica despised herself when she realized how petty she sounded. This man had a perfect life; he couldn't begin to fathom how horrible Annette had made hers. Yet she didn't want to complain about her past. She just wanted to enjoy tonight.

"I'm sorry. I swear I'm not bitter. It's just..."

"It's personal. You don't have to apologize for that, Veronica. Not with me."

She wanted to believe him, but she had a sinking feeling he wouldn't want to stick around when this all got messy. He was in this for the fun, not the drama. Veronica took a massive gulp of her wine.

Thad reached across the table and captured her

hand. His fingers were long and elegant, his palms large and strong. A surge of heat shot through her body like a wire suddenly alive with electricity. Or maybe it was just the wine.

"Please don't be nervous," he said.

It sounded so simple, yet impossible. The man was every fantasy she'd ever had, and yet she felt shards of guilt about wanting to move on after Parker. She had every right to move on, to fall in love again... She just wasn't sure she could. What if she made a mistake like her father and fell in love with someone who would hurt Lyra the way her stepmother had hurt her?

But Thad made her long to give love a second chance, so much so that it scared her.

"I know I shouldn't be nervous but you're just so..." She didn't dare finish.

Thad shifted closer to her on the circular booth seat, a teasing smile flirting with his lips. "The fame thing isn't really real, you know."

Veronica smiled. That did take some of the pressure off. Then she realized something. "Wait, did you just quote *Notting Hill*?"

Thad smiled almost as wide as Julia Roberts. "Sorry, it's one of my favorite scenes."

"So are you just a boy, standing in front of a girl..." The nervousness came back in full force since there was no way in hell she was finishing that line.

Thad chuckled, no doubt realizing the corner she'd

painted herself into. "Do you know the best way to become less nervous about something?" He was close, so deliciously close.

"What?"

He raised her hand to his lips, offering a courtly kiss on the backs of her fingers. "Repeated exposure." The definition in his upper body could be seen beneath his sweater as he moved slightly in the booth.

"What kind of exposure?" She shouldn't have asked. That was a dangerous question. He leaned in, his nose brushing against her cheek and then her throat.

"This kind..." He didn't kiss her, just nuzzled her, holding her hand in his. Small tremors of arousal began to build inside her, making her head fuzzy. Was it the wine, or was it possible to get drunk on a man?

"Thad..." She whispered his name.

He hummed a soft response, as though he too had been intoxicated by the moment.

"*Kiss me*, before my brain convinces me it's a bad idea."

Thad chuckled. "There is no such thing as a bad idea when it comes to kisses."

He cupped her face, angling her toward him for those last few inches, his mouth brushing against hers, letting her have a heartbeat to change her mind before he kissed her.

✣ 6 ✣

Veronica's world went up in flames, burning her with it. She clung to him, needing a universe of him, of more with him The tiny spark of her feminine desire began to smolder, growing and burning deliciously until it became a roaring fire. In one single kiss, a kiss that had yet to end, Veronica had become a girl of eighteen again, her heart tapping a wild Morse code. Shivers of need, of hunger, of basic primal urges rippled through her as she moved closer to him.

Thad's mouth worked a strange and wondrous magic, making her forget about the world around her, and the harsh realities that warned her against indulging in this fantasy. She simply lived in this moment.

She reached out to touch his face, familiarizing herself with him. The lines of his jaw were hard beneath her exploring fingers. A man's face. Oh, how she'd missed touching one.

In one slow and easy move, he gathered her in his arms and pulled her onto his lap. The sudden intimate position drove her wild, and she curled her arms around his neck. His arms wrapped around her body, holding her close, making her feel safe and yet full of a sexual excitement. She had missed kissing so much. The sweet passion between them built to an uncontrollable need.

After a moment, Thad broke the kiss. His warm breath fanned her face. She gasped for her own breath. Shocked rippled through her as she remembered what she'd asked him to do and how she'd responded.

"Are you okay?" he murmured, still cradling her in his arms. He pressed his forehead to hers, his breath quick and rough. He rubbed a hand over her back, his palm soothing as he touched her. It almost made her burst into tears, to feel that caress of comfort. It had been so long since she'd been touched by a man like that.

"I... I think so." She buried her face in his neck, holding onto him. If she pulled back now, he'd see her, and everything she was desperate to hide would be written across her face. All she wanted was to stay on his lap forever, but fate had other plans. The door to their private room opened and Angelo came in, holding two plates of food. He smiled politely as Veronica slid off Thad's lap and sat back in her seat, making no comment on what he'd seen. She pressed a hand to her reddening face and tried not to look at Thad.

"Dinner is served." Angelo bowed and left, giving them back their privacy. An awkward moment of silence passed.

"So..." Veronica began lamely.

"Why don't you try the carbonara? Let me know if it tastes as good as it looks."

Thad's suggestion was a welcome subject change, letting her neatly off the hook. They wouldn't have to discuss the kiss or how it had been earth-shattering. She twirled her fork into the pasta and tested it. The rich flavors and spices exploded on her tongue.

"Do you want to try some of this?" He wound some of his spaghetti onto his fork. He leaned forward and offered it to her. The intimacy of the moment caught her breath. She was going to politely refuse, but the strains of music on an accordion just outside their room seemed to sweep her away. It was the song from *Lady and the Tramp called* "This is the night" that Lyra loved. Whoever was playing knew the tune perfectly. It didn't sound cheesy, at least not right then.

With the music as her inspiration, Veronica decided she was going to live in the moment. She closed the distance between them and accepted the spaghetti off his fork. His eyes lit up. A flash of primal hunger shot through his gaze as though a current of lightning had passed between them.

"Do...do you want to try mine?" she offered shyly.

"I would love to." Thad's eyes still gleamed, but his soft smile lessened the predatory feel to them. He'd gone from a lion ready to pounce to one lounging in the sun, no less dangerous, but for the moment, content. He accepted a bite of carbonara and grinned. "Now I can tell Angelo I've had something other than spaghetti and meatballs, and you're my witness."

The door to their private room opened again and a rotund man in black pants and a red polo shirt carrying an accordion stepped inside. He grinned at them as he began to play "This is the Night" again on his accordion. Thad and Veronica ate and watched him play. The man leaned close to Thad to whisper loudly.

"That is a beautiful girl." His accent was clearly real Italian, nothing fake about it.

"She certainly is," Thad agreed.

The man nudged Thad's shoulder. "In the old country, we kiss girls like that."

At this Thad blushed and cleared his throat. Veronica was already red-faced from all the teasing. The accordion player began to hum along with his song and Veronica's gaze locked on Thad's. This really was a magical moment. She had forgotten her grief, abandoned her sorrow, and just lived in the moment with Thad tonight.

Tears misted her eyes and she blinked them away. Thad reached for her hand, and just as his fingers caressed hers, the private door opened yet again as Angelo came inside, scowling.

"Uncle Luigi!" Angelo chastised the accordion player. "You should be playing in the main dining room."

Luigi shot Veronica a mischievous smile before he turned to his nephew. "Hey, *everyone* needs music tonight, Angelo."

Angelo gripped his uncle's arm and ushered him toward the door. "Yes, well, these two want their privacy."

"But they haven't shared the meat-a-ball yet—" Luigi's protests were silenced when Angelo closed the door.

Suddenly, Veronica was laughing. The moment had been so unreal, and yet it had happened. Thad tried to hold back his own laughter but soon joined her.

"Angelo really has an Uncle Luigi?" Veronica asked between giggles.

"He does," Thad confirmed.

"Oh, God." She couldn't stop laughing. "My life really *is* a Disney movie."

Thad's laughter was now a deep chuckle. "What do you mean?"

"It's silly... I was just talking to a friend and told her my life was not a Disney movie, but right now? It kind of is." She nodded at the meatball on his plate.

"I hate to disappoint you, but I don't think I can roll the meatball to you with the tip of my nose quite as artfully. You'd just see my face covered in tomato sauce."

Veronica wiped tears from her eyes as *that* mental image hit home.

"I like seeing you happy," Thad's eyes gleamed with a flash of emotion. "It's a lovely sight."

Veronica felt like she was rarely happy anymore. Stressed, busy, worried, panicked, all the things a single mother who ran her own business had in spades. But happy? Aside from Lyra, there wasn't much to make her happy.

"You did this," she admitted.

"I wish I could take credit," Thad said. "I believe you're already full of joy, but things in your life are burying it. Believe me, I've been there. All I want to do is unearth that happiness in whatever way I can." He spoke so honestly it made her tremble with the gentle force of that desire.

"How are you this nice?" she asked before she could think better of it.

"What?"

"Guys like you usually don't act like this. I guess I'm just confused about why you're being so nice to me. There are so many more beautiful women out there, ones with uncomplicated pasts."

"Hey, right now the woman I most desire... I see her right in front of me." The look he gave her left no question as to the truth of that statement. He *wanted* her. "I admit, complicated used to scare me off. I'm man enough to own that. But you make it feel worth exploring."

Veronica nearly blurted out she had a daughter just then, but feared it would ruin this perfect night. No, that particular complication had to be held back for another day.

"Now, do you want dessert?" Thad still held her hand, his fingers playing with hers. "I know the tiramisu here is to die for."

Veronica let out the breath she'd been holding as she fell back into the moment with this beautiful man and this beautiful dream. "Okay."

THAD WATCHED VERONICA LICK HER SPOON CLEAN OF the last bite of the tiramisu. She had relaxed again after he had told her he wasn't afraid of complicated. Until tonight, he would have run from complicated in any form. His business life was complicated enough without adding it to his personal life, too. But there was something about Veronica that made him want to embrace the challenge.

He'd always like to care for women, even the ones who were strong and capable and had no need for any help. Even brave, fearless women deserved support. Jared would have teased him since usually Angelo was the most suited of their trio to play the white knight, but Thad had accepted that role now, at least in regard to Veronica. Not that he would ever tell her. The last thing he wanted was to look like some condescending asshole when, in reality, he cared about her. How that had happened so fast, he had no idea.

"You ready to go?" he asked as Veronica collected her purse.

"Yeah." She slid out of the booth and he helped her into her coat.

"What about the bill?" she suddenly glanced around, clearly looking for it.

"It's taken care of. Angelo has my card on file."

"Oh... I guess that makes sense. You probably take dates here a lot."

Thad smiled at the unspoken question there. "Hey, forget what you think I would do with other women. You are different, *good* different. I tossed out the rule-book with you, okay?"

"Why? I'm not—"

He pressed a finger to her lips. "Every time you say you're not special, I'm going to have to kiss you to prove otherwise."

And he did just that, leaning down and replacing his fingertip with his lips. She opened like a flower to him as he deepened the kiss. Her lips parted and he took advantage, slipping his tongue inside her mouth. Veronica's sweet mouth made him dizzy. He curled an arm around her waist, desperate to hold her close, afraid she might melt away like morning mist if he didn't. Every time he kissed her, it left him with a bittersweet ache in his chest for more.

Her mouth was like velvet and he groaned at the way she pressed against the length of his body. She was short enough that he would have to pick her up and set her on the table to get as close as he wanted... But not now. Not yet. He had to hold back for thirteen more dates. Not because he had any real pride where it came to winning the bet, but because somehow, the more time he spent with her, the more he felt that rushing to the bedroom would jinx things. He wanted to enjoy Veronica, wanted to spend time with her and not have it all be just about sex. Things were going well by playing it safe, so he would keep being the gentleman for as long as he could stand it, even though she was tempting him like hell to be anything but.

He broke their kiss a second time that night, but he could have kissed her all night and never tired of it.

"There, let that be a lesson to you," he teased. Her eyes were still full of secrets, but right now he would take every small victory he could get. "Let's get you home." He texted Simon to have the car out front for them.

When they got in the sleek black sedan, Veronica gave Simon her home address. Thad cuddled her close to him during the drive, enjoying the way she fit against his side. When they reached a nice apartment building, a block from the Chi-Bean, he walked her up to the glass doors of the lobby to make sure she got safely inside.

"Thursday night," he said. "I'll sing for you." *And only you.*

She ducked her head and bit her lip. "See you Thursday." Standing on her tiptoes, she pressed a kiss to his lips, a brief and over-all-too-soon kind of kiss that made him realize waiting four days to see her again wouldn't be easy.

He stayed outside the apartment lobby, watching to make sure she got on the elevator before he returned to his car.

"How was dinner, sir?" Simon asked.

"Good, very good." Thad leaned back in his seat. "Take me home."

Simon smiled and pulled out into traffic. "Yes, sir."

VERONICA STOPPED IN FRONT OF THE DALTON apartment and rang the bell. A moment later, Michelle's husband, Steve, answered the door, roaring like a medieval dragon, complete with a pair of scaling horns attached to a headband on his head. Two small children clung to his legs, giggling wildly. Sam and Lyra smiled up at Veronica.

"Oh, hello Ronnie," Steve said with a laugh while

removing the horns and gently shaking off his tiny leg weights.

"Mommy!" Lyra ran to her and Veronica hoisted her up in her arms.

"Thanks for watching them, Steve."

"Any time. Seriously. Lyra wears Sam out and then Michelle and I can have a few minutes to ourselves without the energizer bunny jumping into our bed to throw dinosaurs at us." Steve stepped back so Veronica could come inside.

"Hey, Veronica! Sam! Get over here and pick up your toys." Michelle nudged Sam toward the stack of spilled toys in the family room. "Half of those are probably Steve's fault," she added.

Veronica shooed Lyra in the same direction. "Go help Sam pick up."

"Well, how was it?" Michelle whispered so the kids wouldn't overhear.

"Great, really great."

"Oh! You'll need this." Michelle retrieved a magazine off the counter. "Read it tonight after Lyra's asleep."

Veronica took the magazine from her and blinked in surprise at the sight of Thad on the cover. *GQ*.

"Trust me. It's a real page-turner."

Steve rolled his eyes. "She didn't read it. She just looked at the pictures. I think she's looking to upgrade."

"Oh hush." Michelle elbowed him. "You know I love you."

He snickered and stole a kiss. "Damn right." He snickered and stole a kiss before heading to help the kids.

"So it really went well?" Michelle asked more seriously.

"Yeah, it was really nice. We had a private dining room all to ourselves."

"And?" Michelle always could read her too well; she knew there was more.

"And we kissed... a couple of times."

"How was it? Tell me his kisses are as amazing as his looks."

Veronica's face heated. "They are." One of these days she would learn how to control her blushing.

"Thank God. If he'd been a bad kisser, it would've been a crime against humanity."

Thad's kisses had been everything she'd been missing for the last four years. Lyra was her world, but she'd be lying if she said nothing was missing in that world. She'd thought she was broken after losing Parker, but tonight had proven something.

I'm not broken. Part of me was simply buried.

Thad had been right. The grief, the pain, the stress, it had all hidden the part of her that needed light, that needed joy. Somehow Thad had given her back some that light, but the amazing part was that it wasn't his light. It was *hers*. She wasn't relying on him to feel alive again; he'd simply reminded her of the freedom to let that part of herself crawl out of the darkness and shine.

"You're seeing him again." It wasn't a question. Michelle was ordering it.

"Thursday." Veronica couldn't stop the sudden grin that spread across her face.

"Good for you." Michelle reached out and grasped her hand. "You deserve this, honey." She tapped the magazine. "You deserve Mr. Gentleman of the Year."

Veronica clutched the magazine to her chest as Lyra came rushing up to them with her backpack slung over her shoulders.

"Okay, sweetie. Time to go." She clasped her daughter's hand and thanked Michelle and Steve again.

She and Lyra caught a cab back home. By the time they got there, Lyra was asleep in the back with her small body pressed against Veronica's side. Veronica leaned down and kissed Lyra's cheek, then got out and carried her daughter inside and up the stairs.

After putting her daughter in her own bed, Veronica got into hers and finally opened the magazine. She flipped through the other articles and advertisements, pretending to care about everything but the article concerning Thad.

She turned to a spread of Thad in a gray suit, his hands in his trouser pockets, and the edge of his coat pulled back in that sexy power pose men in suits always look so hot doing. The words *Modern Prince of Thieves* —

this year's Gentleman of the Year stretched across the top of the spread.

"Prince of thieves?" Veronica muttered. She started to read the article.

It seemed Thad Worthington was Prince of thieves for two reasons: He knew the best ways to steal a deal in business, and he was notorious for his large donations to a different charity every year. The city of Chicago had benefited a lot from his generosity. Taking from the rich and giving to those in need was Thad Worthington's style. Or, at least, how the magazine chose to spin it. He was fierce, he was handsome, he was brilliantly educated, and he was single. A different socialite or model accompanied him to every different society function, but no one seemed to claimed his heart.

The photographs told the story, each more captivating than the last. But it was only one side of him. She'd seen another side of him as he held her, kissed her, and spoke of how he felt when seeing her happy.

For a moment, Veronica let herself believe that maybe, just maybe, she was special after all. And that she had reason to look forward to yet another date with Chicago's most charming prince of thieves.

⁂ 7 ⁂

By Thursday night, Thad was obsessed with seeing Veronica again. He'd texted her, even talked briefly once on the phone to see how she was doing, but it wasn't the same as *seeing* her. He'd had Simon drive by the Chi-Bean twice just so he could get a look at her through the windows. Once, he'd even asked Simon to park so he could watch her. He loved seeing her smile as she worked while talking to customers. It was obvious she enjoyed being involved in their world and he loved seeing that side of her.

"You have it bad," Jared crowed. He and Angelo sat across from Thad in the Vol. 39 bar. As per their tradition, they'd reserved a couple of hours a week, post-dinner, to meet and catch up before resuming their lives.

"It's not like that." The lack of conviction in his denial made his friends hoot with laughter.

"Tell me about the *meat-a-ball*," Jared said. He'd only been given the gist of what happened.

"Well, poor uncle Luigi was there serenading them and using his best fake Italian accent, trying to reenact that scene from the movie *Lady and the Tramp,*" said Angelo. "I rescued them before Luigi could embarrass them even more." He chuckled. "I am sorry, Thad. I didn't know he would barge in there."

"It was fine. We had a good laugh about it. More importantly, Veronica didn't get upset."

"So, that's two dates down in less than a week. You planning on dating her at this breakneck pace to get to number fifteen?" Jared asked.

"No, she has a full work schedule. Being a manager of a coffee shop doesn't pay enough for her to take a lot of breaks. Tonight is their Thursday night open mic night, so it's a little easier for her to sneak away for an hour."

Angelo fixed Thad with a knowing look. "You're going to sing tonight, aren't you?" It wasn't really a question. His friends knew him better than almost anyone.

"I plan to. I sang last week. It was liberating." He could still feel the rush of letting his voice carry through the coffee shop and the quiet hush that followed a second before the applause. It was almost as good as kissing Veronica. *Almost*.

"We've never heard you sing," Angelo added, his gaze pensive now. "You've always avoided it whenever we asked."

"I think I heard him once when I dropped by his place early," said Jared. "He shut right up as soon as I walked in. Said he'd had the radio on."

A prickle of embarrassment mingled with guilt. He wanted to trust them, but he couldn't face their laughter if he wasn't any good. Angelo had heard him singing once too, in the shower back in their dormitory at prep school, but the acoustics in the shower hadn't been good and he'd heard Angelo laughing outside the door. After that, Thad had kept his singing private, too afraid to let anyone *really* hear him.

"I'm not going to start serenading you two just for kicks."

"What if we paid you?" asked Jared.

"The two of you combined don't have enough money to afford me."

"Oh, Jared, I don't think we need money," Angelo pointed out. He shared a look with Jared, which Thad, after years of being friends with them, read easily enough.

"No, *hell* no. You two are not going to show up tonight."

"Will you walk out if we do?" Angelo asked, his eyes glinting with mischief.

"I told Veronica I would sing. I'm not breaking any promises to her. She's been through enough."

"What has she been through?" Angelo asked.

If these two hadn't been his best friends, he wouldn't

have said anything, but he knew he could trust them. Thad shifted forward in his chair. "She's a widow. She got married at eighteen and her husband died when she was twenty."

"Shit," Jared murmured. "That's rough."

"She mentioned losing both her parents. I think the only family she has is a stepmother who makes her life miserable." Thad took a sip of his beer, but the taste didn't soothe him the way it usually did. He couldn't get the thought that some woman out there despised Veronica so deeply out of his head. It made no sense. How could anyone hate her? She was so sweet, so hard working, so undeserving of such treatment.

"Have you met her stepmother?" Angelo asked.

"No. If I had, I would have been tempted to do something."

Jared and Angelo knew what he meant. No one crossed Thad. No one. He could break a person's career if he wanted to. It was a power he used sparingly and respectfully and only on those who really deserved it.

"Open mic night, that's going to make it date number three?" Jared took a sip of his scotch and eyed Thad over the rim of his glass in challenge. Jared wasn't not going to let him get away with any uncounted dates.

"Yes."

"You really are holding up to terms of the bet? No hanky-panky?"

"Hanky, but no panky."

"What's that supposed to mean?"

"Nothing that qualifies as sex." Thad had gotten close at the restaurant on Sunday, but aside from the bet holding him back, Veronica hadn't been ready. She deserved a slow, sweet courtship full of heart-shaped boxes, hundreds of flowers, and private orchestra serenades, not hot sweaty sex on a restaurant table.

Thad checked his watch. "Well, gents, this has been fun, but I've got to go."

"Go on then, *loverboy*." Jared's laughter seemed to follow him as he rushed to call Simon to pick him up.

JARED AND ANGELO GRINNED AS THEY WATCHED THAD bolt from the room in his haste not to be late for Veronica's open mic night.

"So, you've met Veronica?" Jared asked.

Angelo chuckled. "I have. She is just as beautiful as your *principessa*, my friend, and just as sweet, I think." Angelo had liked the look of Veronica Hannigan. She was fresh, lovely, sweet, a real woman in the best way.

"How did you find her?" Angelo asked.

"Honestly? I just glanced around and saw this woman who was totally frustrated and flushed, smacking the hell out of some smoothie machine and I knew she was perfect. The woman clearly had more on her plate and a life of her own. I knew Thad wouldn't find it so easy to sweep in with that devil-may-care grin of his and woo her instantly. She even tried to turn him down when he asked for her number."

Angelo laughed. "She was smacking a smoothie machine?"

"And yelling at a customer service rep who tried to deny her a warranty return."

Angelo's laughter slowly faded. "You think he knows?"

Jared finished his scotch and leaned forward in his chair. "Knows what?"

"That he's falling in love with her?"

Jared's slow smile told Angelo everything.

"That's the beauty of it, right? She's going to completely change his world. I predict by date fifteen, the poor bastard won't know what hit him. Even if he doesn't end up falling madly in love with her, it's shaking him out of his bad habits. He's been playing games with fashionistas and heiresses for so long that he's forgotten what the real world...and what real relationships are like. No matter what, this wakes him up and gets his head in the game for really settling down and being happy"

"But have you thought about her?" Angelo asked. "She's a very young widow and has had a difficult life. You are putting her in a bad position by throwing Thad at her when he might just break her heart."

"Felicity didn't have an easy life either. You remember that tiny apartment she lived in before we got married? She had no hot water, lived in a sketchy part of town, and she walked in on a man robbing her place while she was pregnant with our daughter. I was ready to move heaven and earth to help her," Jared replied with the confidence of a man who'd already won the battle for his wife's heart, but seemed to have forgotten the battle hadn't been so easy.

"You already knew you loved Felicity. But Thad... well, you know he's always been stubborn." Angelo finished his beer and collected his coat from the chair.

Jared sighed. "Time to go already?"

"You don't want to go home to your baby and beautiful wife?" Angelo teased.

The lawyer grinned. "Actually, I'm looking forward to it. What about you? You haven't dated in a while. Maybe I need to make a bet with you, too."

Angelo laughed. "Between you and my mother, I will be married in a year. No, I need to get back to the restaurant."

"All work and no play—"

"—Is exactly what you used to do," Angelo finished for him. "And right now, it's all I need."

VERONICA HELD HERSELF STEADY BY LEANING AGAINST the counter while she took an order from a customer. Something wasn't right. It had started about an hour ago with a slight dizziness that she hadn't been able to shake off, and it was only getting worse. At first, she'd assumed she just needed to eat something, so she'd nibbled on a cranberry muffin and drank half a bottle of water. But the dizzy feeling came and went over the last several hours.

Veronica finished taking the woman's order and looked around for Zelda, who was about to introduce open mic night. Her other employee, Zach, was filling the orders she'd taken.

Breathe. You're just tired. You've worked hard this week, that's all.

On Monday, the school had called for her to pick Lyra up—the whole class had been sent home early with flu symptoms. Even the teacher had gotten sick. Tuesday, Wednesday, and all day Thursday, Veronica had pulled true double duty: wiping every surface of the apartment with sanitizers and pulling espressos in the coffee shop while a baby monitor helped her watch over a sleeping Lyra and an extra part-time employee covered the times she had to run upstairs to be more hands on. Meanwhile, the coffee shop seemed busier than usual, and she was forcing herself to palm vitamin C every few minutes to make sure she didn't come down with the flu herself. She couldn't afford to get sick now.

You don't have it. You're not sick. You're fine...

You're delusional.

Normally she was great at lying to herself, but not

now. God, she probably did have the flu. She closed her eyes, focusing on breathing deep. She didn't have a fever and she didn't have a cough, but she'd keep herself slightly distant from the customers just in case. It could also just be exhaustion, which was totally possible given her schedule this week. She needed rest, that's all. Just needed to lay her head down on the counter for a minute...

"Veronica?" Thad's deep voice sounded like a wonderful dream. "Veronica?" A note of concern entered dream Thad's voice, which puzzled her. She drowsily opened her eyes and saw Thad standing in front of the counter. He looked damn good in jeans and a navy blue crew neck sweater. His hair was in that same artfully messy style as before. How was it men could have such great hair and do absolutely nothing to it?

"Oh, hey." She tried to smile but she was tired, so tired. Her limbs were as heavy as lead.

"You okay?" he asked. "You look a little pale."

"Yeah, I'm fine. I'm just a little run down." She put all of her energy into her smile this time and he relaxed.

"Any requests for tonight?" He leaned against the counter, a smile so sweet and seductive on his face that for a second, Veronica didn't breathe.

"Requests?"

"What do you want me to sing?" His look of excitement gave her back a tiny bit of her own energy.

"Sing anything you want. You could sing the ABCs and it would go platinum."

"Well, maybe not that. Hmmm... What to pick..." He chuckled; his eyes lit up with mischief. "Can we go grab a drink after?"

"Sure." She agreed even though her body was quick to betray her the second he turned away. She suffered another wave of dizziness, this time with nausea along for the ride. *Lovely*. She didn't want to miss out on a date with Thad, but she was starting to fear she couldn't power through this.

A few people got up to sing first. Veronica watched them while she helped fill coffee orders. Zelda returned behind the counter.

"Ronnie, you look bad. *Really* bad." Zelda put the back of her hand against Veronica's forehead. "You're burning up. You need to go rest. Zack and I can close up."

"Thanks, but I need to stay." She nodded toward Thad, who sat quietly at the table, watching the current singer finish up. He flashed her a warm smile and applauded as she stepped off the stool. The girl blushed and rushed back to a table of other college girls who were all clutching their pumpkin spice lattes. Then Thad stood and walked toward the stool.

Zelda's brows drew together. "Damn girl, you have it bad for him, don't you?"

Veronica watched him take a seat and pick up the guitar. "I think maybe I do."

Thad settled the guitar in his lap and strummed a few notes. Then he looked straight at her and began to sing. It took a moment for her to recognize the song, "Let You Go" by Illenium. His smooth voice seduced her as he sang of being a fire in the cold rain and how he would hold her in the dark nights and never let go.

She was so lost in his voice she was barely aware of Zelda pushing her away from the cash register so she could take an order. As the song died away and applause filled the room, he nodded at the crowd and murmured a thank you before passing the guitar off to someone else. He didn't go back to his table, however, but headed straight for her.

"You ready to go?"

"Sure. Just let me grab my purse." She removed her apron, only to gasp as a sudden wave of nausea swept through her. Her apron missed the peg on the wall and fell to the floor. As she bent to retrieve it, the dizziness hit her even harder than before. She pitched forward, collapsing on her hands and knees.

"Veronica!" Thad called out.

"I'm—okay." Her hands gripped the fabric of the blue apron as she struggled to stand. She managed to lean against the wall, catching her breath, just in time to see Thad before she collapsed again. She was too tired, far too tired to do anything but sleep.

❄

THAD'S HEART LURCHED. HE VAULTED OVER THE counter, sending Zelda and Zach scattering as he raced to catch Veronica.

He was a second too late. She crumpled to the floor. His mind ran in frantic circles before everything went silent inside his head and fear took over. He put his fingers on her neck, checking her pulse. It was steady, but she was so pale. If anything happened to her, he'd... he stopped that train of thought before it could go any further.

"Oh my God, Ronnie!" Zelda joined Thad, kneeling next to Veronica.

"What's the matter? Does she have any medical conditions?" Thad pulled his cell phone out of his pocket. He was hovering over 911 but Zelda stopped him.

"I think she has the flu. It's been going around." Zelda let out a relieved sigh as Veronica's eyes opened, but they were glassy.

"Am I on the floor?" Veronica asked, her voice soft and confused.

"Yes," Thad said. "You aren't well. We need to get you home." He turned to Zelda. "I can take her home if you and Zach can handle the store."

"Er..." Zelda shot a furtive glance at Veronica. "I don't think—"

"She'll be safe with me, Zelda."

"Oh, it's not that. It's just... oh hell. I'll grab her keys." Zelda called for Zach to handle the counter while she fetched Veronica's purse from the storage room.

"Veronica, I'm going to help you sit up, okay?" Thad brushed her hair back from her face.

"I really don't feel—" she suddenly rolled over and threw up on the floor, her eyes filled with tears as she lay flat on her back again and wiped at her mouth, gasping softly. "I'm sorry—"

"Hush. It's okay. This not your fault. Everyone gets sick." He tried to reassure her.

"Not you, Mr. Perfect." Her exhausted reply was almost a grumble.

He would have been tempted to laugh if he wasn't so worried about her. "Clearly you never knew me in college."

"Shit." Zelda grimaced. "I'll have Zach clean that up." She held up Veronica's keys. "Perks of seniority."

"I think my driver has her address," Thad said.

"Address?" Zelda frowned. "She lives upstairs."

Zelda's words didn't immediately sink in. "Pardon?"

Zelda pointed a finger straight up at the ceiling. "She lives upstairs."

"But... I dropped her off at an apartment a few blocks away on Sunday."

"I don't know anything about that. Maybe she didn't trust you yet, but she lives here. Come on, I'll show you." She nodded toward a door marked *Restricted Access* that Thad already knew led to the upstairs living space he'd toured with Mrs. Becker.

Thad lifted Veronica into his arms, cradling her against his chest.

"Thad, the room... it's spinning." Veronica mumbled against him.

"Close your eyes," he whispered as he followed Zelda upstairs. His mind was still stumbling over the realization that Veronica lived in his dream apartment, the one he planned to buy. That complicated things. Or perhaps more accurately, it simplified them. There was no way he was buying this place now. As they reached the top of the stairs, a teenage girl met them.

"Mrs. Hannigan?" the girl asked in fear as she saw Thad carrying Veronica.

"She's got the flu." Zelda explained. "Zach and I will close up. Let me get you some money and you can go home."

"Thanks, Zelda. Text me and let me know she's okay."

"Will do."

Thad's arms stiffened around Veronica as a tiny voice spoke up from somewhere near his knees.

"Mommy?"

He backed up a few steps and saw a tiny little girl who couldn't have been more than four or five staring up at him. Her bright blue eyes were exactly like Veronica's, but the golden curls were nothing like her mother's raven colored hair.

"Mommy..." the child said again.

"Lyra, sweetie..." Veronica moaned, her eyes still closed. "Mommy is very tired, and she needs to rest awhile."

"*Mommy?*" Thad's own vision was spiraling as the entire messed up scene sank in.

Veronica was a mother. She had a kid.

Zelda motioned for Thad to follow. "Her bedroom is this way." He was glad to move again, to have something to focus on, rather than think. Because right now he couldn't think about much except that Veronica hadn't told him she had a child. She'd mentioned her husband dying but hadn't mentioned kids. Wouldn't she have said something? Why hadn't she?

The master bedroom he'd toured a few days ago with Mrs. Becker turned out to be Veronica's bedroom, only now it didn't look like a sterile and staged showroom. It was cozier with pictures on the dresser, a few bits of clothing draped over a chair, and a faint dusting of glitter where her child had clearly done something artsy on the bed. Zelda pulled back the covers of the bed and Thad laid her down, careful to cushion her head on the pillow.

"She's too sick to leave alone," Zelda said quietly. "I've got the keys; I could probably stay—"

"No, I'll do it," Thad said, even though he had no clue what to do about the kid.

Zelda stared at him a long moment, her eyes hardening. "If you do anything to hurt her, emotionally or otherwise..." For a cute college kid, her voice was frighteningly serious.

He raised his palms up in a surrendering gesture. "I would never hurt her in any way."

"And Lyra?" she pressed.

"Or the kid," he replied, his voice firm even though his heart was racing at the thought of having to take care of a child. He glanced instinctively toward the bedroom door where he saw a tiny face watching him. Her face disappeared a second later as she realized she'd been spotted.

"Okay. I'll get Veronica into some PJs. You stay in the hall," Zelda ordered.

Worry still gnawed at his gut as he left the bedroom. He ran smack into the little girl and caught her by her shoulders to keep her from falling.

For a long moment, they sized each other up. Her big eyes moved over him from head to toe, then suddenly looked hopeful.

"Are you my new daddy?" she asked.

"Your what?" Thad choked out.

"My new daddy. I asked Alexa for one." She pointed to the smart speaker next to the TV in the living room.

"No shi—I mean, no kidding." Thad stared at the device and then the child. She was cute, he couldn't deny that, but she also kind of scared him. He didn't know a thing about kids. Lyra continued watching him, clearly expecting an answer. He opened his mouth but closed it again. What was he supposed to say?

"Are you my new daddy?" Her face was now an open book of confusion, fear, and worry, just like her mother's often was.

Zelda stepped in the hall, saving him from putting his foot deep into his mouth. "Veronica's changed and under the covers. I'll put Lyra to bed." She waved a hand at the girl. "Come on, sweetie. Time for bed. This nice man here is Thad. He's going to take care of you and your mom for a while. I'll come and check on you tomorrow, okay?" She looked at Thad. "If you need me before closing, just call."

Thad nodded. "Doesn't she have any—?" He stopped as he remembered her parents were dead, and her stepmother did not sound like the kind of person he should call for help.

"She doesn't have any what?" Zelda asked.

"Family," he said. "I just remembered."

"No, she doesn't. Only the evil sea witch," Zelda said.

"The who?"

"Annette Becker, the sea witch," Zelda repeated. "It's what we call Veronica's evil stepmom." Zelda murmured this to Thad as Lyra absorbed their exchange with wide, innocent eyes.

Annette Becker. The name hit him like a punch to

the gut. The woman who was trying to sell him this house and the floor below...was Veronica's stepmother.

"We can't tell the sea witch anything," Lyra said, thinking she was part of the conversation.

"Yes, that's right. Now bedtime for you, kiddo." Zelda took Lyra into the other bedroom. He let Zelda handle the child and went to check on Veronica. She lay tucked up under the covers, her face still pale, but at least she looked more relaxed. He eased himself down on the bed beside her and gently tucked her hair away from her face

Her eyes opened. "Thad?" She sounded shocked and exhausted.

"Yeah, honey?" He smiled.

"You're still here..." She wrinkled her nose, her brows knitted in confusion.

"Yes. I'm going to look after you tonight."

She tried to sit up. "But... Lyra..."

"Lyra, too." Thad promised. His fingers pressed into her arm, urging her back down. He needed to ease the fear he saw in her eyes. He gently pushed her back against her pillows. "Zelda's putting Lyra to bed right now. I'll take care of everything the rest of the night. Don't worry."

Her eyes are closed again as though she'd lost the last bit of energy and collapsed into the pillows. "Do you hate me?"

"No—why would I?"

Her eyes opened slightly under her dark lashes. "For not telling you about Lyra. I thought you'd be angry."

Thad was wondered what in her life had made her so certain he would be angry. Keeping that to herself while she got to know him was logical. If he'd been a single father—which was hard to imagine, granted—he would probably have acted the same way.

"I'm not angry, Veronica. I mean, it *did* shock the hell out of me; I'm not gonna lie." He chuckled dryly. "We'll figure it out, okay?"

"You mean you still—?"

"You think some cute four-year-old is going to scare me off?"

"You must be crazy," Veronica said dreamily, and without another word she drifted off to sleep.

Thad pulled the covers over her and turned to leave. Zelda was in the doorway, watching him. He joined her in the hall.

"Okay, Mr. GQ. I'm going to trust you on this, but I'll be back here first thing in the morning. Here's my number." She handed him a scrap of paper with a cell phone number on it.

"Thank you, Zelda."

She gave him a hard stare. "Look, Lyra is desperate for a dad."

"So I noticed."

"Yeah, well, I was all for this when it was about Veronica getting her groove back. But up till now, Lyra didn't know you existed. Try not to get her hopes up, okay?"

Before Thad could reply, Zelda exited, leaving him alone with a sick woman he cared for and a four-year-old he knew nothing about.

He felt the faint vibrations of music from the coffee shop below as he tried to figure out what he was supposed to do next.

He glanced at the little girl's room when he heard something creak. It was exactly the kind of sound he would expect to hear if a child was moving around restlessly in her bed.

He was not ready to be anyone's dad. He wasn't ready to settle down. He was barely ready to take dating more seriously. What the hell was he supposed to do?

8

That pulled out his cell phone and walked into the kitchen where he could talk without being overheard. The walls were filled with family photos that hadn't been there the day he'd toured the place with Annette Becker. She'd hidden this whole world from him when she'd staged the house for the showing. He paused in front of a photo of Veronica holding a baby in her arms, kissing the child's head. He blew out a slow breath as the tightness returned to his chest before he refocused on what he needed to do.

He added Zelda's number into his contacts, then dialed Jared.

"I'm guessing since you're calling, the open mic night didn't go so well?" Jared asked with concern the second he answered.

He closed his eyes and rubbed them with his thumb

and forefinger hard enough to see stars. "That would be an understatement."

"What happened?"

Where to begin, Thad thought dismally. "Veronica has the flu. She collapsed before we could leave."

"Whoa, is she okay?"

"She's all right for now, but she has it bad. I took her home." He paused. "And you'll never guess where she lives."

"Well, don't kill me with the suspense," Jared deadpanned.

"You remember that brownstone residence just above the Chi-Bean?"

"The house you said you were going to have me look over the lease agreements on."

"She's the tenant."

"She's *what*?" Jared's teasing tone was gone. "She doesn't know you sent an offer to buy it, right?"

"Thankfully, no, but that's an easy fix. I'm going to withdraw my offer. The thing is..." He paused a second as he debated how to tell Jared. "She left out a huge detail about her life."

"Bigger than being a widow? She doesn't have a kid, does she?"

"She does, a four year old."

The silence on the other end of the line was not comforting.

"Tell me you're joking."

"I'm not." Thad's shoulders dropped. "And here's the best part. The little girl wants a dad. Apparently, she tried ordering one from Amazon." He leaned against the counter. "Can you put Felicity on the phone?"

"Sure, why?"

"Because I need to talk to a woman about this."

"Ok. Just a sec. Babe?" Jared called for his wife. Thad heard him explain briefly what was going on. Then Felicity came on the line.

"Hey, Thad. How are you doing?" She asked gently, calmly, like he was a man ready to jump off a bridge or something.

"Honestly, not great. What do I need to know about dealing with kids? Really little kids?"

"Jared said she's four?" Felicity confirmed.

"Yeah. She's tiny."

"What's her name?"

"Lyra."

"That's a pretty name," Felicity said.

"She's adorable, just like her mother," he said without thinking. "But that's not the problem."

Felicity chuckled. "Well, kids are pretty tough. She'll be worried about her mom, though. You should be prepared for questions about that. She'll need to have good, healthy meals at least three times a day with snacks in between. No fast food and no sugar."

"Okay, what else?" He searched around the kitchen,

pulling open drawers until he found a pad of paper and a pen.

"Bedtime by nine, I'm guessing. You need to find out if she has preschool, and if so, where and what time it starts and ends."

"Preschool?"

"If she's four, she's probably in some kind of school or daycare at least a few days a week."

Thad wrote *preschool* on the notepad and underlined it twice with a question mark.

"Veronica will need some Sprite and a bowl in case she gets sick. Since she has a little kid, you could check the cabinets or fridge for electrolyte drinks which would be even better than Sprite. You need to keep an eye on her all night but check on Lyra, too."

"Right." He would order some Sprite and other groceries to be delivered first thing in the morning.

"If Veronica isn't better in a few hours, you'll want to have someone come stay with her when you go to work. Unless you can work remotely, that would be better. You need to take her temperature every four hours, if you can."

Thad wasn't totally clueless. He'd had the flu before, though never so bad that he collapsed from it. He didn't want Veronica to become seriously ill and need to be hospitalized, so he planned to take all of Felicity's advice.

"Thanks, Felicity."

"I have this week off if you need a spare set of hands."

Thad leaned over the kitchen bar and glanced down the hall toward the two bedrooms.

"Wait, do I need to know how to change diapers? That may be above my pay grade," Thad said.

Felicity laughed. "She's four. She'll be potty trained."

He blew out a breath. "That's a relief."

Felicity snorted a laugh. "Text me where she lives, and I'll come by tomorrow to check on you if you want me to."

"Thanks." Thad ended the call, and the hairs in the back of his neck began to rise. He leaned over the kitchen bar again. Lyra's door was cracked open and her tiny face now peered at him from the darkness. For a moment they just stared at each other, neither knowing what to do with the other.

"Lyra?" He said softly. It was an unusual name. He would have to ask Veronica where it came from later.

"Daddy?"

"Thad, kiddo. My name is Thad." He left the kitchen and approached her door.

"Dad," she said as if echoing him.

"*Thad.*" He emphasized the "th" sound.

Lyra just stared up at him.

"You should go back to bed."

"Is mommy okay?" Something deep inside Thad's chest fluttered at the way she asked him.

"She's not feeling well. She's got the flu."

The little girl's eyes widened. "I had the flu." She told him in a loud whisper.

"Did you now?" Thad crouched down so that he was eye level with her. Lyra gave a big, exaggerated nod. "So Veronica must have gotten it from you."

Lyra's eyes grew wide. "I made mommy sick?"

"What? No... No, it's not your fault." He reached out and awkwardly patted Lyra's shoulder. The girl suddenly pressed her tiny body against his chest, her arms curling around his neck. Before he could stop her, she'd burrowed into him like a trembling kitten. Poor kid...

Thad froze as a wave of unexpected protectiveness hit him, and, just as he had when he'd kissed Veronica, he felt a shift deep inside.

He slowly stood, still uncertain of what to do, as he lifted her into his arms and carried her back to her room. He nudged her door open wide so he could carry her through. He lay her down on the bed and made her comfortable.

"Your mom is going to be fine. You were sick, but you got better, right?" he asked her. God, he wished he knew the right thing to say in this situation. He just wanted Lyra to feel better, but he had no idea what the magic words were.

She nodded, her bottom lip quivering. "Yeah."

"That's what's going to happen with your mom. She'll

be sick for a while, but you and I will take care of her, won't we?"

"Okay," Lyra scrunched her fists against her eyes and yawned. When she reopened them, her eyes were solemn as she stared up at him.

"Will you sing me a song?" she asked.

"Which song?" Thad racked his brain for something a child would like to hear.

"Sing the *Frozen* song," Lyra said she as she cuddled beneath the covers.

"I haven't seen that movie." He knew that it was a Disney song about a movie with ice and princesses, but beyond that, he was clueless on the lyrics. Sure he'd heard "Let it Go" a few times but not enough to just wing it from memory.

"Sing something, please." Lyra's tone grew softer as he tucked the blankets up around her neck. Her little face was so like Veronica's it made him grin. It reminded him of dinner with her and Luigi with the accordion, and more importantly the song which had made Lyra's mother giggle with delight.

He cleared his throat and started to sing "Bella Notte" from *Lady and the Tramp*.

Lyra's eyes closed. She smiled and made a little kittenish sigh. "The puppy dog song," she murmured before she fell asleep. He kept singing, letting her drift deeper into dreams before he finally rose from the bed and went to check on Veronica.

❄

THE WORLD AROUND VERONICA WAS HAZY AND nauseating. She drifted restlessly in and out of sleep as hot flashes were replaced by cold sweats that soaked her clothes until she was freezing. Her teeth chattered and her body quaked with violent shivers hard enough to make her teeth and bones rattle.

"It's okay. Just relax," a deep voice soothed when she started to whimper. "You're okay, honey." A thermometer was pushed into her mouth.

"A hundred..." The voice murmured with concern. "Do you feel hot or cold?"

"Co—cold—" she stammered.

A second later, a hard warm body was beneath the blankets with her, holding her. Eventually the shaking ceased, replaced with aches that nearly numbed her to everything but the pain.

"Thad..." she whispered.

"I'm here," he assured her.

This had to be a dream. A fevered hallucination. There was no way he was here holding her, taking care of her.

"Is Lyra okay?" she whispered. She hated this, hating feeling too weak to care for her child.

"Lyra is safe. She's in bed. I sang her to sleep," Thad said and tucked her hair back from her face as he tried to soothe her.

Definitely a dream. Veronica thought as she went blissfully still in his arms.

She wasn't sure how long she slept, but sometime before dawn she needed to use the restroom. Only she couldn't move. She was trapped in the cage of Thad's arms.

Not a dream.

He'd removed his sweater and had only a white T-shirt on. Her cheek was pressed against his chest, her skin warmed everywhere it touched him. His heartbeat was strong and steady against her face. She'd forgotten the feel of a man's heartbeat, the way it made her feel... safe. The last thing Veronica wanted was to leave her bed and Thad's embrace, but nature could not be ignored. She pushed gently against his chest. He didn't stir.

"Thad," she said.

"Yeah?" he grunted.

"I have to use the restroom." She was more than a little mortified to admit it.

His eyes opened. They looked even darker in the dim light.

He sat up. "Let me help you."

The room spun as she was tilted upright in his arms. She would have protested, but with the way everything had gone all tilt-a-whirl, she didn't think it would be a good idea. He scooped her up in his arms and carried her to the bathroom. Her sink was cluttered with feminine hair care and skin care products she desperately wished she'd put away.

"Call me if you get dizzy or need help." He made sure she had a grip on the countertop before he turned his back and shut the door between them to give her privacy.

When she was done, she took a few unsteady steps back to the sink to wash her hands. She stared at herself in the mirror. A pale-faced creature with sweat-soaked locks of hair hanging about her shoulders stared back at her. She looked like death warmed over. The last thing she wanted was for Thad to see her like this.

Maybe he hadn't seen her looking so bedraggled when he brought her in here. She grabbed the hairbrush and dragged it through her tangled hair, then saw that wasn't going to help so she pulled her hair over one shoulder and hastily braided it. Then she doused her face with cold water to try and bring some color back before moving toward the door. Thad was waiting for her, an exhausted but hopeful look on his face. God, even tired, he still looked a thousand times better than she felt on her best days.

"Feel any better? Worse?"

"Less nauseous, but really tired." She gasped as he lifted her up in his arms and carried her back to bed.

They settled beneath the blankets and she moved without thought, seeking his warm body and curling up against him. When she realized what she'd done, trying to establish such small, yet so meaningful, intimacy, she started to retreat.

"Hey, it's okay. Don't pull away." Thad brushed her hair with his fingers, and the sensation felt so exquisite that she trembled.

"I'm sorry. I haven't been in bed with someone like this since Parker died. It was instinct."

He ran the back of his fingers over her cheek. "If I can ask you to do one thing, it's to stop apologizing. Never apologize for reaching for me in bed. You'll hurt my feelings." His laughter was low, like a man just waking up from a long slumber. She remembered what it was like to feel that kind of laughter as it rumbled through her body. A man's true delight... She'd missed that.

She scooted back into his arms, her head resting on his chest. "Aren't you worried you'll get sick?"

"I had a flu shot last week. And even if I do, I'll have Simon and my assistant to take care of me. I even have a butler that handles the penthouse where I live."

"A butler?" She tried not to laugh. For some reason she pictured an adorable old Alfred sort of man who helped Thad in his real estate Batcave.

"Are you laughing at me?"

"A little." She giggled. "So what does your butler do?"

"He buttles."

Veronica giggled some more.

"Mainly he sees to things being repaired, has guests

brought up, handles small things like having clothes pressed, buttons sewn back on—"

"Buttons sewn back on? Do you lose a lot of buttons?"

"Er... yes, I do." Thad cleared his throat. "Sometimes...in the bedroom, things get... you know."

"Of course." She remembered what it was like, to be swept away with passion so strongly that clothing became a casualty. Those memories made her bite back a smile.

"So they rip your clothes off?" Veronica asked. She couldn't deny the thought appealed to her to. Thank God she was too weak, and he was wearing a T-shirt, because right then she was tempted to do it herself.

"Yes," Thad admitted. "Some of my best suits have been ruined."

"You poor baby." She stifled a yawn, her eyes closing. Thad continued to stroke her hair as she drifted back to sleep.

When she woke again, she was no less tired than before, but something drew her from her weary sleep.

"Mommy..." Lyra's voice was a bare whisper.

"Sweetie?" She rolled away from Thad, waking him up as she faced her daughter. She had her Princess Elsa PJs on and was leaning on the edge of the bed with big hopeful eyes.

"I'm hungry," Lyra said. Her gaze strayed to Thad then back to Veronica.

"Okay. Let me just—" Veronica was halfway off the bed when Thad pulled her back down.

"Uh uh. You need to stay in bed. I'll take care of this." Thad slid out of bed and waved at Lyra. "Come on kiddo. Let's get you some breakfast."

Veronica desperately wanted to go with them, but she knew if she stood she would probably fall right back down. She blinked at the clock on her nightstand. Lyra always woke up around six, like clockwork. Normally Veronica would have already been up, showered, dressed, and ready to open the coffee shop.

The coffee shop! The panic that thought brought on sent her reaching blindly for her phone on her nightstand, but it was nowhere to be found. She'd find it later. For now, she wanted to make sure Thad didn't accidentally burn the apartment down.

It took every ounce of her strength to leave the bed and move toward the door. She leaned on the walls as she stepped into the hall, hearing the sounds of Thad and Lyra in the kitchen.

"What do you want? Frosted Flakes? Or it looks like your other choice is Rice Crispies?"

Lyra bounced in her seat at the little kitchen table. "Crispies!"

"You got it, kiddo." Thad retrieved the box of cereal from the pantry.

"Dad?" Lyra asked.

"*Thad*," Thad corrected her. It was an unexpected

shock for Veronica to hear Lyra calling someone dad. God, she hoped Thad didn't get the wrong idea about that.

"Thad?" Lyra said with a confused frown.

"Yeah?"

"Can I have extra milk, please?" she asked.

"Of course. Say when." Thad leaned over the her bowl and poured.

"When!" Lyra squealed as the cereal rose and threatened to spill. Lyra was so clearly overjoyed at Thad's presence, which worried Veronica as to what would happen when Thad got tired of taking care of her.

"Mommy!" Lyra giggled with a mouthful of cereal. Thad turned and frowned.

"Hey, you need to stay in bed." He set the milk back in the fridge and started toward her.

"Please, let me stay. I promise I'll rest.".

Thad scooped her up and after a moment, he nodded and gently deposited her on the couch. He covered her with the thick fleece blanket that had been draped over one arm of the couch.

"She's fine," Thad whispered to Veronica as he leaned in and kissed her forehead. "Let me handle it."

"Thank you." Veronica murmured and caught his hand before he could pull away. "I need my phone."

"It's okay. Zelda is going to be here in ten minutes to check on you and Lyra," he said. "She said she'll open the store today. She's got your other two employees to work extra hours until you feel better."

Veronica simply stared at him as he returned to the kitchen. When was the last time she'd been able to let someone else handle all of her worries? Not in a long time. Lyra looked between them, smiling and kicking her little feet where she sat at the table.

Completely torn between the comfort of the couch and her own anxiety, Veronica wasn't sure what to do. It felt like she could actually relax for the first time in...she wasn't sure how long. Yet there was a danger to feeling this free, to letting Thad take control over this part of her life. She felt like she was flying, but what if she suddenly realized she was actually free falling...

"Thad, could you bring me my purse? I still need to check my phone."

"Here you go." He brought her purse to her and she dug through it until she found her cell. Then she lay back on the couch and groaned as she checked her calendar.

Thad sat down beside her on the couch. "What is it?"

"Lyra has a birthday party... I should call and tell them she can't come."

"What time is the party?"

"Four. After her preschool gets out."

"Who takes her to school?"

"My neighbor, Katie. She's in high school. She walks

Lyra to school and back. They usually get home around three-thirty."

Thad stroked his chin. "I need to check my schedule, but I think I could take her."

"No, Thad, please. You've done enough already. I can't have you become her nanny."

The playboy winked at her. He leaned in and whispered, "Maybe we can think of a fun way for you to make it up to me? A dozen kisses, perhaps?"

A dozen kisses? She would give him a hell of a lot more than that if he wanted.

She held out a hand. "Deal."

"Deal." He shook her hand and then stood. "I need to make a few calls first, and it sounds like Zelda's downstairs, so I'll go check in with her."

Just like that, he was gone. The apartment felt empty now without his strong, calm presence. Veronica had a terrible feeling she could get used to him being here far too easily. And that was the last thing she could afford... to fall in love with a man destined to break her heart.

9

That stepped into the stairwell that led down to the coffee shop and dialed Simon's number.

"Good morning, sir," Simon greeted.

"Simon, I need you to do me a favor. I stayed over at Veronica's last night. She came down with the flu and has no one to look after her. I'm going to call Winston over at the Gold Circle. He'll pack my weekender bag and bring it down to you."

"Yes, sir."

"And I'll need you to do another favor."

"Name it."

"I have two young passengers, a high schooler and a four-year-old who need a ride to school at seven-thirty, then back from school to the Chi-Bean around three."

"Easily handled, sir."

Thad hung up and descended the stairs to let Zelda into the shop. She was waiting outside the store in the dark, bundled up in a heavy coat and woolen hat. He unlocked the front door and let her in.

She removed her gear and looked over him critically. "Well, you look like you're in one piece. Glad to see you survived the night. Did she?"

"Everything went well," he assured the petite blonde. He didn't tell her how his neck and back were stiff as hell from his awkward sleeping position or how his head throbbed from a lack of proper sleep.

"You look like you need coffee," Zelda said as she stepped behind the counter. She started prepping a machine to make him a drink.

"I wouldn't turn down a cup," he admitted with an exhausted smile. "Veronica's a little anxious about the shop today. You said Zach and Beth were able to help out for a few days, right?"

"Yeah, they can work more hours. Zach should be here in fifteen minutes." Zelda poured him a fresh cup of coffee, which he accepted gratefully. Caffeine was going to be his best friend today.

"Do you want to go up and check on Veronica?" Thad asked.

"I might when Zach gets here. Still got things to do here."

He nodded. "I'll be working remotely today so I can stay and help her out."

"Thanks for that." Zelda passed him a fresh cup of coffee. "I'm glad she has someone watching out for her."

Zelda's words made him realize just how much Veronica needed someone, at least at times like this, and he was glad to be there for her.

When he went back upstairs, he found Veronica passed out on the couch. Her dark hair was plaited in a long loose braid and one of her hands draped off the couch. Her face was smooth with sleep, yet even in her dreams she still looked worried, with a hint of a frown.

Thad gently tucked her hand back under the blanket before he braced one of his own hands on the armrests and leaned over to brush the backs of his fingers over her cheek. He pulled the blanket tight around her. Her nose was a little red and her skin a bit too pale, but she didn't feel hot to the touch like she had last night. Suddenly, a little body pressed next to him.

"She fell asleep while you were gone," Lyra said in a whisper.

"Yes, she needs to sleep. Gives her body time to get better. So you and I will need to be quiet while we get you ready for school. Do you have a backpack or something you take to class?"

She nodded and held up a green sparkly princess backpack.

"Good. Let's figure out your clothes." They went into her bedroom and he eyed the closet and dresser, totally lost. "What do you usually wear to school?"

The girl tried to open the top dresser drawer. Thad helped her. Inside were neatly folded rows of little leggings and shirts. He did his best to find what matched, but decided it was time to get Zelda involved.

"Stay right here," he commanded, perhaps a bit too seriously. The girl giggled as though he was the funniest thing in the world and crawled onto her bed. He opened the door that led to the Chi-Bean below and saw Zelda had left the bottom door open.

He called down the stairs, "Hey Zelda!"

Her face appeared in the doorway. "Yeah?"

"Can you help Lyra change for school? I can watch for Zach to arrive."

"Sure."

She and Thad passed each other halfway on the stairs. Thad waited by the front door of the coffee shop for Zach to show up. When he did, Thad let him in and hurried back upstairs.

Zelda laughed as she met him halfway down the stairs again. "All done."

"Thanks. If you see my driver, let me know. He'll be taking Lyra and the neighbor girl to school."

"Katie too? Okay, I'll tell her when I see her."

"That be great, thanks."

Half an hour later, Thad was pulled in a dozen directions as he marshaled Lyra and a blushing teenage girl out the door into Simon's care. He'd already had his driver figure out what sort of car seat he'd need for her age and had the driver pick it up before coming over.

His driver had raised his eyebrows at being introduced to Veronica's daughter but didn't say anything, for which Thad was grateful. Thad grabbed his brown leather weekender bag from Simon and slung it over his shoulder before heading back inside.

Veronica had slept through all of it, even the two conference calls he'd conducted at the kitchen table.

By lunchtime, Thad needed a shower. He checked on Veronica one more time. She was still sound asleep, so he collected his shower kit from his weekender bag and stepped into the guest bathroom. He hoped Veronica wouldn't mind.

He ran a palm over his jaw and winced at the thick stubble. He normally never let himself go this long without a shave. Once he was stripped out of his clothes, he reached into the stall and turned on the hot water. As he got inside, the steam eased the ache in his muscles. He sighed and placed a palm on the glass door, drawing in slow deep breaths as he took a minute to process all that happened in the last twelve hours.

What was he doing? He was playing nurse to a sick woman and nanny to a kid?

This was so not him. Yet, he didn't want to leave. He felt responsible for them somehow. He chuckled at the strange thought and shook his head beneath the spray of water.

Jared was right. Going out with Veronica was different, so very different than he was used to. It was messy, chaotic, and yet he found it all strangely irresistible. After just one week, she'd tilted his world onto a completely different axis. This past day was one step short of total chaos, but he didn't regret it. The only thing that bothered him was what came next. He wanted Veronica, wanted her to the point of madness, but Lyra was now part of the equation. He didn't know the formula to solve this particular problem. He knew how to date single women, but a single mother? He was out of his depth here.

Thad scrubbed shampoo in his hair and relaxed. He knew he was alone, since Veronica was asleep. He couldn't resist testing the acoustics of the bathroom, so he opened his mouth and started to sing.

A BEAUTIFUL SOUND PULLED VERONICA OUT OF pleasant dreams. Somewhere, someone was singing. She sat up in a daze on the couch. She vaguely remembered Thad putting her here and tucking her in. She'd fallen asleep, listening to him and Lyra talk, hadn't she?

She picked up her cell phone from the floor to check the time. 2:30. There was no sign of Lyra. Had Thad found Katie and gotten the girls off to school? Veronica wrapped the fleece blanket around her like a shawl and moved through the apartment in search of the music. As she got closer to the guestroom, she recognized the baritone. It was Thad singing. Hearing his voice was like drinking the smoothest of whiskeys and it was coming from the guest bathroom.

Don't do it... Don't...

Screw it.

She opened the door and the heat of the humid air curled around her, chasing away the chill in her bones. The glass was fogged, but only barely. She could see the outline of Thad's tall, muscled form all too clearly as he showered. Thad's palm appeared on the glass as he tilted his head back beneath the nozzle, and something primal stole through Veronica.

She dropped the blanket around her and walked toward the shower. She was too shy to remove her clothes, but she wanted so desperately to be near him, to touch him. In that moment, his presence called to her like a star's gravity pulling her into his orbit.

Veronica opened the shower door and his voice died away. His dark gold hair hung in slightly wet curled tendrils against his ears and the back of his neck as he faced her. She swallowed hard and swept her gaze down his body. Every inch of him was perfect. She stared below his waist and was not at all disappointed. In fact, his size was actually daunting. She raised her eyes back up and saw that he was watching her with a relaxed perusal of his own.

A dark spiraling tribal style tattoo of a bird covered part of his right shoulder and pectoral. It was the only thing that marked his perfect body.

"You want to join me?"

Thad's invitation was impossible to resist. "Do—do you mind?"

"Not at all." He moved back half a foot while she removed her boxers and panties but left the long T-shirt on. She wasn't ready for that next step, but she was close. He didn't say anything about her choice.

"What is your tattoo of?" she asked as she closed them both inside the shower. He moved so the hot water covered her, soaking her shirt and plastering it to her skin. She reached up and traced the beautiful design with her fingertips.

"It's a phoenix. Symbolic of rebirth among the ashes. I like the idea that even if you burn up you can still get a second chance."

Veronica kept her hands on his skin, now stroking the hard planes of his chest until her fingers circled each of his nipples. "It's beautiful. When did you get it?" He huffed at that caress and a rush of power filled her. She was affecting this gorgeous God of a man with just her touch.

"I got it when I turned twenty-four... I may have also lost a bet with Angelo and Jared and I *may* have been more than a little inebriated. I don't regret it, though." He hissed out another breath as she dragged her nails lightly down his abs to the V-shaped muscles of his hipbones.

"Fuck, honey," he groaned as she continued to touch him with teasing strokes. "Keep it up and I'll embarrass myself."

Veronica wanted him to kiss her, wanted it so much it hurt. But she was still sick, and Thad didn't deserve to get the flu after everything he'd done.

"I shouldn't be here. I don't want to get you sick."

Thad smiled. "Well, I got a flu shot recently, remember?"

"Those aren't a hundred percent effective."

"Maybe I'm willing to take the chance." She sighed as she turned to face the water, so it splashed down her chest. He rubbed her shoulders, his strong fingers digging into the knots she didn't even know she had.

"Oh God, of course you have magic fingers," she moaned and leaned back against him. His chuckle sent ripples of arousal through her, building up and making her long desperately to go further than she'd planned with him today.

"Just wait until you see all the things these fingers can do." His teasing only made her desire burn hotter. Veronica clenched her thighs together. She felt safe in this warm enclosed space with him, as though anything she said in the quiet sanctity of the shower would be protected. "Thank you for taking care of me. Of us."

"You deserve to be looked after." His voice was gruff,

as though he was annoyed no one had been there before to do it. She turned in his hold and his arms slid down her back, his fingers clenching the fabric of her soaked T-shirt just above her bottom.

"It's been hard," she confessed. "I want to say that everything's been easy, that I have it all together, but I don't. I barely get by. Every day I ask myself if I'm hurting Lyra if I don't give her everything she needs. Then I get so stressed I can barely breathe—" She choked on the rest of her words and he simply pulled her deeper into his embrace.

"Hey, lean on me," he whispered in her ear. "It's okay. Let me ease your burdens, honey. Please." His voice was so soft, so smooth and reassuring.

"And when you leave?" She dared to ask. She rubbed her cheek against his chest, her arms twisting about him.

"I don't plan to leave anytime soon, so don't worry." His arms were like twin bands of steel holding her together. He made it all sound so easy, to not think about that day when he'd eventually get tired of her. But Veronica spent all of her life grounded and knew better than to keep her head in the clouds.

"Just promise you'll warn me before you leave."

Thad was silent a long while before he answered. "Neither of us know where this is going, but I understand what you're saying. You want to be realistic. You have to be. I will always be honest with you, no matter how things end up."

His answer stung, but they both knew this was only temporary. He wasn't ready to settle down yet, and she couldn't afford to attach herself to anyone, not unless she went all in, and she wasn't sure she would ever be ready for that.

Thad let go of her and reached for the shampoo bottle. "Turn around."

She gave him her back and he washed her hair. When she was ready to wash the rest of herself, he pressed a kiss to her forehead and stepped out of the shower, giving her some privacy to remove her t-shirt. He seemed to understand that she still needed time before she was ready to be intimate with him. Given that they'd only gone on a few dates, they'd already leaped light years ahead of most couples.

When she emerged from the shower, he handed her a fluffy white towel, which she wrapped around her body. He stood at the sink, filling up a face brush with shaving cream. The crisp, tart-scented cream brought back memories of watching Parker shave. A bittersweet ache filled her as she saw Thad move the razor over his jaw and chin in slow measured strokes, taking time between each to run the razor under the water and clean it off. Halfway through, he noticed her watching him.

"It's been a while since I've seen a man do that," she admitted. It had been a while since she'd seen a man do a lot of things up close. Now more than ever, she realized how deeply she'd buried her loneliness.

"You can watch me shave anytime." He finished shaving and flicked his wet fingertips at her. She squealed and grabbed her wet t-shirt from the floor of the shower and flung it at him.

Thad lunged for her. She laughed as she tried to evade him, but he caught her by the waist and pulled her flush against him. Their laughter slowly died as he held her in his arms, their bodies separated only by their clean towels. Their faces were close, but not touching, their gazes locked.

"This is crazy, isn't it?" she asked.

He cupped her cheek with one palm, and she leaned into him.

"Maybe it is, but I like this kind of madness."

Thad leaned in and kissed her. She tensed, trying to push him away. "You'll get sick."

"I won't, but even if I do, it'll be worth it," Thad said and covered her mouth with his again. In that moment, she released all her anxiety about the last day. The kiss started soft, but soon hardened in the most delicious way, as if he wanted to devour her. She sighed in sweet pleasure as she explored his mouth, embracing the sharp need for more. She trembled, her knees knocking into each other as she envisioned his body mimicking the gentle thrust of his tongue between her lips. She lost count of the hours or perhaps days this moment seemed to last. When their mouths finally parted, she was clutching his shoulders and he was holding onto her tightly.

"Unfortunately, I've got some work to do before Lyra gets home, and you still need to rest," he said with reluctance, as though he wanted to say something more. Doubt soon crept into her mind. Had he truly wanted more, or was he already losing interest? And how pathetic was she to already be worrying about that?

"We need to go slow. I don't want to rush this," Thad said, answering her unspoken fears.

"You mean that?"

He traced her lips with his fingertips. "Yes, I do. Sometimes fast is fun, fast is easy, but everything about you is different. I want to take my time with you, even if it kills me." He flashed her that charming grin that made her belly flutter.

"But maybe not too slow?" She found herself asking.

"Not too slow," he agreed and playfully slapped her bottom. "Go and put on something comfy. I want you either in bed or on the couch. I have some soup for your lunch. All right?"

"All right." She thought she would never want to eat again after last night, but her appetite was coming back with a vengeance. By the time she'd changed, brushed her teeth again and came out into the living room, Thad was unpacking a bag of food.

"You didn't need to order in. I had soup cans in the pantry."

He scoffed. "Cans? You need homemade soup.

Angelo makes the best chicken noodle." He set the soup out on a small tray and brought it over. She couldn't help but admire his long, lean form and how relaxed and sexy he looked in his jeans and moss green Henley top. He looked good in everything, especially if a camera was pointed at him. Just looking at him revved Veronica's body back up, but she was too exhausted to really do much about it. And a part of her agreed with him: now was not the time to rush into anything.

She finished her soup while he worked at his computer and over the phone. Veronica was fascinated seeing him in his element. He was ruthless at times, pushing his terms as he negotiated deals over Zoom meetings. He always smiled as he finished a deal, even the people who caved to his terms sounded happy to be doing business with him. He really was a beast in the boardroom, and it was surprisingly hot to watch.

His phone vibrated and he checked it. "The kid is on her way up. Simon just dropped her and Katie off."

Veronica sat up on the couch, too tired to move any more than that. It was like she'd just had that one brief flare of energy during the shower. Now she was back to feeling half dead. But she did feel better after Angelo's chicken soup.

Katie and Lyra barged in, talking excitedly to each other, and in each of their hands was an ice cream cone which, given the cold weather outside, made Veronica laugh. Only kids could enjoy ice cream in the winter.

The driver, Simon, came in behind them with Lyra's glittery, green backpack slung over his shoulder.

"Ice cream, Simon?" Thad asked, raising a brow.

The driver blushed. "Sorry, sir. Everyone needs ice cream sometimes." Simon's gaze drifted to Veronica. "I hope you're feeling better, Mrs. Hannigan."

"Thank you, Simon. I am much better." She opened her arms for Lyra, who bounded up to the couch and crawled up to sit beside her.

"Thanks for picking them up, Simon. I'll text you in a few minutes when Lyra and I are ready to leave for the party."

"Yes, sir."

Only then did Veronica remember that Thad had agreed to take Lyra to a birthday party.

"Oh, Thad, really. I think I can go—"

"No, you won't. Relax, I've got it covered." He smiled that wolfish smile that made her hot all over. She kind of liked it. No, she *really* liked it when he got bossy. What was wrong with her? She never thought she was that kind of girl, but there was something about Thad's easy self-confidence that made everything he did deliciously wonderful.

"You have it covered?" She echoed with a smile of her own and a shake of her head. "You have no idea what you've just agreed to, do you?"

He gave a shrug of his shoulders. "It's just a kid's birthday party."

Boy, you are in trouble, Veronica thought. She didn't dare warn him otherwise. The only thing better than casual self-confidence was seeing it given a reality check now and then. A reality check that came in the form of wild screaming children, cake icing stains, and total exhaustion was even better.

10

Thad was in trouble.

He stood just inside the entrance of a giant kids party place called Razzy Tazzy. Hundreds—not dozens— *hundreds* of children were running around and screaming like banshees. Inflatable slides almost a story tall gleamed beneath bright ceiling lights and dozens of arcade games flashed as sirens went off every time they spat out tickets to young, screeching kids.

"Holy shi—" he stopped himself short as a tiny hand squeezed his. He looked down at Lyra, who wore a bright pair of red leggings and a green shirt, beside him. He'd chosen something he'd thought at the time would make her easy to spot, but all the kids dashing about wore clothes that were just as bright. She was going to blend in, so he couldn't risk letting her out of his sight.

"You ready for this, kiddo?" he asked her. She'd been talkative before they'd left for the party and during the car ride over, but now she seemed overwhelmed by the chaos around them.

She gazed out at the wild party scene and shook her head. When she leaned against his leg and clutched at his jeans, his heart clenched and something soft and sweet grew within him. He squeezed her hand back.

Glancing about the chaotic scene, he had sudden visions of Lyra diving into a ball pit where he'd never be able to find her.

"Stay close and don't let go of my hand." He navigated his way through the chaotic scene toward a party room that had six large picnic tables covered with snacks and presents. Each table had a banner with a child's name printed in balloon-shaped letters hanging above it from the ceiling. Thad looked at each one until he spotted the name *Sam Dalton*.

Parents sat around the table, exhausted, beleaguered and frazzled. It made him think of a war movie, where a group of soldiers might try to get a moment's rest while shells rained down all too close to their location. And the party had only just started.

Others hovered about the table, setting out gifts and handing out snack packs to children who shot past them like heatseeking missiles. Another group of parents slouched in uncomfortable chairs, nursing plastic cups and staring off into the distance, trying to imagine themselves being anywhere else.

Thad had a bad feeling about this.

Thad and Lyra approached the table. He took a moment to study the couple who seemed to be in charge of the party, a woman who was cutting up a large birthday cake.

"Mrs. Dalton?" Thad asked. The woman looked up at him and froze, her lips parting as she stared at him. She dropped the knife and rushed to smooth her hair back and offer him a flustered smile.

"Oh my God, she wasn't kidding..."

The man behind the woman stepped forward. "You're Thad?" the man asked.

"I am." He motioned to Lyra. "I'm here for Veronica. She's got the flu."

"I'm Steve Dalton. This gobsmacked woman is my wife, Michelle. Ronnie said that you'd be coming. Glad to meet you." He and Steve shook hands.

"You'll have to walk me through this whole kid's party thing." He held out the bag filled with brightly colored tissue paper to Steve. "I've got Sam's present."

"Thanks. This is your first time at Razzy Tazzy, I take it?" There was a glint of humor in the man's eyes.

Thad glanced around. "Yeah." His ears rang with children screaming as the sounds bounced off the concrete walls of the play place. "Tell me there's a place I can get a drink, I've got a feeling I'm going to need it."

Each time he moved, some kid screamed, usually knocking into him. He ran a hand through his hair and took a deep breath.

Steve sighed in sympathy. "Well, that's the bad news. The closest place to get a beer is two blocks away and we need all hands on deck to watch over these little monsters." Steve bent to ruffle Lyra's loose blonde curls. She beamed up at him with trust and adoration. He wondered if she would ever look at him like that.

"The best we can do," he continued. "Is to survive until after cake and opening presents in two hours. The kids usually wear themselves down in the bouncy houses and not even the sugary cake can resurrect them."

Michelle finally seemed to get control of herself and spoke again. "Wow, you really came."

Thad raised a brow at the question.

"Oh, God. I'm sorry. That was rude. It's just when Veronica texted me today, I didn't really believe her."

Thad continued to stare at her. "Did you think Veronica made me up?"

"No! No. It's not that."

"It's a little that," Steve interjected.

"It's just after losing Parker... Well, Veronica is crazy protective of Lyra. She's only known you a week—"

"—assuming you were real—"

"—and she's ready to let you take her daughter to a birthday party alone? It's just—"

Steve rolled his eyes. "What my wife means is it's

nice to meet you, Thad, and we never thought you were an imaginary coping mechanism for Veronica. We're glad you came." He looked down at Lyra. "Why don't you go find Sam? He's in the arcade over there." Steve pointed out a little boy next to a giant whack-a-mole game.

Lyra held firm to Thad's jeans.

"I'll be here if you need me, okay?" he told her.

"Promise?"

"I promise, kiddo." He put a hand on her small shoulder and gave it a gentle squeeze.

Lyra's big blue eyes were like something out of a Margaret Keane painting. She slowly let go of his pants and moved toward Sam. She stopped after fifteen feet and looked back at him. Thad waved encouragingly, keeping his gaze on her until she safely reached the birthday boy.

"She so small," Thad murmured. "Most of the other kids are much bigger than her." He looked at Steve. "Is it safe for her to play on this stuff with them?"

"For the most part, yeah, but we'll keep an extra eye on her. The teenagers who work here aren't exactly motivated by quality performance." Steve jerked his head toward a pair of pimply-faced teens manning the prize counter with glazed expressions.

"Swell," Thad muttered. "I feel so safe knowing my kid is being looked after by those guys."

"Your kid?" Steve chuckled.

Thad's rubbed the back of his neck. "You know what I mean." he amended.

"So, you and Ronnie. Can I ask how serious it is?" Steve's question was casual, but Thad could hear the protectiveness in the other man's tone.

"I'm not sure. This is all new to me. I don't usually..." He couldn't tell this man that he didn't usually date women like Veronica. That made him sound like an asshole.

"I get it, man. I've seen the article." Steve poured him a Diet Coke in a red Solo cup and grinned. "Cheers."

Thad knocked his cup to Steve's. "Cheers. So if you read the article..."

"My wife has too, obviously. She gave it to Ronnie a few days ago."

So Veronica had finally read it, and probably knew more about the public side of his life than was probably wise. Had that changed her opinion of him?

"She's a good person, so whatever you think about her reading the article, she's nothing like the women you're probably used to," Steve said after a moment. "Michelle and I met her at Sam's daycare last year and we hit it off. She's had a hell of a time raising her kid alone."

Thad wondered if he could get Steve to tell him more about Veronica. "She told me about her husband, about how he died."

"Did she tell you she was eight months pregnant when he died?" Steve volunteered this.

That caught him by surprise. "No, she didn't." His heart gave a strange lurch as he pictured a young pregnant Veronica burying her husband, knowing she'd have to face so many things alone. He didn't want to think about the fact that Parker had died before ever meeting his child. Christ... he couldn't even begin to imagine how strong Veronica would have to be to get through that.

"Yeah, they'd been getting along okay, but losing Parker. She had to use all of her savings to open the Chi-Bean, and her stepmother is a real piece of work. She's always trying to sell the house out from under them."

Steve's words hit him like a right hook. He'd thought she had the right to live there, with a tenant contract that protected her and Lyra.

"They aren't tenants with a lawful contract?" Thad kept his voice calm, but a black pit was churning deep inside his stomach.

"That brownstone is her childhood home, but her dad left it in a trust that won't end until she's thirty. Until then, her stepmom can do whatever she wants as long as she puts the money into the trust for Ronnie."

Thad started to panic, something he hadn't felt in a long time. By asking to see the brownstone, he'd given Veronica's stepmom encouragement to sell Veronica's home. Even if he backed out of the sale, she'd be shopping it around elsewhere. He'd become the catalyst for one of Veronica's worst nightmares.

"Not that the trust is doing her any good," he added. "Ronnie tells us that her stepmom never pays her enough during her monthly distributions. And if the Chi-Bean does well, she lowers the amount, then never quite raises it back as high when things get slow. So, until Veronica reaches thirty, she's struggling to get by."

"But why?" Thad asked.

"Control. Spite. Take your pick. Whatever her reasons, it's Machiavellian as hell. But that's always been and will always be Annette's way. Or so I hear."

Thad felt that dark pit rising and swirling inside him until he was nauseous. No wonder Annette had been so eager to show him the house. Well, the joke was on her. He wasn't going to buy the house.

Hell. He'd forgotten about Brandon and how he'd asked him to send off his offer.

"Could you watch Lyra for a second so I can make a quick call?" he asked Steve.

"Sure."

"Thanks." He walked back to the Razzy Tazzy's lobby and dialed Brandon.

"Yes, Mr. Worthington?"

"Brandon, don't send that offer for the brownstone to Mrs. Becker."

"Oh, Mr. Worthington, I'm so sorry. I just emailed it off five minutes ago." Brandon apologized.

Thad pinched the bridge of his nose and cursed under his breath. Shit. This was the only problem with Brandon. He was too good at his job.

"That's okay. I'll call her to withdraw the offer verbally and send a follow-up email."

"I'm sorry, Mr. Worthington—"

"It's not your fault. I just changed my mind, is all. Call or text me if anything comes up." He tried to keep his breathing deep as his vision tunneled. If he couldn't get the offer rescinded before she accepted, he'd be facing a difficult conversation with Veronica.

"No problem. Your father has some blueprints for you to look over, but he said there wasn't any rush."

Thad ended the call and immediately dialed Mrs. Becker. His head started to ache as he waited for her to answer. He ran over all the ways this conversation could play out and how to make it work to his advantage. It was exactly how he always handled his job, yet this felt more important than any business negotiation he'd ever had.

"Annette speaking," she answered.

"Mrs. Becker, this is Thad Worthington."

"I just received the offer from your office—"

"I'm afraid I need to rescind it. I'm not quite ready for that investment yet."

"Oh..."

"I'm very sorry," he added. "I am very interested in sending a new offer in perhaps six months." It was an age-old tactic: lie to prevent the other side from selling to a third party. "I'll probably pay half a million above asking at that point if you don't mind being patient."

"Well, I suppose I could wait a bit longer." She sounded more excited now. "I will wait to hear from you."

Thad waited until he ended the call to exhale. He'd managed to buy himself some time, but he wouldn't be able to do it forever. Still, he basked in the relief of knowing he'd kept the brownstone from changing hands anytime soon. With that taken care of, he returned to the game room to keep an eye on Lyra.

While the stalling tactic had bought him some time, it would only convince Annette to hunt for another buyer if his offer fell through. He needed to come up with a solution and fast, one that wouldn't make Veronica hate him.

VERONICA LAY ON THE COUCH, DEBATING WHETHER she should bother Michelle during Sam's party. She'd let a virtual stranger take her child to a party, after all. She had to know how Lyra was doing, and she was dying to know if Thad was surviving the party. There's no way he knew what he was getting himself into. She quickly dialed Michelle before she could talk herself out of it.

"Girl, why are you torturing that gorgeous man!" Michelle asked the second she answered.

"Oh no... What happened?"

"You sent *GQ's* Gentleman of the Year to the Razzy Tazzy, that's what happened. The man is dressed like he just walked out of the magazine and has found himself in the toddler version of Mad Max. The poor man is struggling to survive in a world where everything is loud, noxious, and sticky." Michelle said. "God, kids are so grubby."

Veronica held back a laugh. "Seriously, Michelle, how's he doing? How is Lyra doing?"

"Seriously? They're both fine. Lyra was clinging to his leg when they walked in. She's so darn cute and he's very protective of her. Enough to make my ovaries squee. Seems like he and Steve hit it off too."

Veronica couldn't hold back a laugh this time. But it soon turned into a wheezing cough.

"Have you slept with him yet?"

"Michelle, please tell me no children are near you." Veronica sipped on the hot tea she'd had just enough energy to make a few minutes ago. The soothing honey and chamomile left her calmer than she otherwise would have been.

"Naw, all the kids are going down that huge inflatable slide right now. Now answer the question."

"No we haven't slept together, but he did stay the

night. I was so sick... I couldn't take care of Lyra. It was frightening, I've never been this sick."

The other end of the line was quiet, except for the screaming children in the background.

"Michelle, are you there?" Veronica asked.

"Yeah, I'm here," Michelle finally answered. "He stayed the night? Like to take care for you?"

"Yeah. He put Lyra to bed and made sure she had breakfast in the morning. He even carried me to the bathroom. I'm feeling better now...just exhausted."

"That's so romantic. I swear when men get sick, they think it's the end of the world, but when we get sick, it actually *is* the end of the world and they don't care for us like we do for them. I mean, Steve is amazing, but my old boyfriends? They were the worst." Michelle chuckled.

"Thad really is wonderful. He even ordered home-made soup from his friend, the chef over at the Italian village."

"The place where he took you to dinner on Sunday, right?"

"Yeah. They're best friends, apparently."

"That's pretty classy. Best friend who's a chef? Your wedding will have the best catered food ever."

Veronica rolled her eyes. "Michelle, don't talk like that. We've only been seeing each other for a week."

"Don't wreck my fantasy," Michelle said. "When I close my eyes, I see you marrying this gorgeous man. I will be your matron of honor, obviously, and it's one of those insanely lavish weddings on some private tropical island somewhere. Oh, and you'll have a ton of adorable kids." Michelle's dreamy sigh over the phone filled Veronica with her own wistfulness.

She remembered her rushed City Hall wedding with Parker. All she had was a baby blue sundress to wear, but the day had been filled with unspeakable joy. Parker had bought her a bouquet, even though they didn't really have the money. She'd held those flowers tight, spoken her vows, and meant every word. But it didn't stop her from having dreams of a bigger wedding, or a dress that a princess would envy. Those kinds of dreams had been around since she was a little girl. But Thad wasn't the marrying kind.

"You'll call me if anything happens, right?" Veronica asked.

"You know I will. But she'll be fine. Now, I need to go make sure no one steals any of the cake before it's time to blow out the candles."

"Thanks." Veronica hung up and settled back onto the couch. As she drifted to that place between awake and asleep, she dreamed of wearing a white gown and running through a snowy dark forest, the frost biting into her feet.

She could hear an evil laugh all around her, a cold, cruel laugh that sounded very much like Annette's.

❄

THAD AND STEVE STOOD AT THE BASE OF THE GIANT inflatable slide, watching kids scream down it like bombers on an attack run. The two wore forced smiles as they kept an eye on the smaller kids, even the ones they weren't responsible for. The massive rubber slide looked dangerous as hell, and neither Thad nor Steve felt comfortable leaving anyone unsupervised.

The teenage attendants, on the other hand, looked completely disinterested. This either meant Thad and Steve were overreacting, or the teens were terrible at their jobs. Both assumed the latter.

Thad's heart jumped into his throat whenever he saw a kid Lyra's size go down. When Lyra's tiny face finally appeared at the top of the slide, she searched the crowd of adults and children down below looking for him.

"You can do it, Lyra. I'm here to catch you." Thad called up to her, stepping toward the slide, but a pimply face barred his way.

"Sorry, sir. You'll have to stand back."

Thad wondered how hard it would be to get this kid fired.

A huge grin curved her lips as she spotted him and waved. She looked like a blonde-haired version of her mother, only shrunk down to pocket size. The few times he'd been around kids since boarding school, he hadn't exactly enjoyed the experience. He'd felt unsure what to say to them, how to interact, and they seemed just as uncomfortable around him. But Lyra was special. She was sweet and shy and so God damn cute it actually caused a painful twitch in his chest to look at her. She crept to the top of the slide and was about to sit down when a much bigger kid shoved her hard. She screamed and tumbled down the slide.

Thad's heart jumped into his throat. He shoved the attendant aside and surged over the inflatable death trap to catch her. She was in a rigid curled up ball of terror as he scooped her up into his arms.

"Thad, is she okay?" Steve called out. He'd leaped over the barrier to grab the kid that came down next, the same little monster who'd shoved her.

"Let go of me!" The boy tried to kick Steve in the shin, but Steve had a death grip on the boy's shirt.

"Lyra, honey, are you hurt?" Thad asked as he carried her to a nearby chair and sat her down on it.

"My arm hurts," she said.

"Let me see." He knelt and gently examined her arm. She had a slight reddened mark. It looked like she'd skidded on the rubber of the slide when she came down wrong.

Thad pointed to the attendant who'd blocked his way in the first place. "You. Get a first-aid kit." He then looked at Steve. "Hey, can you get a glass of water for her?"

"Sure." Steve stared down at the kid he still held and then back at Thad.

"I'll take care of it." Thad made sure Lyra was okay on the chair before he went over and bent down to be eye level with the boy.

"If you hurt me, I'll tell my dad!" he snapped.

Thad grinned darkly. "Oh, I don't need to hurt you. If you ever hurt another kid, I'll know... And when I find out... I will buy the house you live in and throw you and your parents out on the street. Do you want to live under a bridge with rats?"

The kid's eyes went wide as he shook his head.

"Then quit being a bully and you'll be fine." Thad stood and nodded at Steve who released the kid. The boy took off at a blind run to escape him.

"Damn, you even scared me." Steve laughed. "Would you really do that?"

"Make him live under a bridge? No, probably not, but he doesn't need to know that."

"I like your style." Steve clapped a hand on Thad's shoulder. "I'll go find that kid looking for the first aid kit. He's probably lost in a broom closet somewhere."

Thad returned to the chair where Lyra was still holding her arm. She had a tiny cut on her elbow but didn't seem to realize it was there. Her hair was a mess of blonde curls. He got on his knees and straightened her little shirt.

"You are one brave girl," he said.

"I was scared when I fell," she admitted.

"I was too. But being brave doesn't mean you aren't scared. You did the right thing by curling up like that. That was very smart. I'll be sure to tell your mom how smart and brave you are." Even as he said it, he feared he was going to be in deep trouble when Veronica found out what happened.

Steve returned with the teen attendant and a first-aid kit. Sam was tagging along. "Is Lyra okay?"

"Yeah, she's fine," Thad said, liking how the little boy cared about her.

Sam held out a chunk of neatly folded tickets he'd won from a game to Lyra. "You want some of my tickets?"

"Can I?" Lyra asked Thad.

"Sure," Thad looked at the little boy. "You're a good kid, Sam."

"He's the best," Steve said, bright with pride for his son.

They treated the cut on Lyra's elbow and then put some burn cream on her small burn before he handed the kit back to the attendant.

"Next time, pay more attention to what's going on," Thad warned. He tturned to the kids. "You guys ready for cake?"

Lyra nodded, her face a bit less pale as she followed them to the party area.

"On a scale of one to ten, how much in the doghouse

do you think I am for her getting hurt?" Thad asked Steve.

"Don't worry about it. It wasn't your fault that kid was a dick. You handled it well and I'll tell Ronnie that."

"Thanks." Thad slid his hands into his pockets and watched the kids sing happy birthday to Sam before they all started diving into the cake like a pack of wild raccoons. He chuckled when Lyra got frosting on her nose and didn't seem to notice. She waved at him and he saw that her little fingers were covered with cake. His heart stuttered in his chest and he finally saw the look he'd been hoping to see, the one that meant she liked him and trusted him. Hell, he was falling in love with both the kid and her mother. This was getting dangerous.

He was starting to get way too attached to Veronica and her daughter, which begged the question: what was next? He didn't want to hurt them if things didn't work out, but he also didn't want to back away just because he was afraid of things not working out. He wanted to see where things would go, but not if it meant people got hurt at the end of it all...

For a moment, the future seemed scarier and more uncertain than the slide Lyra fell down.

11

As the party wound down and the sugar high turned to a crash, the crowd at the Razzy Tazzy became more subdued. Thad rubbed his temples as a dull throb began just behind his eyes.

Steve handed him two pills and Thad raised a brow.

"Aspirin. Trust me, take it now before the pain really sets in."

Thad downed the pills with some water. "Thanks. What's next on the agenda? Chasing them through the fire swamp?"

Steve nodded toward the prize counters, where dozens of kids were waving long streams of tickets. "Prize time."

Lyra held back from the crowd, her small stack of tickets in her hands. Thad held out his hand to her.

"Want to get a prize?" he asked.

She smiled and nodded, placing her tiny hand in his. Every protective instinct in him was still on high alert from what had happened on the inflatable slide. Their hands were still locked together as they reached the ticket counter.

"What do you want?" The teenage boy asked in a bored tone.

"The teddy bear." Lyra pointed a tiny finger at a giant russet furred teddy bear that was as tall as she was. It had a large blue satin bow tried around its neck.

"That's a thousand tickets."

Lyra handed the teenager her small pile of winnings. She had no more than fifty tickets. The teen humored her by running the tickets through counting machine.

"Sorry, you've got only forty-six. How about one of these pencils and erasers?" The kid behind the counter gestured to an array of pathetic consolation prizes.

Crestfallen, Lyra studied the erasers and pencils. The look on her face hit Thad like a punch to the gut. She didn't cry or whine, she just looked so sad and it only made Thad want to spoil her all the more.

"She's only four years old. Can't she just have the bear?" Thad leaned in to whisper to the teenager.

"Sorry man, rules are rules. I could get into trouble."

Thad glared at him. "My kid got hurt today. Some little punk shoved her down that slide—"

"All parents have to sign waivers. We aren't liable for injuries."

"That's not what I... nevermind." Thad pulled his wallet out of his jeans and thumbed through his bills. He pulled four bills out and flattened them under his palm so that the teen could see.

"I'll buy the extra tickets necessary to get it. Give me the bear and you can keep the change."

The boy's eyes widened at the four $100 bills before hastily nodding.

"Sure thing." He plucked the giant bear off the shelf and handed it to him. Lyra watched with wide eyes as Thad lowered the bear to her.

"Is he too big for you to carry?" Thad asked, knowing the answer, but he wanted to see joy fill her tiny, adorable face as she held the bear in her arms. He pulled his cellphone out of his pocket and snapped a quick picture to send to Veronica later.

"No, I can carry him." Lyra curled her tiny arms around the plush teddy inside like a contented kitten as she hugged the bear.

"Thank you, Mr. Dad," she said.

"No mister dad. I'm just Thad to you, honey." He ruffled her hair and his heart swelled as she valiantly held her toy up so the bear's feet wouldn't drag on the ground, marching proudly back to the party room.

Steve winked at him when they returned to the seating area. "Fifty tickets go a lot farther than I remember."

Thad grinned but said nothing.

"Oh my goodness, Lyra. Look at your bear!" Michelle gushed. She turned to Thad and whispered. "How did she get that?"

"I figured after what happened today, she deserved something nice."

Michelle gave him a long look that he couldn't read, but then smiled. "I've put some extra cake in some Tupperware for you to take home." She handed him a small sack filled with party favors and clear plastic tubs.

Thad nodded in appreciation. "I'll make sure Veronica gets it." He turned to Lyra. "You ready to go home?"

She nodded enthusiastically. Presumably she had big plans for her new stuffed friend.

They said their goodbyes to Sam and the others and took their leave. Thad kept a hand on Lyra's back as he guided her safely out of the continuing chaos.

"Why don't you let me carry the bear? You can carry your party favors. There's some cake in here for you and your mom." He swapped with Lyra, keeping the ridiculously huge bear under one arm. Simon pulled alongside the curb and got out to open the door for them.

"Thank you, Simon."

The driver put the bear in next to Lyra while Thad buckled the girl in her car seat. Thad got in the front with Simon to give Lyra and her bear more room in the back.

"How was the party, Miss Lyra?" Simon asked the girl.

Lyra kicked her tiny feet, leaning against her bear. "Great!"

Simon glanced toward Thad. "And you, sir? Did you have a good time?"

Thad's lips twitched. "Give me a board meeting discussing a hostile takeover any day."

"That bad, huh?"

"I survived. Still, watching her have fun was worth it." He looked back toward Lyra. She had already leaned her head on the bear like a pillow.

It was a twenty-minute drive home and he was pretty sure she would be asleep by then. The thought made him smile.

IT WAS ALMOST DINNERTIME WHEN VERONICA HEARD A knock. She got up from the couch and opened the door. Thad was there, but instead of Lyra, she saw only a massive brown teddy bear with a blue bow around its neck.

"Where's—?"

Thad put a finger to his lips for silence as he turned to face her. Her child was fast asleep in the other side of his arms.

"Let's put her in bed," Veronica whispered.

Thad followed her into Lyra's room. She pulled the covers back and removed Lyra's socks and shoes. Thad set her down and Veronica tucked her in. But as she was pulling up the sheets, she noticed a bandage and scrape on Lyra's arm. She looked at Thad, who motioned for them to step into the hall.

"What happened?"

Thad gently took one of her hands and led her to the couch. He collapsed onto it, pulling her down with him as he let out an exhausted sigh.

"Thad? What happened?" she asked again.

"Some little jerk shoved her down an inflatable slide. Didn't even apologize. I wanted to shove that kid down a slide," Thad growled, but his words softened as he spoke again. "Lyra was tough. She didn't even cry. Steve and I bandaged her up."

Veronica relaxed against him and rested her head on his shoulder. "These things happen. One time she fell off a see-saw and landed on another kid running by. Chaos is the default setting of playtime." She looked back to Lyra's room where the enormous teddy bear had been placed. "So what's the bear's story? There is no way she got enough tickets for that. Did you hustle someone for it?"

Thad's rumbling chuckle warmed her to her toes. "Not exactly. I *may* have paid the kid running the ticket counter for it. It was the one thing she wanted, and I wasn't about to let her walk out of there with some stupid eraser or pencil."

"Oh God, you didn't. I'm afraid to ask how much."

"Not much."

"Thad, how much?"

He was silent a long moment. "Four."

"Four dollars?"

"Four hundred."

"Four *hundred*!" She almost shrieked as she jerked up to stare at him. "I'll pay you back."

"Oh, come on. It's a gift. She's a great kid. After a fall like that, she needed something."

Veronica lay back down against him. "If you pay out four hundred bucks every time a kid hurts themselves, you're going to be broke by next year,"

Thad laughed at that.

"Besides, you know that spoiling a kid is bad, right?"

"Yeah, but a good kid deserves good things. She worked hard for her tickets. She was so much smaller than the other kids, so much younger. She couldn't ever have gotten the tickets she needed."

Veronica bit her lip as a riot of emotions warred inside her. Thad was being so nice, and in a weird way, his actions scared her. She couldn't shake the feeling he was enamored with the novelty of her life, not the reality of it.

"You feeling any better?" he asked as he yawned.

"Quite a bit. How are you holding up?" She placed a

hand on his chest, feeling the warmth of his body through his sweater. A dark, spicy scent clung to his clothes, reminding her of when she'd watched him shave. His cologne added to the natural scent of his skin, making her deliciously aware of how masculine he was.

"I'm dead on my feet, honey. Dead." He closed his eyes and let his head fall back on the couch. "I never get this tired," he grumbled. "And I've held eight-hour board meetings."

"You know they ran an experiment once, having an entire football team try to follow around a bunch of preschoolers all day to see who would last longer? Kids wiped them out."

"I can believe it."

"Just rest," she suggested. "You earned it."

"Only if you rest with me." He shifted on the couch to lay lengthwise with just enough room for her to join him. She had no desire to argue. Lounging beside him felt wonderful. She settled in and closed her eyes, sighing as he stroked her hair and she drifted off.

She woke to the sound of Thad's cell phone vibrating on the coffee table. Thad woke at the same time, surging up, but kept an arm around her as he fumbled for his phone and answered it.

"This is Thad," he said before he yawned., "Oh, hey, yeah. I forgot today was Friday." He listened to whoever was on the other end of the line. "Well, actually, I can't make it tonight." His hazel eyes flicked to hers. "I've got plans. Can we reschedule? Thanks." He hung up.

"You missing something important?" she asked.

"Not really. On Fridays I sometimes have dinner with my parents. Usually a social engagement, a party, a gala, that sort of thing. They have something going on almost every week. I go with them to find new business deals and new clients. But tonight, I'm right where I want to be."

She couldn't resist smiling and brushing her fingertips over his face. "I guess I really owe you," she said in a teasing whisper.

"You might," he agreed. "I seem to remember something about kisses."

"I seem to remember something about that too. What do I owe you?" This man made her giddy and she adored him for it. It felt so good to flirt, to tease, to just feel like a woman in the arms of a handsome, wonderful man who desired her back.

"Hmm, a dozen? Maybe two? I also accept alternative payments of a sensual nature." He gave a lazy grin that set fire to her blood.

Sensual payments. God how she wanted to pay him back for all the things he'd done to help her and knowing she'd enjoy owing him kisses only made it hotter.

He lowered his head to hers and she didn't pull back as he captured her lips. She was still worried he might get sick, but if that happened, she would take care of him.

His lips parted, his tongue seeking hers and she opened to him, heat rushing through her as he kissed her hard and hot. His desire seemed to mirror her own. Thad was kissing her like she was the only thing that could sate some dark hunger. His hands gripped her hips, pulling her against his hard body. Her legs parted as she shifted more fully on top of him. The press of his arousal in his jeans rubbed against her own body, reminding her how much she'd missed the intimacy of sex.

She wore only a pair of black leggings, which made her feel practically naked. He shaped her hips with his hands, then cupped her bottom, squeezing hard enough that she moaned against his mouth. How could this classy man kiss in the dirtiest and best way? An unfamiliar excitement lit her belly, and a throbbing pulse went straight to her clit as she rocked against him.

"That's it, honey. Ride me. Just like that," he encouraged in a rough voice that only heightened her arousal. She didn't care that she was dry humping him like a horny teenager in the back of a car. She only knew that she needed his hands on her, his body against hers and his mouth doing all those wickedly wonderful things. She lost all track of time as she lived in the moment, until a climax hit her and she clung to him, gasping softly.

He held her still over him, his eyes dark with passion. "God, you're beautiful when you come."

She ducked her head, embarrassed. He spoke so openly of passion, but she'd gotten used to always watching her language around Lyra. She'd forgotten how intoxicating it was to be with a man like this, to feel like this.

"How long has it been?" She tilted her face up so that their eyes met. She felt like she was a mortal looking upon a God.

"Since...?"

"Since you had an orgasm?" He splayed his hands over her lower back, and she felt wonderfully small and feminine. It made her want to tell him everything that lay in her heart.

"A few months... and it happens sometimes while I'm dreaming in my sleep." She wouldn't have told anyone else that, but something about Thad, after everything they'd been through and all he'd done, she trusted him, even with embarrassing, private things.

"God, honey, that's too long. I want to do so many things to you." There was a sweetness to the determination in his tone, as if he'd made it his life's mission just now to do exactly that. Veronica couldn't deny how amazing he made her feel.

She laid her head on his chest and sighed. "I think I want that too."

"But I want you to be sure you want it to. We'll take

our time." He massaged her body until she was nearly boneless on top of him. Her stomach rumbled.

He chuckled. "You want dinner?"

"Yeah, but I should shower first." She still had that tired, dirty feeling about her, even though she'd showered that morning.

With a smile, she left to shower, and by the time she dried her hair and put some light blush on her cheeks to combat the paleness, she found Lyra had gotten up and was in the kitchen with Thad.

"Cheese!" Lyra said.

"Nothing else?" Thad asked.

"Just cheese," Lyra said confidently.

"Cheese it is then, but how about we get half of what your mom likes too?"

"I guess we can." Lyra sounded slightly doubtful.

Thad saw Veronica lingering in the doorway to the kitchen. "Ah, there she is. What do you want, honey?"

"If you're talking about pizza, sausage is my favorite, but only get it if you like to eat it too."

At the mention of sausage, Thad's eyes lit with a sexual light, but he shot his gaze to Lyra and she realized the joke he'd likely wanted to make had to go unsaid. She bit her lip to hide a smile. She liked that he wanted to tease her, but she also liked that he kept it away from small, innocent ears.

"So you like a lot of sausage? I think I can give you

that." Thad winked at her before he tapped a few things on this cell phone.

Veronica shot a look to Lyra who clearly thought nothing of the innuendo Thad had just made.

"Pizza should be here in about thirty minutes." He slipped his phone in his back pocket

"Lyra, why don't you watch a movie?" Normally Veronica tried to make Friday and Saturday nights game nights, but she was too exhausted to try to entertain her four-year-old.

Lyra shot a pleading look at her mother. "Can we watch *Frozen*? Thad hasn't seen it."

"Honey, Thad doesn't want to watch something like that. I'm sure he has work to do."

"Actually, I don't mind. Apparently, I am missing out."

Veronica smiled. "You know she's going to make you watch the second one."

"There's two?"

"And then there's the shorts. *Frozen Fever. Olaf's Frozen Adventure. Once Upon A Snowman...*" Veronica walked up to him and patted his chest. "You've got a lot to learn about little girls and their princess movies."

Thad's eyes heated and he caught her wrist, gently bringing her fingers to his lips so he could kiss her knuckles.

"I'm willing to learn."

❄

WHEN THE PIZZA ARRIVED, THAD SETTLED THE GIRLS on the couch before he turned the movie on. The first movie. He insisted Veronica and Lyra both drink Pedialyte mixed with Sprite. Veronica needed the hydration and sugar and Lyra, well, the kid deserved a bit more sugar after the nasty fall she'd had.

As he turned the movie on, he could hear Lyra telling her mother all about the party and how she'd gotten her bear.

"And then he said, 'Give her the bear.'" Lyra's voice went deep as she tried to imitate him. He felt that tightening in his chest again. When he turned, he saw Lyra nestled in her mother's lap, the bear beside them. And he knew that had been the best four hundred dollars he'd ever spent.

Veronica watched her child talk, her pale face relaxed and her lips in a half smile. Love emanated from her weary features in a way that look stole his breath. She loved her child fiercely and unconditionally. It was a beautiful thing. He'd understood but never personally experienced how people could be so captivated by their children. He had an amazing, loving relationship with his parents, and he'd seen how Jared and Felicity mooned over their baby but seeing Veronica and Lyra together...it all became less of an abstract concept to him and something more tangible, more desirable. He was finally glimpsing behind that mysterious curtain. It scared him to think of loving someone like that, but as much as it scared him, it also fascinated him.

Veronica patted the spot beside her on the couch. He joined her, curling an arm around her shoulders as she stretched the blanket over their legs and propped his feet up on the ottoman.

The screen filled with Nordic men hauling ice from the lake and singing. Thad let himself relax for the first time in what felt like forever. Halfway through the movie, Veronica laid her head on his chest and her breathing deepened as she fell asleep. He smiled down at her and glanced toward Lyra. She'd stopped watching the movie and was watching him instead.

"She's really tired," the child said solemnly.

"Yes, she needs lots of rest to get better."

"You will take care of her?" Lyra asked, the question asked so seriously that it made him think carefully about his response.

"Yes, I'm going to take care of her."

"And me too?" the child asked.

"You too, kiddo," he promised. He understood now that Lyra and Veronica were a package deal. And while that intimidated him on some level, he was not the sort of man that let anything scare him off for long.

Lyra settled back to watch the movie. "Good."

The music was actually pretty good. He made a note to find the guitar sheet music for it so he could practice for Lyra. As the movie ended, he noted with bemusement that Lyra was still awake, albeit barely. She yawned with a tiny fist curled against her mouth.

"Let's get you in the bed," he whispered. He carefully left the couch so as not to wake Veronica. He lifted Lyra up and carried her to the bathroom where he helped her brush her teeth and change into her PJs, then he tucked her in bed with her new teddy bear and kissed her forehead before saying good night. He was closing the door when her soft voice stopped him.

"Good night, Thad." He was about to correct her about his name, then realized she'd called him Thad. Only a part of him had heard "dad" nonetheless. It made him think. He wasn't her dad, but in that moment, he wanted to be.

He closed the door and returned to the family room where he collected Veronica in his arms next. She stirred with the movement as he carried her.

"Is the movie over?"

"Yes. Lyra's in bed." He set her down on her bed but hesitated. "I want to stay the night again, if that's okay with you"

"I want you to stay, too."

"I have my bag. I can sleep in the guestroom—"

"It's okay. You can stay here in my bed." Veronica sounded more awake now and he smiled. Her big blue eyes glowed in the moonlight from the window and a soft desire filled her face.

"Well, if you insist." He tried to tease her with his words, but they came out rough with emotion as he came toward her.

"I certainly do." She scooted over to one side of the bed. Thad stripped down to his boxers and got in beside her, then pulled her into his arms, relishing the way she felt. There was nothing better than this.

"Bet you had no idea how crazy asking me out that day was going to turn out." Veronica chuckled as she lay her head on his chest. Still, he heard the uncertainty in her tone.

"Oh, *hell* no. But I wouldn't change a thing about it all." He kissed the top of her head.

She rubbed her cheek against his chest and his heart beat a little faster. Laying in bed with women was nothing new to him, but this was different. This made his heart race in a way those other moments never had. He was beginning to suspect he knew what it meant too.

12

Thad was finally back in his apartment after a long weekend spent at Veronica's. She was back to her regular, flu-free self, which was a relief, because he knew she couldn't afford to miss any more work. He also had dozens of meetings this week that he couldn't skip, plus a few crucial negotiations he couldn't do over the phone.

Dropping his weekender bag on his bed, he changed into his running clothes before he went to the private gym in one of the spare rooms of his penthouse. He could feel the proverbial cobwebs blowing away as he ran for the first time in several days, but the pleasant relief was short-lived.

After half an hour, he slowed down to walk, breathing harder than normal. He'd pushed himself too far this week, and as much as he loved spending time with Veronica and Lyra, it had worn him out. He was starting to understand what parents meant when they said kids were work. But when he thought of Lyra's face as he'd put her to bed last night, he didn't regret a second of it. He walked another ten minutes before he called it quits and showered for work.

By the time he got into the office, Brandon had a mountain of contracts for him to review. Jared must have spent the weekend redlining every document Thad had sent him over the last two weeks. As he worked for the next several hours, he found himself wishing he had a picture of Veronica on his desk. He didn't even have a picture of her on his phone to look at and he wanted to see her face as he worked.

What was the protocol these days about photos? He was not a fan of selfies, but maybe the next time he, Veronica, and Lyra were out doing something, he could ask someone to take a picture of the three of them.

Brandon stuck his head in Thad's office doorway. "Sir, is it okay if I leave for the evening?"

Brandon checked the time, though he hardly needed to. It was clearly past office hours. "Of course, have a good night."

Thad pulled himself out of his daydreams. The stack of contracts he'd gotten back from Jared was only halfway done. Shit. He'd been thinking about Veronica way too much. He needed to get back into work mode and not let anything else distract him.

It was nearly nine when he packed up to leave. His father was still in his office and Thad checked in with him on his way out.

"Don't work too late," he told him.

His father chuckled at that. "I won't. Oh, your mother and I missed you this weekend."

"Yes, sorry, I..." He almost didn't tell his father about Veronica but changed his mind. "I met someone and was spending some time with her. She got the flu this past weekend, so I kept her company."

His father's eyes brighten with interest. "Do your mother and I know this girl?"

His parents had spent the last couple of years awkwardly placing him in situations where he could meet young women they approved of. Smart, classy, kind women from well-connected families. They'd all been lovely, but none felt right, and he hadn't been curious enough to go on a second date with any of them.

"You don't know her," Thad said. "But I think you'd like her."

"Are we going to get a chance to meet her?" Timothy asked with a polite tone, doing his best not to push him into anything.

"Eventually. It's new," Thad admitted. "I think she might need some time before we add any additional complications."

His father quirked a brow. "What is complicating this relationship?"

Thad felt a flush of embarrassment. "She's a widow and... a single mom. She's got a four-year-old girl."

He waited for his father to react, to say anything. Timothy took his time before answering. "Thad, you've never dated a woman like this before have you?" He hadn't. They both knew it. "Are you sure that you are ready for an obstacle like that?"

Thad fought off a prickle of irritation. His parents would love to see him married, but with a widowed single mother, his father was suddenly hesitant?

"Honestly, I don't know. But right now, I want to be with her, and her daughter."

"*And* her daughter?" His father's eyes softened with understanding. "That's good. How about dinner in a few weeks?"

"I'll ask her, but she still may not be ready."

"Of course, but it can't hurt for you to ask," Timothy said with a smile.

"Good night," Thad said.

"Don't forget the meeting tomorrow with Bob Sayer and his legal team."

"Right." He left the office and had Simon pick him up outside.

"Where to, sir? The Gold Circle or Mrs. Hannigan's?"

"The Circle tonight."

Thad had spoken with Veronica that morning about needing to go back to his own place for a few days and she'd agreed. He wanted to be there with her and Lyra, but before, with other women, he'd always needed time in his own space. He was worried that spending too much time with her might make him claustrophobic, or perhaps she would think he was overcommitting himself. So forcing himself to take a few days away from her would be a good thing. It would give him time to clear his head.

His butler was at the hotel front desk waiting to greet him when he arrived, handing him a stack of mail.

Winston smiled. "It's been quiet without you here this weekend."

Thad chuckled. Poor Winston, all those mornings he'd had to come collect clothes in need of repair or have the housekeeping staff cleanup from an exciting night. Yes, he'd been very quiet lately in some ways, though not in others.

The night before last, he'd been playing board games with Veronica and Lyra, the whole affair had been noisy and chaotic in the best way. Lyra knew how to play the card game Uno and absolutely loved shouting "Uno!" whenever she won. Her excitement had him and Veronica laughing.

Right before Thad stepped into the elevator, his cell phone rang. He frowned at the name that flashed across the screen as he pulled it out.

Annette Becker.

He waved for Winston to let other guests take the

elevator first and he headed for the bar to answer the call.

"Mrs. Becker?"

"Mr. Worthington, I'm glad I reached you. There's been another offer on the house. I wanted to give you a chance to counteroffer since you are so interested in the property."

So she didn't even wait for his offer to fall through before shopping it around. "Yes, I'm still interested. How much has the other party offered?"

"They've offered 3.5."

Thad sat down the bar on one of the tall, black bar chairs and waited for the bartender to get his favorite cocktail.

"That's quite a bit above the listed value," Thad said coolly.

"But it's what you were planning to pay," she reminded him.

Thad accepted the gin and tonic the bartender placed in front of him and nodded silently in thanks.

"Mrs. Becker, are you using my previous offer to encourage this other buyer to overpay?" He was certain that was exactly what she was doing. No wonder Veronica called her the evil sea witch.

"Of course not," Annette said. "Mr. Covington, the other party, met me at a fundraiser this evening. When he learned you were interested, he said he couldn't help himself."

"Roarke Covington?" Thad tried not to growl at the name.

"Yes, that's him."

Thad downed half of his gin and tonic in one gulp. "I will make a counteroffer. Give me an hour."

"Certainly." Annette's tone was full of sugary sweetness. He ended the call and dialed a phone number he wished he didn't know by heart.

"I wondered when you would call," Roarke chuckled as he answered.

"You have a minute to talk in person?" Thad asked.

"Actually, I do. Are you at The Circle?" Roarke asked.

"Yes, in the bar."

"Perfect. I'll be there in two minutes." Roarke hung up.

Thad finished his gin and tonic and waved for another. If there was one man he truly hated dealing with, it was Roarke Covington. Roarke had also been at the same prep school where Thad met Jared and Angelo, but Roarke was as blueblood as they came and had all of the prestige, good looks, and money you'd expect from that background.

He was also, aside from Jared, one of the best real estate lawyers in the city, and more often than not ended up on the opposite sides of the negotiation table. Timothy sometimes joked about hiring Roarke so they could stop fighting him on contracts. Thad couldn't stand the idea of working in the same office building as him, let alone directly with him.

He'd just finished the second drink when Roarke strolled into the bar. He grinned as he spotted Thad and pulled up a seat beside him.

"Drinks on a Monday night? Don't mind if I do." He got the bartender's attention. "A glass of your best scotch and put it on this guy's tab." He slapped Thad's shoulder as though they were friends rather than business rivals.

"Roarke, I know you put an offer on a brownstone on North Astor Street."

"I'm not surprised you know about it. That Becker woman was only too happy to hear about my interest in you. She told me you had made an offer but withdrawn it."

Thad pushed his empty glass away and glared at Roarke. "I need you to withdraw your offer."

"Why?" The smile was gone from Roarke's face and he was all business. "What does that house mean to you? You've got the best penthouse in Chicago and can easily afford any other home twice as large."

"What it means to me isn't important. What is important is that you walk away from it."

"You know me better than that. I have no intention of doing that unless you tell me why."

It went against everything inside him to expose any

weakness to Roarke. But the man's pockets were as deep as his own, so Thad had no choice but to risk it.

"It's personal."

"So this isn't some big development score you're lining up?"

Thad shook his head.

"Details, or I close the deal as soon as I leave."

"If I tell you, when I'm done, you'll call Becker and withdraw the offer in front of me."

Roarke was grinning again. "Fine, fine. Color me intrigued. Scout's honor, I'll rescind my offer."

"You weren't a Boy Scout," Thad snapped.

"Was too. Eagle Scout and everything. I finished before high school." Roarke fired back, clearly offended.

Thad was tempted to ask him why he was such an asshole when he'd supposedly been a Boy Scout, but he held back the retort.

"So, what is it?" Roarke pressed.

"That house belongs to a friend. It was their childhood home and Becker, unfortunately, has control of it as a trustee."

Roarke was silent a moment. "You used a possessive plural pronoun to conceal the gender, so this friend must be a woman. I know where your friends live, so it must be someone new in your life, and that means you're dating her." Roarke looked like a kid who discovered Christmas had come early. "Oh this is priceless.

Worthington, you've gone and fallen in love." He started laughing.

Thad gripped his arm. "This isn't funny, Roarke. She's been through hell these last four years because Becker is her stepmother. That woman is trying to sell that house so she can kick her out."

Roarke stopped laughing. "Evil stepmother? Christ, you sure know how to pick them. Will this girl of yours turn into a pumpkin at midnight?"

"It's the coach not the girl that turns into a pumpkin."

"And Frankenstein's the doctor, not the monster. I know. I'm just saying, what kind of woman holds *that* kind of grudge?"

"Hell if I know. But I told you the why, now it's your turn. Make the call."

Roarke slid his cell phone out of his pocket and dialed Annette.

"Mrs. Becker? Yes, this is Roarke Covington. I'm sorry, but I need to rescind my offer. I just realized I'm closing on a property in Colorado this month. Yes, I'm very sorry. Good luck." He hung up and looked at Thad with a thoughtful expression. "You want my honest advice?"

"As long I don't have to pay you a legal retainer fee, counselor," Thad joked grimly.

Roark smiled, but only briefly. "That woman is serious about selling. When I met her tonight, she was telling everyone about that property and clearly trying to get anyone she could to make an offer. I steered clear of it until I heard you were the first person who'd been interested. Naturally, I thought you had some kind of scheme cooking, and figured making a counteroffer might let me flush out what it was. I have to say, this was the *last* thing I expected."

"Honestly? I was originally planning to move in, make it my new home."

Roark seemed surprised. "That place? Never thought you for the quaint brownstone type. Well, if you love this girl, you'd better buy it tonight. You want any more love advice, I'll be happy to reduce your retainer fee." He tossed back the rest of his drink and with a cocky grin got up from the barstool and left.

Thad watched the other man walk away before he called Annette back. As much as he hated to admit it, Roark was right.

He leaned back against the bar and watched the people laughing and drinking beneath the glow of the glamorous hotel chandeliers as he dialed Veronica's stepmother.

"Mrs. Becker? I'm officially extending my offer again. Asking price, all the same terms I previously offered." He didn't tell her he knew Roarke had withdrawn.

"Well, I'd love to accept but the asking price is now 3.75."

Thad took a deep breath and suppressed the need to

tell her to go to hell. He reminded himself that the money would go to Veronica's trust and that Annette couldn't touch it. In six years, Veronica and Lyra would have it to live on. That was good enough for him.

"Fine. I'll pay it. I'll have the paperwork sent over tomorrow morning, but I would like a formal written acceptance of my offer from you via email tonight. I would also like to remind you that in my initial offer, I required privacy for this sale. I understand you have tenants, so they are not to know my name."

"I will do that immediately. Thank you, Mr. Worthington. I'll be delighted to see what you do with the place when you move in." Her voice was so smug it made him sick to hear it.

Thad said nothing to that. If she learned he didn't plan to move in and kick Veronica out, she might try to get out of the sale. And if she couldn't, she might tell Veronica who bought the house if she suspected Thad knew Veronica. He didn't want her to think he was "white knighting" her until he had a chance to explain he wasn't out to make her owe him for this. He would have to be careful with how he revealed this to her and resolved it so she owned her home and not him.

"Good night, Mrs. Becker." He dropped a twenty in the tip jar before heading upstairs. The house was safe. Now he just had to make sure that Veronica didn't find out he'd bought it, at least until he could find a way to tell her without upsetting her.

His phone rang again as he stepped into the penthouse. It was Veronica. A sudden flash of panic swept through him. Had Annette already called her to let her know that someone had bought her home? He had to get control of himself a moment before he answered.

"Hey, you okay?"

"Yeah, feeling so much better." She hesitated. "Um... Lyra wanted to know if you could sing to her. I know it's late and I told her I would ask but that you might be busy."

"Too busy to sing for her? Not tonight. Is she in bed?"

"Yes." Veronica laughed. "Lyra, he's going to sing, but you can't have him do this every night, okay? He has important things to do."

"Okay." Lyra's voice was slightly muffled, but Thad heard the disappointment in it.

"You can put me on speaker," he told Veronica. Already the distaste of dealing with Roarke and the evil sea witch was fading.

"Thad?" Lyra called out.

"Are you all tucked in bed?"

There was a little giggle. "Yes!"

"Good." He settled on his couch and picked up his guitar. Then he put his phone on the table and hit the speaker button. He strummed a few notes testing to see if the guitar was tuned.

Then he began to sing "Africa" by Toto, which he'd

learned Lyra liked. He had to sing in a higher octave than normal, and he knew it would make her laugh when he hit the really high notes. He sang about the rains in Africa, longing for company and loving a woman so fiercely he could not be dragged away from her. It was such an intense set of lyrics, yet it had the bounce and catchiness of an 80s love ballad. When he finished, he could hear Lyra giggling. Veronica was laughing too.

"Oh Thad, you should see her. I think she might make that her new favorite song over anything from *Frozen*."

"Glad she likes it. We need to get her into more of the classics."

"We do, do we?" Veronica sighed. "Bedtime, Lyra." He heard the click of the door closing and she spoke more softly. He could picture her lingering in the hall outside.

"Thank you for that. She really loves music."

"She gets that from you, I think. I saw your music collection. All those old vinyl records."

"Yeah. Music was the only way I survived losing Parker before she was born. Even before that, music was always part of me."

"Music can be a powerful healing tool. When my mother was a young resident doctor, she always encouraged her patients to listen to music. She swears it helps heal people."

"A positive state of mind does wonders," Veronica

said. "Well, I'm sure you want to enjoy the rest of the night off."

Thad laughed. "You say it like I'm on vacation from you two."

"Well, I mean..." Veronica's voice trailed off, embarrassed.

"Hey, it's okay," Thad said, his tone serious. "I was only teasing."

"I know." She exhaled. "God, I just don't know how to do this."

That sounded like red flag. He stilled, holding his breath. "Do what?"

"Be normal. Have dates while I have a kid." She laughed nervously. "It's going to take some time for me to figure out how to adjust to three people in my life."

Thad felt a wave of relief. "I think you're doing just fine. And for the record, I don't know what I'm doing either. Before you, life was uncomplicated. I was used to being just alone. My relationships were basically a series of one night stands and convenient hookups."

"You *never* dated anyone seriously?"

Thad was quiet for a long moment. "Well, I did, a long time ago. She was the daughter of a friend of my parents."

He didn't like to think about Victoria. She was in the past, so much so that he buried all thoughts of her as deep as he could.

"What happened? If you don't mind me asking?"

He expected the question, and he knew in all fairness that he owed her his story given what she told him about Parker.

"I was twenty and I met her at Princeton. Our parents were friends. Her name was Victoria. She was beautiful, passionate, intelligent, driven. I'd never met anyone like her. I thought at the time that I understood love and what it meant to share my life with someone. I put it all on the line for her." He still remembered how foolish he felt when he proposed on one knee in a five-star restaurant and how she looked at him with pity.

"What happened?" Veronica asked quietly.

Thad closed his eyes, trying to keep the past from coming back too strongly.

"She reminded me about the world we were born into, the expectations, the demands, how fairytales didn't happen for people like us. She wanted to be a federal prosecutor and was bound for Pepperdine Law school and then DC. I wasn't. Our paths were designed to keep us apart. Two workaholics who would never see each other."

"Oh no..."

"I tried to argue the point, said I'd give it all up to be with her. I was too blind to see the truth of it, but she wasn't."

Thad could still remember the weight of the ring box in his trouser pocket as he walked out of the restaurant, never to see her again. That small blue box from Tiffany's weighed a thousand pounds that day.

He hadn't hated Victoria for turning him down, and in time, he even appreciated the fact she cared for him enough to be so honest. But that experience had closed off his heart and he'd been afraid to expose himself to those feelings ever again.

"Sometimes you have to lose something to know what it really meant to you," Veronica said. "I loved Parker and he loved me, but it wasn't until he was gone that the depth of what I'd lost hit me."

It nearly killed him to think about her hurting like that, of losing that love. No, of having it ripped away. "I can only imagine," was all he could say.

She sighed. "It's okay. There are tough days, sure, but then I look at Lyra and I remember instantly what it felt like to have spent those years with Parker. I see him in Lyra's smile, hear him in her laugh. He may be gone, but he left part of himself behind in her. I'm so lucky for that."

Thad realized with a small amount of surprise that he wasn't jealous of Parker or worried about his ghost standing between him and Veronica. If anything, he was grateful. Grateful that Veronica had been loved by a good man and that Lyra was living proof of that love. If anything, it made Thad feel all the more protective of Veronica and her little girl.

Thad cleared his throat. "You should get to bed. You still need your rest. I'll call you tomorrow if that's okay?"

"That would be great." She drew in a deep breath. "Good night, Thad."

"Good night." He ended the call and walked over to the sofa, collapsing onto his back. He dropped the phone to his chest and gazed up at the ceiling.

What he hadn't told Veronica and what he was too afraid to admit even to himself, was that he already cared more for her than he ever had for Victoria.

13

Thad leaned back in his chair in the board room, facing off once again with Roarke Covington on a large real estate deal. Roarke smirked at him from across the expensive mahogany table. Thad rarely took the bait. He defeated Roarke more often than not, but the two of them were always counting points on who won a particular round. He wasn't a cocky bastard like Roarke, but winning still mattered.

His father sat on Thad's right and Jared was on his left. The rest of the chairs were filled with various other employees who handled financial matters for Thad's company. Directly across from them was Leslie Newton, the man they were here to negotiate with. The man Roarke was representing in this real estate deal.

"Shall we get started?" Newton said as he eyed Thad.

Newton was the owner of three old mansions on Long Island that had recently been listed in the mansion section of the *Wall Street Journal*. The mansion section was an excellent place to advertise a property because the feature page always discussed the properties' history and any recent work done. Normally it was movie stars or other big names putting up their ten million dollar Malibu beach houses or the like, but every now and then some real gems showed up in the section.

"Since the *Journal* featured one of these properties recently, there's been a lot of interest..." Newton began a lengthy presentation to the dozen or so people involved in the potential transaction.

Thad was pulled out of his thoughts as Jared poked his hand on the table with his legal notepad. He glanced at Jared, who gave a subtle nod to the pad. He looked down at what Jared had written.

What # are you on?

Thad almost laughed. This made him think of grade school where boys and girls sent little notes to each other asking if they liked a certain guy or girl. He picked up his pen and calmly scratched out a reply, acting as if he was taking notes.

1 — Drinks at Vol. 39

2 — Dinner at Italian Villa

3 — Open mic night

4/5/6 — Spent the weekend with her and Lyra. That counts.

He slid the notepad back to Jared. While this exchange was going on, both were still listening to the presentation. Over the years, he and Jared had become adept at multitasking, even in important meetings. Jared wrote something and slid the pad back.

That doesn't count.

Thad rolled his eyes, scribbled a response, and slid it back.

You weren't there. Trust me, it counts.

Jared took a bit longer to respond this time.

Fine. You taking her to the gala Friday? We got a sitter for Haley. You could have her look after Lyra too.

Christ, he'd forgotten all about the Met. The tickets were sitting in his office and he'd just completely spaced on it. He was invited every year and always went because it was a great place to make business contacts. But if he took Veronica, he might actually enjoy himself.

He hesitated a second before writing out his reply.

Maybe. Need to ask her.

He returned the pad to Jared and focused back on Newton's presentation. Thad soon realized Roarke was watching him. Gone was the smug smile, and in its place was cold-hearted determination. The man's gaze flitted to the notepad in front of Jared, then back to Thad, betraying Roarke's thoughts.

He thinks Jared and I are planning a play on the negotiations.

The truth was, he and Jared had already planned

their strategy long before the meeting started. This meeting was simply a formality. Thad let Newton finish discussing his view of the properties' worth, then took control of the negotiations by opening, as he always did, with his vision for the land.

"Mr. Newton, picture if you will, these three mansions completely revamped. Everything returned to their original splendor with plumbing, kitchen, appliances, and electrical components completely updated. Then, the rooms open into guest rooms and the houses themselves become half of the attraction, the other half would be commercial interests with wedding destinations, hotel services, etc. Yet the integrity the property would still be completely retained."

Newton had been expecting a pitch like this, but Thad knew the man had better offers for the property. He had to really sell it.

"We'd like to offer twenty million, Mr. Newton, for the three properties."

Newton glanced toward Roarke, who gave a subtle shake of his head to his client.

"My client has received many similar offers, including one yesterday that's double that," Roarke said.

"I imagine so. I'm sure some condominium companies are beating down your doors for this. They could put new condos right next to the ocean, and we all know how valuable beachfront property is. But let me ask you this, Mr. Newton." Thad leaned forward, resting his arms on the table. "Do you want more money today, or to be known as the man who helped create a lasting cultural legacy for your children and grandchildren?"

"Legacy?" Newton's eyes lit up. "But how? If I sell to you..."

"We provide an incentive for you to buy back in. I'll increase our offer to twenty-five million, and you buy back into the investment on the property in thirty days after we close to become a partner. Consider that five million extra your buyback. With that, we name the properties in your honor and donate a hundred acres of the non-developed land to become a park in your name, promoting conservation for the future."

"A buyback?" Roarke snorted. "Leslie, don't fall for that. It's just a way for him to make you think you're getting more but you're still leaving that five million in his pocket."

Roarke's argument was entirely valid, and as money was all that mattered, Newton would've left the room at Thad's first offer. But Thad knew how to read people, to figure out what mattered to them. Newton was already rich, but he was at an age where he was all too keenly aware that he wasn't going to be around forever. He wanted immortality, but in a positive way. Condos wouldn't get him that. But a legacy that honored these Gold Coast homes, yet also made them protected and open to the public? That was a form of immortality he couldn't resist.

"Mr. Worthington, would you mind giving me and my attorney a minute?"

"Of course." Thad and his team left the conference room. Jared, Thad, and Timothy remained in the hallway, while the other employees that had been present for the pitch went back to their offices.

"I think you got him, son." his dad said. "You knew *exactly* what to offer him."

Thad smirked. "We did a bit of sleuthing. His charitable donations are above average, and all the charities he gave to provide some kind of public recognition in exchange. It was clear what Newton liked. Jared found it and I merely made the sales pitch."

Jared chuckled. "Did you see Roarke's face? I thought his eyes would fall out of his head and roll onto the table."

Thad slid his hands into his pockets and studied the closed conference room door, wondering how long Roarke would try to talk Newton out of the offer. "Today's the day he learns that money is *not* the answer to everything."

A few minutes later, Newton opened the door and they returned to the conference room. Roarke stood by the tall windows overlooking the city, his arms crossed and a deep scowl hovering over his face.

Newton held out a hand. "Mr. Worthington, we have a deal."

Thad grinned and shook it. "Fantastic. Let's talk specifics."

By Friday, Veronica was finally feeling like herself. She felt safe enough to be around her customers without worrying about passing on the flu. Before that, she'd spent the last few days staying in the storeroom or her office.

It had been much easier than she'd expected to survive the week thanks to Thad's help, but his staying over hadn't felt like an imposition. He'd just somehow seamlessly fit into her world as though he'd always been there. Yet, she was still hesitant about trusting him, despite the safety she felt.

"Hey boss, your boy toy is here!" Zelda hollered way too loudly.

Veronica came from the storeroom to find Thad leaning against the counter smirking.

"Boy toy?" he asked her.

"That's all Zelda. I *swear* I do not call you that."

Thad leaned over the counter and kissed her. "I'll be your boy toy anytime, sweetheart." Veronica's face heated and she smiled foolishly at him.

"What are you doing here?" She had missed him last night at open mic night. He told her he'd had a ton of paperwork to do and warned he wouldn't be able to make it.

"Well, I know this is last minute, but I have something to ask you." He looked adorably sexy when he got all bashful.

"Ask me what?"

"There's this thing going on tonight and I would like for you to be my date."

"Okay... I might be able to get Katie to babysit."

"Actually, Jared and Felicity have hired a sitter and are happy to share with us."

"Oh?" She had met Jared only the one time, but he seemed nice and it would be fun to meet his wife. Thad often spoke highly of her.

"Yeah. We could take Lyra to Jared's house and then head to the airport."

"The airport? What exactly are we going to be doing?" What event could Thad have planned if it required a jet to get there?

"We are going to attend the gala at the Met."

For a moment it didn't sink in. The Met? The only Met she knew of was the Metropolitan Museum of Art? When that hit home, she finally found her voice.

"In New York?" she gasped. "But we wouldn't get back until..."

"Early in the morning, I know." Again that bashful boyish look was getting to her.

Veronica nearly said no immediately but stopped herself. Thad had a way of making her want to say yes.

"The sitter can stay until we get home. We can come back and crash at your place and sleep in since it will be Saturday."

"But Saturday mornings are so busy for the Chi-Bean."

"I can cover it, boss." Zelda jumped in. "Zach is looking for more hours. I bet he can handle a full day on Saturday, and Beth and I have tonight covered. Go let the boy toy whisk you away to New York."

"Okay, wait just a second." Veronica sometimes got the feeling Zelda and Thad arranged these moments just to gang up on her. "Even if I did want to go, and assuming Lyra was fine with a sitter she didn't know, I have nothing to wear for a gala at the *Met*."

"Not a problem." Thad whipped out his phone, where he already had a calendar marked up with a clear timetable for the rest of the day. "We have four hours until we need to take Lyra to the sitter and head for the airport." He scrolled through the calendar page with a single swipe. "After that, the timetable takes care of itself." Thad was smiling fully now, an almost devious expression on his face that warned her she was in for a hell of a surprise.

"You're not suggesting we go...?"

"Shopping." Thad replied as though the answer was

obvious. "I'm going to buy you a dress, shoes, and some jewelry."

"Oh, no you aren't." She already felt indebted to him for helping her while she was sick, not to mention the expense of Lyra's teddy bear. She did not need to add a financial obligation that went beyond the existing list to their relationship.

"Honey, I have too much money and as much as I like my suits, I never get a chance to buy the fun stuff. Let me do this for you."

"Richard Gere wants to do a *Pretty Woman* with you," said Zelda. "How can you say no?"

Thad gazed at her with that irresistible smile that reminded her how much she enjoyed it when he got what he wanted. And right now, his desire was to buy her beautiful clothes and take her to a gala.

In another life, she might have attended a gala like that with her mother and father. In another life, before her mother had died...

"I guess I could... But you can't buy anything too expensive, since I really doubt I'll have a chance to wear it again."

"Fine, I won't spoil you too much." He glanced at Zelda. "You okay to take over now?"

"Definitely. Have fun, boss." Zelda winked at Thad, and Veronica was even more convinced her employee and her boyfriend were in cahoots on this. She'd been cahooted! Her mind stuttered to a stop.

Boyfriend? Did she really think of him that way?

"Grab your purse," Thad said as she removed her apron.

Veronica slipped on her coat and grabbed her purse before she followed him outside where Simon was waiting. Veronica greeted the driver with a smile, which he warmly returned.

"Where to, sir?" Simon asked when she and Thad were inside the car.

"Taylor's, please."

Veronica gasped. That was the most expensive private clothing boutique in the city. They only let people in by appointment. "I thought you agreed not to spend too much?" she reminded him.

"I have an account there and they treat me very well." Thad clasped his hand in hers. "I said not too much, and this isn't too much."

"To you, maybe," she grumbled.

Thad laughed. "You're so cute when you get mad about being spoiled."

"I just don't think you should waste money on me like this."

He raised her hand to his lips and kissed the back of her knuckles. "Nothing is a waste with you. Try to enjoy this, please."

She wanted to enjoy this, to just surrender to him and the glittering world he was taking her into, but the fear that it wouldn't last, that he wouldn't stay, left her on edge. But she forced herself to calm, to push back the negative worries and embrace the delight at the thought of shopping with him.

When they reached Taylor's, Veronica was still fighting her nerves when something occurred to her.

"Wait, you have to have an appointment with Taylor's. How did you know I would say yes?"

"I didn't, but I was hoping you would." After they exited his car, Thad opened the door to the shop, letting her enter ahead of him.

The white carpeted room had several groups of mirrors and dozens of artfully designed racks of skirts, evening gowns, and suits. There was also a table of shoes on display. Each outfit looked like it would cost her a month's earnings at the Chi-Bean.

"Mr. Worthington." A woman in a slim blue suit approached them. Her gray hair was cut just above the shoulders and she looked faintly like Anna Wintour.

"Martha." Thad embraced the woman before introducing Veronica. "Veronica, this is Martha Weiss, owner of Taylor's. Martha, this is my date, Veronica Hannigan."

Veronica shook Martha's hand, feeling wildly self-conscious about her off the rack sweater and jeans.

"We have cranberry mimosas for you both if you'd like to take a seat and enjoy refreshments while we get the gowns ready." Martha gestured to a dark velvet blue couch where a young woman had a pair of champagne flutes waiting for them.

Thad put an arm around Veronica's waist and led her over to the couch. He handed her one of the mimosas as they sat down.

"So how does this work?" she whispered before sipping her drink.

"I told her where we're going tonight. Martha will bring out what she thinks are appropriate dresses. The ones you like, you try on. She's procured all the pieces in your size."

"But how would she know my—?"

His cheeks reddened slightly. "I may have peeked at your closet when you were sleeping off the flu."

Saving Thad from further embarrassment, Martha rolled out a rack of gowns.

"Feel free to let me know which ones you'd like to try on." She told Veronica before she and her assistant began removing the dresses one by one off the rack to show her. The pieces were all elegant and stunning. Some were bright pink, others silver, gold, or purple. But it was the very last one that caught her attention.

"Oh, can I see that one?" she asked.

"Of course. Come this way. We'll see how it fits."

Veronica followed Martha into the changing room where the woman helped her undress and get into the beautiful gown. It strangely reminded her of her first middle school dance when she was fourteen, just before her mother had died. She and her mother had gone to an expensive dress shop and tried on a dozen gowns. She'd felt so carefree then, so unaware of how drastically her life would change in a matter of months.

Now, here she was again, donning princess gown after princess gown and feeling homesick for her mother in a way she hadn't allowed herself to feel in years. She blinked, trying to dispel the tears threatening to form in her eyes. Veronica focused on Thad, on tonight, on the magic and splendor of where they were going together. Before she even knew it, she was smiling as she put on the dress.

"Well? Do you think he'll like it?"

"I think..." Martha said with a winning smile. "That he will be stunned speechless in the best possible way. I know he saw it on the rack, but there's nothing like seeing it on for the full effect. If you like it, let's keep it a surprise for Mr. Worthington."

"Good idea, oh, how much is—?"

"Hush, don't worry about that." Martha waved a hand as though to ward off any discussion of prices.

Veronica swallowed hard. That meant this gown was insanely expensive. Maybe it was better she didn't know. She removed the garment and got dressed again before joining Martha outside the changing room.

"Now, let's talk shoes." Martha showed her a small selection of shoes on the table display. "These are just a few pairs I brought out to match the gowns you looked over."

"Oh. Well..." Veronica thought she could easily use a

pair of shoes from home, but Martha held up a pair of dark blue teal pumps with brocade silver flowers in the fabric on the sides and toes.

"These were designed to match the dress you selected," Martha said. "Try them on."

Veronica took the shoes over to the velvet couch. Thad watched her as she tried on the shoes, a hint of a smile on his lips.

"What do you think?" she asked, angling her leg toward him to show him the pump.

"Lovely," he answered.

Veronica gave Martha a nod, then handed the shop assistant the shoes before putting on her boots and socks.

"Charge it to my account, Martha."

The older woman smiled. "Are you bound for Winston's next?"

Thad chuckled. "We are."

"Winston's?" Veronica asked as they stepped out into the street.

"Harry Winston's," he clarified.

"*Harry Winston's*!" Veronica almost shrieked as they headed for the car. Martha's laughter followed her down the street.

Thad put his arm around her again. "Yes. Now come on." For a moment, she let herself enjoy the feel of him touching her, and did her best not to think about diamonds, specifically the ones from Harry Winston's.

She and Thad stepped into a private viewing office at the back of the Harry Winston Chicago store fifteen minutes later. She'd never been in this jewelry store. Her father had bought her mom a bracelet from here for their anniversary once, but he hadn't taken Veronica with him since she'd been in school. Now that Veronica was inside the store, her mind reeled with thoughts of how much Thad going to spend on whatever he was about to buy for her.

A man who'd introduced himself as Mark Barber gestured for them to sit in front of the viewing table. "Mr. Worthington, I brought out our Icons and Secrets collections for you." Several velvet cloths covered what Veronica assumed were diamonds held securely in special black display boxes. Mr. Barber began to lift the coverings off each one by one. As he spoke about the piece's attributes, he placed it on a black velvet mannequin bust. The sheer volume of glittering stones made Veronica's head ache.

"What do you think? Anything you fancy?" Thad asked her. She stared between him and the diamonds, her mouth dry and her ears ringing a little.

"Thad... These are too expensive. You can't."

"I can and I want to." He turned his focus back to the jewels. "Which one speaks to you?"

She studied the dozens of sparkling necklaces, each stunning in their own way. She saw the desire flaming in Thad's eyes as he gazed, not at the diamonds but at her.

Suddenly, she wanted to enjoy this more than ever, to step into the role of a princess for just one night. Veronica turned back to the necklaces and chose the one that made her heart skip a beat, the one that made her feel the way Thad made her feel whenever he looked at her like he was now. That was the one she wanted.

"The cluster," Mr. Barber confirmed. "Excellent choice. Would you like to try it on, madame? It is the ultimate embodiment of the house's iconic design, with an aesthetic that transforms fine jewelry. The three-dimensional clusters, as you can see in this light, never stop sparkling. It will give you life and movement when you wear it."

Boy, this man knows how to sell diamonds, she thought.

Mr. Barber lifted the necklace with too many diamonds to count, all beautifully clustered together, just as the name suggested.

"Come to the mirror." The jeweler motioned for her to stand up and lift her hair out of the way before he slipped the jewelry around her neck. The slightly larger cluster at the center rested between her collarbones. She stared at her reflection, utterly captivated.

Thad came up behind her, and she saw the hunger in his expression. She imagined herself wearing these diamonds and nothing else as he made love to her. He would claim her with his body and make her his with this possessive collar of the world's most exquisite diamonds...

"We'll take it, Mark. Thank you."

She snapped out of her fantasy and turned to Thad, ready to argue.

"Please, Veronica. Let me do this." He didn't order it, didn't command her to accept it. He asked her to let him buy her one of the most expensive necklaces in the world as though he *needed* to do it.

"Why?" she asked. "I know how much a Harry Winston necklace costs. I don't know if you're thinking clearly. This money could go to better causes."

For brief second, disappointment flashed across his face. "Is that how you think I see you? As a cause?"

She shook her head. "That's not what I meant. I mean there are charities out there..."

"And I give to many of them. Generously. You read the article in GQ. You know what I do. I think I've earned the right to spoil myself a little bit. And I want to do that by spoiling you. You understand, don't you?"

She did. This beautiful Prince of Thieves was handing her a necklace fit for a king's ransom and she'd just insulted him as if he never gave anything away to those who needed it. Worse, she'd implied she was one of those charities.

"I'm sorry, I... I didn't mean—" she stammered. "I guess I just don't feel worthy of this necklace."

Thad's gaze sharpened. "That's where you're wrong." He shot a look at the diamond jewelry. "Every woman is worthy of the most amazing diamonds. Isn't that right, Mark?"

"Yes, quite right, Mr. Worthington. Diamonds belong to women. They were born to wear them. *Every* woman deserves diamonds."

"And I know you, Veronica. You deserve this." He gestured toward the necklace hanging around her neck.

She touched the diamonds as she faced the mirror again. She became lost in a different daydream, not one of diamonds and sultry nights, but sunny Saturday mornings tangled in Thad's arms. She saw a new life with him, a thread of possibility glimmering brighter than any diamond. She wanted to tug on that bright thread and see where it might lead. Her eyes met his again and she smiled.

I'm trusting you, Thad. Please don't break my heart.

14

"Has Felicity vetted this sitter for CPR? Does she know how to set up car seats in case she has to take them somewhere?" Veronica asked Thad as she and Lyra stood next to him facing the door to Jared's apartment.

Thad shot her a bemused look. "If I know Jared, he probably ran a background check on the sitter."

"Are you sure she's going to be okay?"

"I'll be fine," Lyra declared in an adorably sensible voice.

"She'll be fine," Thad echoed just as Jared opened the door.

"Hey, nice to see you again," Jared greeted Veronica with a grin. "Come on in." He bent to see Lyra. "And you must be Lyra," he added solemnly and held out his hand to her.

"I am," Lyra said, as she clung to Thad's leg, pressing her cheek against his knee. She reached out and curled her hand around his fingers and gave it a little shake.

"You really don't mind us sharing the babysitter?" Veronica asked as they followed Jared inside.

"Not at all." Jared turned to call out, "Felicity, they're here."

A woman close to Veronica's age with an hourglass figure and dark auburn hair came from a back bedroom carrying a baby in her arms. A woman in her mid-40s was right on her heels.

"Hi, I'm Felicity, and this is Hayley." Felicity raised the baby in her arms slightly, then nodded toward the other woman. "This is Miss Tuttle, our neighbor." Felicity came over and shook Veronica's hand. "It's nice to finally meet you, Veronica. And this must be Lyra."

"Is that your baby?" Lyra asked Felicity with less shyness than she'd greeted Jared.

"Yes, this is our daughter Haley. Will you help Mrs. Tuttle watch her tonight?"

Lyra nodded and Veronica hid a smile. Her daughter was at an age where she loved babies.

Felicity motioned for them to come deeper into the apartment. "Let's get our girls settled." Lyra took to Mrs. Tuttle right away and it wasn't long before Veronica was hugging her baby goodbye as she and Thad left with Felicity and Jared.

Simon drove them to a small private airport outside

the city. Veronica stared wide-eyed at the private jet waiting for them to board. She'd always considered herself a rich kid growing up, but she'd never had the sort of money Thad threw around.

As Veroinica sat down in a plush white leather seat, Thad and Jared moved to the back of the plane to fix some drinks.

Felicity sat down across from her. "It's kind of *a lot*, isn't it?"

"That's an understatement," Veronica said. "Today he just carried me off to the most expensive dress shop in Chicago, then Harry Winston's. After, it was just 'Let's fly to the Met Gala in New York tonight' as if that's something he does every weekend." She closed her eyes and took a deep breath before she spoke to Felicity again. "Don't get me wrong, this is amazing, but I keep wondering..."

"When the other shoe will drop?" Felicity finished. "When you'll wake up? When *he'll* wake up?"

"Yeah, exactly. There's a lot of uncertainty involved. If it was just me, that would be one thing, but this isn't just about me. Lyra has asked for a father since she could talk. What if she gets too attached to him and he walks away? How do I protect her from that?"

"I get it. Uncertainty is a real bitch, pardon my language, especially with a kid in the picture. But if it's any help, I've known Thad for a while now, and in my opinion, there's a huge possibility that this could work out," Felicity said. "He's so different around you."

Veronica winced. "That worries me even more. People don't change overnight. You know how they say that weather isn't the same as climate? Weather changes constantly, but climate is more consistent over a long period of time? The same is true for mood and personality. He's high on a mood right now, but at some point, personality will take over and he'll want to go back to his old life."

"No, listen, Veronica. What I mean about different, I mean he's *better*. Before you came along, he had this sort of hard edge to him that scared me a little. He was always a caring man, a perfect gentleman, but there wasn't the softness I see in him now. He hasn't changed so much as he's opened up. Let his guard down."

Veronica and Felicity stopped talking as the men joined them.

"Shirley Temple?" Thad teased as he handed her a glass that looked suspiciously like a real Shirley Temple, right down to the gleaming red cherry.

She tasted the cocktail and laughed. There was only the faintest bit of vodka in it. "That's all you're giving me? Seriously?"

"Seriously," he echoed. "It's better to drink once we get to the event."

"That reminds me, where are we going to change?" Veronica asked. She didn't like the idea of getting dressed in a small airplane bathroom. It could spell disaster for her and the expensive gown currently hanging in a black garment bag at the back of the plane.

"We'll change at my company's apartment in New York City." Thad put an arm around her as she settled into his embrace while she buckled herself in.

The flight went by fast. Too fast for Veronica to really enjoy it, but she felt cozy and comfortable with Thad sitting beside her with his arm around her shoulders. It was crazy, but she loved that he always seemed to know when she needed to be held.

Felicity had already checked in with Miss Tuttle twice during the flight; the girls were doing well. They'd watched *Frozen*, no surprise there, and had colored in some coloring books and eaten pizza before putting Hayley to bed. They planned to watch another movie until Lyra was ready for her bedtime. It had felt strange leaving Lyra with someone she didn't know while she flew halfway across the country, but when Felicity had handed her the phone and she'd heard Lyra's delighted voice, she relaxed. Everything was okay. Lyra was safe and Veronica could enjoy tonight.

Thad and Jared discussed work, giving Veronica a chance to learn more about Thad's business. He genuinely enjoyed the projects he worked on and while he made a ton of money, he wasn't actually focused on the money, but rather on the vision of each project he took on. It was also fun to see Jared tease Thad the same way Angelo did. It was clear how close the three of them really were. She envied him that. It had taken her a long time to build friendships after she'd left home, and it had been even harder after losing Parker.

Felicity nudged her elbow. "Those boys can talk business all day. I want to hear about the Chi-Bean. Jared said you import really nice foreign coffees."

"We do. It gives us a chance to experiment with the menu," Veronica said. "You work at the Chicago Art Institute, don't you? What's that like?"

Felicity shared some of her experiences about how complex the art world really was.

"You should come by sometime for a private tour with Thad. I can set it up."

"That would be amazing. I haven't been to the museum since I was in middle school, before my mom died." Her mother had loved art and they'd always gone when there was a new exhibit to see. After her father married Annette, they'd stopped going. They'd stopped doing a lot of things.

When they got to Thad's apartment in New York, Veronica and Felicity quickly called Miss Tuttle again to check on the kids. All was well and Lyra had just gone to bed. Felicity and Veronica got dressed in one room, the men in the other. Felicity put on a dark honey gold gown that billowed out much like an old-fashioned ball gown from the 1960s and wore set of slender diamond necklaces that cascaded down her throat in a lazy, splendorous sort of way.

"You look amazing," Veronica gushed. "Like Grace Kelly."

"Blame Jared. He has some Grace Kelly fantasies when it comes to me." She laughed as she slipped into her silver pumps. "Your turn." Felicity opened the massive garment bag and gasped. "Oh my God... Is this a Marchesa gown?"

"Yes, isn't it unbelievable?" Veronica still couldn't wrap her head around the designer dress she was getting ready to wear. She stepped into the gown and pulled it up before Felicity zipped it behind her. After slipping into her shoes, she donned the diamond cluster necklace.

"Wow, you look incredible!" Felicity gushed.

"Thanks, but I still think it's a bit much. Thad definitely spoiled me." Veronica glanced down at the gown, the magic of it filling her with excitement.

"Well he should. Don't go filling your head with doubts tonight. You're wonderful and you deserve it. End of story. Now, you ready to stun the boys?" Felicity beamed mischievously.

Veronica nodded, feeling her confidence return. "Let's do it." Tonight she was a princess, a real one, right down to the enchanted dress. Despite her concerns about the future, she intended to enjoy this evening.

"Jared has already seen me in this, so let me go first.

That way you can really wow them." Felicity opened the door and stepped out into the living room.

Veronica felt the diamonds at her throat; they were no longer a burden, but a gift. And the gown flowing around her was no longer a costume, but part of her. This was her night.

She drew in a deep breath and a smile curved her lips as she thought of how much she cared about Thad. He truly was her prince charming. And right now, she would be his Cinderella.

Veronica stepped into the hallway.

THAD WAS STRANGELY NERVOUS ABOUT THE GALA. HE knew he'd pushed Veronica quite a bit with the visit to Taylor's and Harry Winston's, but he'd wanted this night to be perfect. She deserved magic, and he had the resources to give her a night he hoped they would both remember.

The Met Gala wasn't usually this big a deal to him but tonight was important. He wanted to show Veronica she could not only survive but thrive and enjoy a life with him. That sudden realization stopped him in his tracks as he'd been pacing the length of the living room. A life with Veronica. A future.

He'd only ever imagined a future with one other woman.

Jared seemed to notice Thad had paused in his nervous pacing. "You okay?"

"Yeah, I'm fine," he lied. His heart was beating harder as his thoughts spun down a dozen, no, a hundred paths and he contemplated all the ways he and Veronica could have a future together.

He *wanted* a life with Veronica and Lyra. He wanted them both. Now that he'd faced that desire head-on, it all seemed to suddenly, *easily*, click into place.

The door to the bedroom opened and Felicity emerged. She was a vision in a dark gold gown with strands of thin diamond draped over her collarbones. It enhanced the image of a princess who had carelessly dressed and stepped out of her palace for a night of fun. A year ago it would have been an intoxicating thing to see. He remembered that fleeting desire he'd felt for her back then when he and Jared had both been interested in her, but those feelings were like a childhood memory of some dim dream now.

Felicity came to Jared and he kissed her, grinning like a lovesick fool before they both turned to Veronica's entrance. Thad stared at the darkened doorway with his breath held as he waited for *his* princess.

She moved into the soft golden light of the living room and he almost forgot to breathe. The Marchesa ball gown was a strapless creation in a deep teal hue that spoke more of a midnight blue than the bright teal one would expect. It had two layers that rippled in soft flowing flounces at her thighs and again at the base of her skirt like petals of a flower. A floral print spanned her waist, bust, and hips. A second layer on the bottom of the skirt started at her hips and stopped a few inches above the hem. She looked like a woman who'd cloaked herself in the midnight sky. The floral print was in shades of white, gray and silver, and blended perfectly with the deep teal of the dress. The diamonds at her throat flashed as she drew breath, calling attention to her swanlike neck.

"My God," he whispered.

Her dark hair hung in loose waves, falling over her shoulder and coiling in tantalizing curls along the top of her breasts. Her pale skin was luminescent. She came further into the light and Thad found himself moving toward her before he even understood what he meant to do.

"How do I—?" she began, but he didn't let her finish. He couldn't wait another moment. He cupped her face in his palms and kissed her. She gripped his wrists as though she were hanging onto him the same way he was clinging to her. His lips crashed down on hers, wild and hard. She tasted like winter dreams and felt like a roaring fire in his arms. He lost himself to her, to the possible future that was now emerging from the hazy realms of the land of possibilities.

How had he ever been afraid of this?

Thad found himself smiling as he finally broke the

kiss. His eyes searched hers. Beneath the passion, he saw confusion.

"Thad?" she whispered.

"You look stunning." He shook his head. "There actually aren't words enough to describe you properly." He nuzzled her nose with his and her lashes fluttered closed briefly.

"I hate to interrupt, but we don't want to be late," Jared interjected.

Thad released his gentle hold on Veronica and clasped her hand. "He's right. We'd better go."

They exited the apartment lobby, drawing looks and comments as the four of them stepped out into the street where a limousine waited. Thad had done events like this dozens of times, yet he felt a wild flutter of nerves as he saw his world through Veronica's wide-eyed gaze.

He saw the red carpet that greeted them outside the Met. The flashing lights. The movie stars and models dressed in the best couture money could buy. The inside of the Met was bathed in red; hearts festooned every surface from lights to topiaries to hanging glass sculptures forming chandeliers. The theme of the evening was the Golden of Age of Hollywood with designer gowns and art from the 1920s through the 1960s from major films. Art from hundreds of famous painters and sculptors filled the exhibits throughout the museum.

Veronica gripped Thad's arm as though she feared he

would vanish, and she would be left to navigate this night alone. The eyes of every person fixed on her the moment he'd helped her exit the limousine. Dozens of photographers called for her to stop and she'd done so, reluctantly. She looked like a shy Audrey Hepburn with her large innocent eyes and dark hair.

For the first time since the GQ article had come out, Thad was not the focus of the crowd. He gladly stepped back and let Veronica have her moment. Her shy smile made his chest ache with a flurry of soft emotions he now knew had a name: love. He loved her.

With more than one jealous starlet waiting for their turn in the spotlight, Thad soon rescued his date from the crowd of cameras and ushered her inside.

"Is this what it's like for you all the time?" Veronica asked as they ascended the staircase covered in rose petals.

Thad chuckled. "Not all the time. But it does have its moments." His gaze lingered on her when they reached the top of the stairs. She was so beautiful. Not just tonight, but every moment between the first time he'd met her and now.

"So what do we do?" Veronica asked.

"Mingle, drink, admire art, eat amazing food, maybe dance a bit." He led her to their table, where Jared and Felicity had already settled in.

"Now, after that adventure, let me get you a *real*

drink." He kissed Veronica's cheek and intercepted a waiter carrying glasses of wine.

"Red or white wine, sir?" the waiter asked.

"Red, please." He took two glasses and was halfway turned when he saw a familiar face across the room. How was it that life always seemed to conjure up the past just when you were ready to move on?

He'd expected to feel a cruel twist upon his heart seeing her here. Instead he felt only a strange melancholy, as though the man who'd loved this woman, or believed he'd loved her, was someone from another life.

Then, before he could turn away, she noticed him. She was a vision as always with those dark blonde curls of hair that bounced as she moved, but she no longer moved him, not as she once had.

She placed her hand on her companion's arm and leaned in to whisper something to him before she lifted the skirts of her crimson red gown and headed toward him.

"Hello, Thad," she said as she reached him.

A small lump formed in his throat at seeing her for the first time in so many years. "Hello, Victoria."

She swept her gaze over him. "How are you, Mr. GQ Gentleman of the Year?" her voice held a gentle teasing.

"Good. You?"

She looked like she ruled the world. She hadn't changed and he hadn't wanted her to. Victoria was and always would be a bittersweet memory for him.

"I'm good. Well, better than good." She blushed as she showed him the glint of a diamond ring upon her finger.

"You're engaged?" he asked.

Her blush deepened. "Married. To an investment banker." She nodded over her shoulder at her companion. She seemed both pleased and embarrassed as she admitted this. She bit her lip and met his gaze. "You'd like him. He's a good man."

"I'm happy for you. You deserve a good man." He meant it. Victoria had been his world once. She'd never been cruel, even when she'd rejected his proposal. She'd only been honest. Despite how much that day had wrecked him, he'd never held it against her.

"I thought... I thought you might be married by now," Victoria mused. "Please don't tell me that I—" she halted and shook her head but didn't continue. Her cheeks flushed dark red.

He didn't speak immediately. Like her, he felt almost embarrassed, but there were things he wanted to say now after all these years. "For a while, yeah. After you, I gave up on the idea of love. I decided I didn't want to try again." The truth slipped from his lips, stunning him.

"For a while? What about now?" Victoria asked. "I hope you did try again. You were a man made to love, to be in love. Somewhere out there is a woman who deserves all the love you can give her."

His gaze moved from her to Veronica, who was

walking with Jared and Felicity to look at a nearby sculpture. "I'd like to think I'm ready to try."

Victoria followed his gaze. "I wonder who she is. A number of people are talking about her tonight. That dress and those diamonds... simply stunning. I wonder if she's one of the models that flew in from Europe. Perhaps European royalty. Princess Alexandra, maybe?"

She did indeed look like royalty, a princess born of moonlight and dreams in that blue gown with frosted roses patterned over it. As she glanced about the room, she looked like a girl who'd dreamed of endless gardens and castles in the clouds. But he knew how grounded she was, how hard she worked, how great a mother and a woman she was. And he was desperately in love with her.

"I know who she is," Thad said.

"Oh? Who is she?"

Mine. He thought the word but dared not say it aloud.

"She owns a coffee shop called the Chi-Bean in Chicago."

As if knowing she was being discussed, Veronica's eyes locked with Thad's before she blushed and turned away.

"A coffee shop?" Victoria studied Veronica critically, though not meanly, rather as if she were trying figure out a puzzle laid before her. "Who did she come with?"

"A man who doesn't deserve her."

"Thad," Victoria began, not seeming to realize he'd

spoken about himself. "I do hope you find love and happiness again. You, more than most, deserve it." She touched his arm and with a bittersweet smile, she swept away, the train of her gown gathering rose petals as she moved.

VERONICA TRIED NOT TO STARE AT THAD AS HE SPOKE to the stunning woman in the red ball gown. She also tried to ignore the flash of worry she felt when the woman touched his arm.

"Jared, who's that?" she asked with a discrete nod in Thad's direction.

"Who? Oh—" he cleared his throat. "That's Victoria Lumley, an old friend."

"Is that the one he used to...?"

"Yes." Jared seemed reluctant to discuss it further. Veronica turned away as Thad approached. She didn't want him to think she'd been watching him.

"Here you are," Thad handed her a glass of wine. His smile was genuine, relaxed. He didn't look heartbroken over running into his old flame. That thought eased the knot in her chest, allowing her to relax.

"Thank you." She sipped hers as they studied the rest of the art pieces. She soon lost herself in the magic of the evening as they enjoyed a sumptuous dinner and incredible works of art. Afterwards, Thad held out his hand to her.

"Dance with me?" he nodded toward the dancefloor, now filling with couples.

"Only if you hold me close so I don't fall." She wasn't normally a clumsy dancer but with so many people staring at her, she felt like she might lose her footing.

"I'd never let anything bad happen to you, especially when you're in my arms," he promised. There was such a fire in his gaze, yet a softer, sweeter emotion she was still afraid to name lingered behind that heat.

Veronica was intimidated, but she trusted Thad to not let her trip.

His mouth curved into a seductive smile as she placed her hand in his. Was there anything this man couldn't get her to do?

She gathered her skirts with one hand as That gripped her waist and they twirled and moved in step. It was something out of her dreams, this feeling of floating in a man's arms, and music soothing her soul. She belonged in this glittering world, if only for tonight. It was the world she'd walked away from after her mother died. She didn't regret marrying and loving Parker or having Lyra, but for one night, it was a joy to fall back under the spell of art, culture, diamonds, and flowing gowns.

But the best part of the night wasn't any of those

things. It was the gorgeous man who gazed down at her with such sweet intimacy it made her knees buckle.

"You look happy," Thad said as they finished their second dance.

"I am," she replied. "I'm with *you*." And that was a deeper truth. Tonight wouldn't have mattered at all if she hadn't been here with him.

"Me too, with *you*." He gave her that boyish smile that devasted her heart. "One more dance?" he asked.

"One more dance," she agreed. This time as they moved in waltzing patterns across the floor, she saw Victoria watching them from a table at the edge of the floor. The woman looked sad... No, that wasn't the right word, it was something more complex than that. But Veronica thought maybe she understood. The other woman was seeing what she had walked away from. What might have been.

As the dance ended, Thad pulled Veronica into his arms and kissed her. She forgot about where they were as she gave herself to him, letting him pull her deeper beneath the surface of this wonderful dream.

IT WAS CLOSE TO FOUR IN THE MORNING WHEN SHE and Thad picked Lyra up to take her home. Thad, now dressed in his jeans and sweater, carried the sleeping child in his arms. Veronica held Lyra's overnight bag with her clothes and toys. Miss Tuttle had helped Lyra change into her PJs before putting her to bed in Jared and Felicity's guest room.

Thad cupped the back of Lyra's head in one palm. "Mrs. Tuttle said she had fun." Her little cheek rested on his shoulder as she slept blissfully.

"I imagine she did. Pizza, ice cream, and a movie? That was her Met Gala." Veronica smiled. "Plus, she loves babies right now, so I'm sure being around Hayley made her happy."

Simon picked them up outside. Veronica and Thad got in on either side of the car to buckle in the sleeping little girl. This moment felt so natural between them, yet it was also momentous, as if whatever came next would make every difference in the world for their future.

Her eyes met Thad's and held for a long moment before he went around to the front passenger seat. The ride home was a quiet, dreamy daze of the Chicago night lights flying past her in the windows as she thought about how much she didn't want this night to end.

Once they were home, she followed Thad as he carried Lyra to her bedroom to put her to sleep. After they tucked her in, they stepped back into the hall.

Thad pressed a kiss to her lips, one that lingered and burned in the best way. "I'll see you tomorrow?"

"Yes, that would be nice." Veronica wanted to fold herself into him, to bury her face against his chest and feel the strength of his body as he held her. She wanted so much more than that right then, but she was afraid to ask him. Thad smiled and took his leave.

What the hell am I doing? I want him to stay!

Veronica dashed after him.

He was already at the door when she caught him by the arm. She tried to still her racing heart. Words like "love" and "you" were sitting on the tip of her tongue, but she held them back, afraid they would ruin this wonderful night.

"Stay... *Please*," she said insisted.

His eyes moved to her lips and she knew what he was thinking, because she was thinking it too. She reached up and pulled him down to her by the collar of his sweater. Their lips met, hot and feverish, as she pulled him back toward her bedroom. He closed the door, flipping the lock, and she slipped out of her ankle boots and jeans. He caught her in a fierce embrace as he made love to her with his mouth. Her knees buckled at the wave of desire and desperation that overcame her.

They fell backward on the bed together and he helped her out of her sweater until she was down to only her bra and panties. He leaned over her, his fingertips tracing her collarbones.

"We don't have to do this, not yet," Thad whispered.

His compassion for her and what she was feeling always stole her breath.

"I want to..."

His eyes filled with a fiery lust that quickened her breath. He rolled her onto her stomach, and she lay there, arms bent to pillow her cheek as she felt him undo the clasp on her bra. Then he kissed his way down her bare back and tugged her panties off. he rolled her over again and came down over her. Their lips forged a burning fire as Thad cupped one of her breasts, rolling the nipple with his thumb and forefinger with the slightest pressure. Pains of pleasure shot straight through to her womb.

"You are exquisite," Thad growled between kisses. "I was the envy of every man tonight."

Whatever she meant to say next died upon a moan as he lowered his face to her breasts and kissed the sensitive peak he'd been playing with. She whimpered as he sucked her nipple between his lips. One of his hands slid down her body toward the apex of her thighs. She gasped as he penetrated her with one finger.

"Oh, God." She arched her hips off the bed, seeking a deeper, harder penetration.

He seemed to know just how to drive her mad with featherlight flicks and caresses over her clit, along with the deep thrusting of two fingers. But she completely lost her mind when he slid down her body and covered her mound with his lips. This man was a God when it came to oral sex. There should be a GQ award for that...

Thad sucked on the bud of her arousal and flicked his tongue against her folds until she whimpered and begged him to never stop. A climax crept up on her and when it finally hit, she could only writhe in pleasure as it overwhelmed her. She slumped, exhausted on the bed, too tired to move an inch. She struggled to reach for his pants, but he caught her wrists and kissed her palms before shifting her, so she lay beneath the covers.

"Tonight was about you, honey. Only you." He covered her mouth was his, drugging her deliciously with his kiss. In that moment, she could have died from happiness.

"You'll still stay?" she asked dreamily.

"Yes."

That single word held a world of other promises within that made her heart quiver like a plucked violin string with the note still humming in the air.

THAD WATCHED VERONICA FALL ASLEEP. THOSE SOFT, warm emotions that once frightened him were now held close to his heart. He loved this woman, and he loved her child. He loved *life* with them both, even the wild chaos of it.

Seeing Victoria tonight had driven home to him what his future could be, so long as he was careful about it. She deserved the best, and he could give her that. A woman like her should have a long, slow seduction before he asked her the question that would determine their future.

Then he thought of Lyra and the way she'd fallen asleep in his arms. The fierce love he'd felt for Veronica's daughter while she slept against his chest made him feel whole in a way he'd never imagined. He wanted her to have the world. He wanted to be there for her as a father.

Thad stripped down to his boxers, then unlocked the bedroom door, just in case Lyra needed them during the night. After he joined Veronica in bed, he let his mind wander with exciting plans before he fell asleep. He knew what he would do. It would be the perfect thing for his girls. Both of them.

15

"Disney World?" Veronica was still in shock.

Thad leaned back in his chair at Veronica's kitchen table. "I know it will be a bit cold this time of year, but it'll be perfect because there will be shorter lines for the rides." As he played with the coffee mug, his strong, elegant fingers made her flush a little and she forced herself to not slip into a delightful daydream about what those fingers could do to her.

Veronica sipped her hot cocoa and watched Lyra drawing and kicking her legs in the air on the living room floor as she hummed. It had been a week since the Met Gala, and she and Thad had settled into a cozy rhythm together. They'd sneak away for drinks for an hour, or bring dinner in for themselves and Lyra, then play board games or watch movies.

He'd spent most of his nights here, sleeping in her

bed even though they still hadn't had sex. The intimacy of him holding her had become more precious to her than she could have imagined. Each morning, they sat at the table, having their coffee and cocoa, just enjoying being together.

"She can't go on that many rides though; she's too small." Disney World was Lyra's dream, but Veronica had planned to wait a few years for her to be bigger.

"She can explore all of the worlds and meet her favorite characters. As for the rides, they have the teacups and quite a few rides for smaller kids now. And plenty of tame adult ones. It's A Small World is very tame—"

"Oh God, any ride but that," Veronica begged and tried not to laugh. She didn't need that song stuck in her head or Lyra's.

"Okay, not that one." Thad chuckled as he took a sip of coffee. "But this is a great opportunity. I mean, we'd be staying in Cinderella's castle—they hardly offer that to anyone. I think Mariah Carey was the last invite. Besides, we can always go again when she'd older."

Veronica's heart leapt as she realized what he'd implied by that.

"Well, when you put it that way..." It was hard to say no to a-once-in-a-lifetime event like that. "But I'll need to figure out if I can hire a few holiday workers to help out with the shop."

"We have a few weeks before we have to worry about that."

It hadn't escaped Veronica's notice that Thad continued to say "*we*" more and more often, causing her pulse to shoot into a flutter that was part panic and part joy.

I want this dream to come true so badly.

Thad nodded at Lyra. "You want to tell her?"

"And spoil the fun of seeing you do it? No way. You were able to get this present for her, you tell her." She found his leg under the table with her foot and rubbed his leg with her toes.

Thad's eyes lit up with mischief. It had been only three days since they'd been to New York, and Veronica had fallen asleep after he'd gone down on her. She'd apologized the next morning, but he'd only chuckled and said he was still waiting for the right time and there was no rush.

Maybe in Cinderella's Castle, she would finally get the chance to really be with him. He didn't seem to be in a hurry, and for some reason that worried her. Didn't guys *always* want sex? Parker had never turned down a chance, and he'd initiated a lot of their intimacy mainly because she'd been young and shy about her body and sexuality.

This was new territory for Veronica, to be the aggressive one in the bedroom. Surely a guy wouldn't mind a woman starting something, but Thad had this subtle alpha edge that made her think that if he'd wanted her, he would have already put the moves on her rather than sit back and wait for her to act. Maybe he didn't want her the way he did other women?

She hated indulging in thoughts like that, but after three weeks of dating him, they only ever seemed to get to third base. He was a playboy. He'd had dozens, maybe even hundreds of women. And yet, with her, he appeared to be in no rush. What made this so different for him? What if he didn't see her as someone with a sexual appetite, but rather as comfort food?

"Lyra, come over here," Thad called. "We have a surprise for you."

Her daughter clambered up from the floor and came over, her face lit with expectation and excitement.

"Your mom and I were thinking next weekend we would go to Disney World."

Lyra's eyes widened. "Can I come too?" she asked hesitantly.

"Of course you're coming!" Thad laughed. Lyra giggled and rushed to hug him. Thad embraced the girl and gave Veronica a playful grin that melted her heart.

"See? Totally worth it," he whispered.

Yes, he was right. Giving Lyra memories like these was worth it. Lyra had never traveled outside of Chicago. It would be a huge deal for her to go all the way to Florida.

"Well, I've got to get back to the office. I'll see you

tonight?" He set Lyra down, who immediately returned to her drawing, now sketching out what she assumed was the Epcot Center.

"Of course."

Thad leaned over to kiss Veronica. She sighed against his lips. When he started to pull away, she caught the collar of the shirt and pulled him back for a longer, deeper kiss.

"You had better go," she teased when he didn't straighten back up.

"It's hard when you keep giving me the nicest reasons to stay." He stole one more peck, one of those wicked kisses that Lyra really shouldn't be anywhere near at her age. And she loved it. With a reluctant sigh, this time from him, he grabbed his coat and called Simon to pick him up.

After he left, Veronica saw Lyra off to school and then joined Zelda and Zach down in the Chi-Bean.

"You look happy," Zelda said with a knowing smile. "Have a nice morning with *Mr. Hemsworth*?"

"I did," she admitted, ignoring Zelda's teasing about Thad's name. It was much easier to talk about him now. Early on, she'd been so hesitant to jinx the situation by even mentioning it. "We need to put up some hiring signs on the front door and put some online job notices up. Would you mind helping me with that?"

"We're hiring?" Zelda asked. "Is this for something good or something bad?"

"Relax," she said. "I just need some additional employees by next weekend."

"Okay." Zelda leaned against the counter. "What's happening next weekend?"

Veronica bit her lip. "I'm taking a few vacation days."

"What? No," Zelda gasped dramatically. "You never go anywhere. What's the deal?"

"Well, Thad helped purchase and design a new Disney resort in the Caribbean and they've given him an all-expenses-paid trip to stay in the Cinderella Castle suite for one night."

"Shut up!" Zelda said. "Oh my God, tell me you aren't pulling my leg."

"I'm not," she laughed. "So I need to make sure I have enough people to handle the shifts."

"No problem. It's getting close to the holiday season and a lot of people will need the extra work."

"Thanks." She was so grateful to have Zelda. She needed to find a way to give her a raise.

Veronica spent the rest of the day either filling orders or working in her small office with Zelda to set up open position postings online.

"Uh oh," Zelda said.

"What?" She looked toward the coffee shop front door where Zelda was staring.

Annette Becker stood there, removing her expensive gloves. Her pinched face scanned the room until she saw Veronica.

"What does she want?" Zelda whispered.

"I don't know, and I'm afraid to find out." Veronica approached the counter and Annette's sour expression turned to one of smug triumph.

"Hello, Annette," Veronica said pleasantly, though it nearly choked her to do it.

"I just came by in person to tell you the news."

"What news?"

"That I sold the brownstone. All of it, even the coffee shop." Annette's smug look of satisfaction deepened the sudden dread that hit Veronica in the chest.

For a second, she couldn't breathe. It was as though the world spun violently around her and then came to a sudden stop.

"What did you say?" she asked faintly.

"The house... I sold it. My guess is you will have a few weeks before you have to move out."

"What... But..." Words simply failed her. She'd been dreading this for weeks, but she hadn't wanted to believe that Annette would actually succeed in her evil plot. "Who bought it?"

"No one you know. Besides I was required to sign a confidentiality agreement. Once he assumes ownership, I imagine he will contact you himself."

Veronica's hands clenched into fists as she stared at her stepmother. There was no point in being nice anymore. Annette had crossed the line.

"What did I do to you, Annette?" Veronica asked,

her tone quiet and calm despite the fact that she felt like she was breaking up inside like a ship tossed against the rocky shore.

"What did you do?"

"Yes. What could I have possibly done to you that was so horrible that you've spent every minute thinking of new ways to hurt me?"

Her blunt and honest question caught Annette so off-guard she could only bluster.

"You clearly hate me," Veronica continued. "When you married my father, he needed love. He deserved a second chance at happiness. I wanted a stepmom. I was excited to meet you, but you hated me from that first moment."

"Of course I did! From the moment I married your father, all I ever heard about was you, you, you. It was like he didn't even care about me. I was just someone to share his bed at night."

"He's my father, of course he cared about me," Veronica growled. "And I cared about him. I *wanted* to care about *you*, but you screwed that up by being a hateful bitch."

"I don't have to listen to this," Annette snapped.

"No, you certainly don't. The door is that way. Feel free to never come back here again," Veronica replied with a mocking smile. "Not that you would, because soon I won't even have a home here or even a goddamn *job* anymore!"

Annette looked as mad as a wet cat, ready to hiss and use her claws, but Veronica was done with Annette, done being afraid. The worst had happened, and she would find a way to survive. She and Lyra would start fresh somewhere else. Somehow.

"You'll get everything that's coming to you," Annette warned. "The new owner will throw you out."

As if Veronica hadn't already figured that out. She stared at Annette, a cold raging sweeping through her. "Get out of my shop. Now. I *never* want to see you again."

Annette fired back a glare. "Gladly." Then she left.

Veronica stared at the Chi-Bean's door, her ears ringing.

"Ronnie?" Concern laced Zelda's tone.

Veronica turned. She'd completely forgotten she wasn't alone.

"You okay?"

"Yeah," Veronica said. "I'm... I just need a minute." It took all her strength to get to the storage room and close herself inside. She sank to the floor, put her head in her hands and cried.

She was not okay. It was over. Her and Lyra's life here was done. She'd hoped to raise her child in the home that had given her so many happy memories, the home where she'd once had a complete and loving family. She'd hoped that Parker would have shared this life with her, and she'd lost him. But she'd at least still had the house, and a business she was proud of, and now she'd lost those too. She was failing her daughter yet again.

The stress of the last few weeks came crashing down on her, and she struggled to breathe past the heavy sobs. She fought to keep control, to make sure Zelda didn't hear her while her world collapsed around her.

When she was too exhausted to do anything else, she cleaned herself up and, after a long moment, put on a false cheery smile and returned to work. She would start making plans tomorrow. She would continue to plan for the trip to Orlando next week and hire some workers. The only thing that gave her some comfort was that at least for now, she could lean on Thad.

16

Thad was packing up his briefcase to leave when his father appeared in the doorway.

"Thad," Timothy greeted him with a warm smile. "Haven't seen you in the office much the last few days."

"I've been busy with Veronica and Lyra."

His father nodded. "Your mother and I really want to meet them. Why don't you come over for dinner, all three of you?"

Thad wanted to say no. It was too soon, but his dad looked so hopeful. He hadn't seen that look on his father's face in a long time. Not since he told his father he'd bought a ring for Victoria.

"Let me talk to her. If she says yes, I'll let you know."

"I'll hold you to that." His father left.

Thad pulled out his cell and dialed Veronica's

number. She didn't answer right away, but when she did, she sounded distracted.

"Hello?"

"Hey, is now a bad time?"

"No, it's just busy right now. What's up?"

"So... I know I keep springing surprises on you, but how about dinner tonight at my parents' house?"

She didn't immediately reply. "I would need to find a sitter—"

"Lyra's invited too."

"You sure? I don't want to bring her if she'll be too much for your parents."

"She won't be too much, I promise. You'll be surprised at how chill my parents are. They love kids." He knew his mother in particular would adore Lyra.

"Well, if you're sure she won't be in the way."

"Naw. I'll have Simon come and pick you up at seven. Sound good?"

"Should we dress up or...?" She sounded adorably worried. Thad wished they were having this conversation face-to-face so he could pull her into his arms and kiss the lines of worry away one by one.

"It's not the Met, honey, just my parents. Jeans is fine," he assured her. He hadn't planned on changing, but he would put on some jeans himself the moment he got off the phone. He needed to create the least amount of pressure for Veronica.

"Well... okay. See you at seven." Veronica sounded a little more relaxed.

"See you then." He hung up and dialed his mother.

"Did your father speak to you about dinner?" she asked.

"Yes. Veronica and her daughter Lyra are going to come. But mom, you have to go easy on Veronica, okay?"

"What you mean?" She sounded wounded by the request.

"Just don't ask her a million questions, okay? She scared to death to meet you and dad. She's worried about Lyra and..." He trailed off, realizing he was actually a little nervous, too. He hadn't brought a woman to dinner since Victoria, and that felt like a lifetime ago.

"Your father and I will behave ourselves; we promise. Do they have any dietary restrictions?"

"No, but maybe cook something kid-friendly? Lyra is only a little over four."

His mother cooed in delight. "Oh, she's so little!"

"She is." *So young*, he added silently. So young and deserving of someone who could be a father to her. He dared not mention that to his mother, though. She would start planning the wedding before he and Veronica even sat down at the dinner table.

"I think I know what to cook," his mother said confidently.

"Great. We'll see you tonight."

❄

In front of the Chi-Bean, Veronica and Lyra were already outside waiting when Simon pulled the car up. Thad helped settle Lyra into the car seat and then took the front passenger seat so Veronica could sit next to her daughter.

"Thad, what's your mother's name?" Veronica asked. "I just realized I don't know it."

"Angelica. My father is Timothy."

She repeated the names softly a few times until she seemed confident she would remember them.

When they reached his parents' house, Veronica unbuckled Lyra and handed her to Thad. He swung her about, and Lyra giggled before he set her down on the sidewalk, only to have her comically continue spinning around on her own. The tense expression on Veronica's face seemed to smooth away. For now.

"You okay?" He put an arm around her waist and held Lyra's little hand on his other side.

"I'm fine, totally fine." She promised, but Thad could see the strain on her face return. The sooner they got inside, the better. Once she met his parents, she would realize there was nothing to be afraid of.

The front door opened, and his mother stepped out, his father one step behind her.

"Welcome! You must be Veronica." His mother

locked Veronica in a hug before Thad could stop her. Veronica stiffened for an instant, then relaxed.

His mother released Veronica and smiled down at the child. "And this must be Lyra."

Lyra stared up at his mother then looked at Thad. "She's your mommy?" Lyra asked in a serious whisper.

Thad bent to whisper back. "Yes, and she's a really nice one. So be nice to her, too."

Lyra turned back to Angelica and gave her a small, shy wave. Angelica's face was so full of joy and excitement that Thad knew she would talk his ear off about all of this later.

Timothy waved them inside. "Come in so you don't get cold."

Thad collected Veronica and Lyra's coats and hung them in the closet.

"Who needs some wine?" Angelica asked.

"We do." Thad wound an arm around Veronica's waist and gave her hip a gentle squeeze. She leaned into him slightly and that cottony warmth in his chest seemed to spread. He loved it when she touched him back, when she let him hold her, even like this.

His mother rushed off to the wine cellar wall while Thad escorted Lyra and Veronica into the family room. His mother kept an elegant and well-furnished home, but it never felt stiff or and unlived in, like many homes he visited over the years. The fire was crackling over diamond dragon glass in the fireplace. Framed antique sketches of wildflowers decorated the walls, and a cream satin wallpaper had been painted with climbing vines to make the room feel like an English garden. Lyra's eyes widened as she studied the room, but she seemed hesitant to enter it. Thad knelt beside her.

"You can go in, you know."

"I can?" she whispered.

"Yes." He tried not to laugh as he picked her up and carried her to the large blue velvet couch. He plopped her down on it and crashed next to her, purposely slouching to match her height. She giggled and cuddled up against him. Veronica joined them, smiling.

When his parents returned to the room, Thad's mother's eyes sparkled at the sight of the three of them on the couch. If he hadn't been so worried about Veronica, he would have teased his mother over it.

His father handed him and Veronica a glass of wine and gave Lyra a small plastic cup. "Root beer for the little lady." His father glanced Veronica. "I assume that's all right?"

Veronica nodded. "Yes, of course. Lyra, what do you say?"

"Thank you, Mr. Thad's dad."

"You can call me Timothy." His father winked at Lyra. Her face turned red and she took a sip, smiling back.

"Lyra is a beautiful name. Where did it come from?" his mother asked.

"It's from a book I loved as a child. *The Amber Spyglass* by Philip Pullman." Veronica's eyes fixed on her shoes as she continued. "After I lost my husband, I was facing my childbirth alone. I wanted the name of a strong girl, a girl who could save the world, even if she had to lose the man she loved." Her voice grew rough, and Thad realized she had probably shared a bit more than she'd intended.

"That's beautiful," Angelica cleared her throat. "Names should have meaning. Names should matter. Thad's name is short for Thaddeus, which means 'a brave heart.' I miscarried twice before Thad was born. By the time we made it to the delivery room with him, we knew he had to be brave to survive."

Thad stared at his mother. He'd never known she'd had any miscarriages. He'd begged for years as a boy for a brother or sister and she'd always gently refused. Now, after knowing Lyra for so short a time, he couldn't imagine the pain she felt at losing a child. Twice.

Veronica sipped her wine. "Thad is a wonderful name. I wondered if it was short for Thaddeus."

His mother smiled. "Well, I'm sure you're hungry. Let's go sit in the dining room and I'll fetch the food."

"Please let me help you," Veronica said and started to rise.

"No, that's all right. I'll help." Thad stood and lifted Lyra, along with her now empty root beer cup. He set the child on her feet and Veronica took charge of her, following Timothy into the dining room.

Thad joined his mother in the kitchen as she opened the oven. Heavenly smells of steak and mashed potatoes filled the air. Using her oven mitts, she pulled out a large tray of...

"Is that mac & cheese?"

"Yes." His mother chuckled. "It was your favorite dish when you were four."

"Good thinking." He helped pull out a tray of oven cooked steaks, mashed potatoes and asparagus drizzled with a balsamic reduction out of the oven next.

"Mom," Thad said quietly as his mother began to prepare the plates for him to take into the dining room.

"Yes, dear?"

"Thank you for being so nice." He wasn't quite sure that was adequate for what he wanted to say. His parents weren't the typical stuck up types he imagined other people expected them to be given their wealth. He was damned lucky.

"Why wouldn't I be? She's beautiful, Thad. And Lyra is precious," his mother said, but when she raised her eyes to his he saw a "but" lurking behind them. "She is very hurt, very vulnerable. To lose a husband and to raise a child on her own, that's a great struggle. I pray you never come to know it."

"You don't think I should date her?" he asked, though it wasn't really a question.

His mother leveled a frustrated gaze at him. "That's not what I mean. You don't *date* someone like her. You *marry* someone like her. You have to live a life with her. That is what I mean."

Thad thought over what she'd said. He'd known from the start that this wouldn't be just another fling. Granted, this had all started with a bet, but Jared's wager had simply been the push he needed to put himself out there. To try for something more serious with someone who felt the same way.

Veronica deserved so much more out of life. At first, he'd been worried he wouldn't be able to give it to her. Not with his past. But now...

"I think I want that," he told his mother. "I think I want a life with her."

His mother stopped spooning mashed potatoes on a plate and stared at him. "You mean that?"

"I do. I know it seems fast, but I think I'm ready."

Angelica patted his cheek and chuckled. "You know how many dates I went out with your father before he asked me to marry him?"

"Six months," he said, positive he knew the answer. He'd listened to their engagement story a dozen times since he was little.

She laughed and shook her head. "That's what we told our parents, what we told you. But it was actually three dates. Three dates and we *knew*. It was like lightning. It wasn't just a hormonal love at first sight thing. I just knew your father was mine, the one I wanted to spend my life with. It was attraction, love, belief, hope, and trust all rolled into one. When it hits you, you just know." She snapped her fingers. "Like that."

What she said resonated deeply with him. Everything had clicked in the place exactly as his mother had said. Part of him had worried about it, overanalyzed it, thought maybe he was just infatuated—or worse, trying to break out of a rut—but hearing his mother say this now made him feel less crazy.

She handed him two plates. "Take these. I'm sure you're all hungry." Thad carried them into the dining room where Lyra was telling his father about Sam Dalton's birthday party. Lyra used her hands to suggest a giant slide above her head.

"And then I fell! Down the big slide!"

"You fell?" Timothy asked.

"Actually, a big boy pushed me," Lyra said. "But Mr. Thad grabbed him and scared him real good."

Thad felt his father's eyes settle on him in silent questioning while he set plates of food in front of them.

"I just told the kid not to do that ever again," he explained.

"You said you would make him live by the river with rats!" Lyra giggled.

Jesus, was there nothing a child didn't overhear?

His father shot him a questioning look. "A bit harsh, perhaps?"

"I wasn't *serious*, dad."

"Then he bought me a teddy bear that was bigger than me!" Lyra continued.

Timothy was trying not to laugh. "Did he, now?"

"I didn't have enough tickets, but Mr. Thad made him give it to me."

Timothy arched a brow and Thad knew he would be facing harsh questions about his parenting techniques later.

"And we will be paying him back for it. Won't we, Lyra?" Veronica stared at her daughter, who nodded solemnly.

Thad didn't want to argue with her on that right now, so he went back into the kitchen to grab more plates.

"Look, mommy!" She pointed excitedly at her plate. "Mac and cheese."

"Yes, I see that. Aren't you lucky?" Veronica gave his mother a grateful look as Angelica took her seat at the table.

The rest of the meal went well. Lyra talked about her friends in school and everyone listened with amusement.

"And then Mr. Thad watched *Frozen* and *Frozen 2* with me while mommy was sick."

"It was just the flu," Veronica quickly interjected. "Thad was wonderful. He helped Lyra get to school and back home. That's why he took her to Sam's birthday party. I was too sick to go."

His parents exchanged a look that made Thad fidget

in his chair. He hadn't told them about Veronica being ill when he spent the weekend working remotely.

"Your son is wonderful," Veronica said again, her face as red as he felt.

His mother cleared her throat. "Does anyone want dessert?"

"I do!" Lyra piped up. Veronica frowned at her, and Lyra turned bashful and added more softly, "Please, Mr. Thad's mom."

"Come on then, honey. You can help me." Angelica offered. Lyra slipped out of the chair and followed his mother into the kitchen.

"I should go make sure she doesn't make a mess." Veronica rushed after her daughter, leaving Thad and Timothy alone.

For a moment, they sat silent, father and son, drinking their wine and avoiding the inevitable conversation they both knew was coming for as long as they could.

His father broke the silence. "So, was she ill the night you skipped family dinner? And that whole weekend?"

Thad played with the stem of his wineglass. "She was really ill. She collapsed at work and I really didn't want to leave her alone. I didn't even know about Lyra until then. Then, when I found out she had a daughter, I couldn't exactly leave her alone. She needed me. They both did."

His father was quiet a long moment. "I like her, and her daughter is adorable. I'm just surprised. Not displeased, mind you."

"Surprised?"

"She's a commitment. A real one. You can't walk away now, not without hurting them."

"You're as bad as mom. I'm not planning on walking away," he said quietly. "Truth is, I'm planning on asking her to marry me. I just don't want to rush it."

Timothy smiled and for the first time, Thad saw a different kind of pride in his father's eyes. It wasn't the fierce pride of the father in the board room. It was a more fulfilled expression, something he'd never seen before on his father's face.

"I'm glad to hear it. It's about damn time."

SOMEHOW, DINNER WITH THAD'S PARENTS HADN'T been a disaster.

Veronica still couldn't believe it. She'd not only survived, but actually enjoyed dinner with Angelica and Timothy. They hadn't looked down their noses at her or Lyra. They'd been just like their son, warm and welcoming. The whole evening had distracted her from the fact that she was going to lose her home.

She hadn't told Thad yet. She sensed he might try to do something noble, like get his lawyer friend Jared to sue Annette or something, but she didn't want Thad involved, not if she could avoid it. He was a comfort, but she didn't want to lean on him, not if she didn't have to. She needed to focus on the future, on what good might come out of this, rather than what she might lose. And since dinner wasn't a disaster, maybe Disney World wouldn't be a disaster either.

Veronica closed up the coffee shop for the night. She smiled when she saw Thad still working on his laptop in the corner by the fire. He'd started doing that this week, showing right up before closing, working quietly. She liked it. He didn't seem plagued by the need to be her sole focus; it was more that he simply wanted to be near her. It was sweet and, if she was honest, having him so close all the time kept putting the most wicked thoughts into her head. They still hadn't had sex, not really, and she was beginning to wonder if he was enjoying stringing her along like this.

"I'm off for the night, boss." Zelda's voice broke through Veronica's fantasies.

"Have a good night," she called out as Zelda headed for the door.

Thad packed up his work into his leather briefcase and came over after Veronica had locked the front door. He looked irresistible in his dark gray trousers and white button-up shirt. He'd rolled up the sleeves, exposing his tan, muscled forearms. A sudden hunger for him, so overpowering, made her back away a bit. She moved toward the supply closet while he watched her from the other side of the counter. His eyes held a silent question, and she nodded at him and crooked a finger to encourage him to come closer

He slid over the counter and dropped down next to her. She backed up into the storage room and he followed, stalking her in a way that made her feel like prey.

Thad entered the storeroom with her and closed the door. Her retreat ended as her back hit the far wall. When he was close enough to touch, he raised his hands to cup her face and gazed down at her, his eyes ravenous. She tilted her head back and bit her lip as she imagined all the things she wanted to do with him.

He savored the moment before he bent his head to hers and their lips met. The kiss was packed with all the lust and desire they'd both been feeling for weeks.

"God, I want you." He moaned and pressed her tighter against the wall.

"Then take me," she said as she sought to undo the buttons on his shirt. She loved the way he stole her lips, a conquering king with his every touch, and she adored it when he got a little rough, as though his desire was too much for him to rein in.

Thad threaded his hand in her hair, coiling a strand around his fingers. She arched against him, moving her lips down to his throat, kissing him and licking his skin. When he cursed, she giggled.

Then she gripped his shirt with far too much delight and ripped it the rest of the way open. The buttons popped and scattered, and he let out an amused chuckle before he went back to kissing her. She started giggling even more.

"I'll bet your butler is glad he isn't here..." she played with the frayed thread where a few of his buttons had been an instant before.

He chuckled. "It's Winston's lucky day."

Her hands roamed around his chest and her fingers memorized the feel of the hard planes. He tilted her head back and kissed the corner of her mouth, then down along the line of her jaw, before he flicked his tongue against the pulse point of her throat.

A throbbing need built deep inside her as she tried to clench her knees together, but he pushed one of his legs between hers. She clenched his shoulders as he pressed against her core, just where she needed him the most.

He pulled the sweater off of her body and tugged the cups of her bra down below her breasts. Thad cupped one with his large hand and squeezed gently. He rolled her nipple, and she threw her head back, gasping. He then captured her nipple with his lips and Veronica cried out, the sharp sound loud in the enclosed space of the storage room. Somehow this frantic sexual exploration in such a small room, with her heavy breathing and soft sounds of pleasure, only made everything hotter.

He sucked on one breast before turning to the other and she whimpered as her body filled with need.

"Please, Thad..." she begged.

He released her nipple and raised his head from his crouched position. His eyes were dark with passion and desire, making her body tremble.

"*Please*," she begged again.

A bright flame filled his eyes as he now towered above her and spun her around to face the wall. He touched her body with such firm possession that it made her knees nearly buckle. She liked that he wanted to show he was in control, that he was so lost in his desire as he took command of the situation to give them both what they needed.

Thad reached around to the front of her jeans and unzipped them, then jerked them down past her knees. He caressed her belly before sliding a hand beneath her panties to her soaked folds. She hadn't been this aroused, or this hungry for a man's touch in such a long time. She'd almost forgotten the wild thrill of it all. Now, Thad was ensuring she never would forget again by burning himself into her memory with every scorching look and branding touch of his hands.

One finger teased her clit, nearly making her shriek before he penetrated her with one digit, then another, stretching her and filling her. His lips caressed her ear as he began to whisper.

"You have no idea how much I want this, how much

I want you. How I want to sink my cock into your tight little body. You're killing me." He bit her earlobe in just the right spot before he began pumping his fingers into her hard, almost brutally. She thrust her ass back, pushing hard against his shaft, which was still trapped by his pants. He was going to kill them both with these games. Why wouldn't he just fuck her?

But it seemed he wanted to torture her with pleasure instead. He nibbled on a sensitive spot between her neck and shoulder blade that made her entire body seize with arousal until she reached the point of no return. When the orgasm hit, she screamed as she came hard on his fingers. Her legs trembled and she collapsed, barely able to use the wall for support. Thad curled an arm around her waist, holding her up against him. He pressed more kisses to her neck, ear, and cheek.

"You okay?" he asked.

"Oh God, yeah." She smiled for a long moment before she realized he hadn't come inside her.

She turned in his arms and nearly tripped since her jeans were down around her ankles. "But you didn't—"

"No, but that's okay." He smiled at her so sweetly it nearly killed her.

"No, it isn't." She suddenly wanted to cry. Why did he keep pushing her away? What kind of man rejected sex? "Am I so undesirable that you'd rather have blue balls?" She snapped.

His frown twitched into a ghost of a smile. "Blue balls?"

"Yeah—" She halted as she realized what she'd said and was mortified. She sounded like a teenager.

"Honey, everything I do with you is for a reason." He cupped her face. "I want to make love to you at the Cinderella castle in Disney World. I want our first time to be truly magical." He suddenly laughed. "God, I bet that sounds so corny, huh?"

She stared at him, stunned. "You...want to make love in the Cinderella Castle?" She had to be imagining this.

"Yeah..." He looked away, his cheeks coloring with embarrassment.

"That is..." She cupped his face so they were both holding each other. "...one of the most romantic things anyone has ever said to me." She didn't care that her pants were around her ankles or that the buttons of his shirt covered the floor; all that mattered was that she tell him right now how cherished he made her feel.

"You don't think it's silly?" he asked. "Maybe you'd rather go to Paris or—"

"No, Cinderella's Castle is perfect." She pulled his head down to kiss him and smiled against his lips. "Now, why don't you come upstairs and shower with me after we put Lyra to bed." She trailed her hand down his chest.

"That sounds nice," he admitted.

"And..." She added what she hoped was a sultry look.

"I would like to return the favor." She gazed meaningfully down at his erection.

"Well..." Thad chuckled. "I won't say no to *that*." He kissed the tip of her nose, then her mouth, the lingering sizzle of that connection making her dizzy. She wasn't just falling for Thad anymore. She'd fallen. *Hard*.

17

"Mommy, look! Princesses!" Lyra squealed in joy as she rushed ahead of Veronica and Thad through the crowds at Disney World.

"Stay close sweetie!" Veronica shouted, but she didn't need to worry. Her daughter had frozen in her tracks in front of Queen Elsa.

"Hello there," Elsa greeted with a bright smile.

"H...hi," Lyra breathed in shy excitement.

"Lyra, let me take your picture with Elsa." Thad held up his phone and motioned for Veronica to join them. Elsa stood next to Veronica and Lyra was in front of them, her face lit with such joy. He snapped a few pictures. Veronica thanked Elsa and then Lyra ran toward Princess Anna, who was waving at children.

"How about one with Anna?" Thad asked Lyra as he caught up with her.

"Yeah, but you need to be with me!" She reached for his hand and he followed her to stand beside the very accommodating Princess Anna actress. Thad placed his hands on Lyra's shoulders and smiled as Veronica took their photo.

"You think you can keep up with her all day?" Veronica teased.

Thad laughed. "Yeah. Something about seeing her here is actually giving me energy." He curled an arm around Veronica's waist as they started down the cobbled path with Lyra just ahead of them.

They hadn't seen their rooms yet, but Thad knew it would be incredible. They had arrived that morning and met a man for a private tour of the park while their luggage was taken directly to the castle suite. Now they had the rest of the day to enjoy the park.

Tonight Lyra and several other children visiting for special occasions were to attend an exclusive performance in another part of the castle while the adult special guests had romantic dinners on their own. Once the kids were—hopefully—tuckered out from the day's adventures, the parents could enjoy some alone time.

Thad was especially looking forward to that alone time with Veronica. Ever since they had "the talk" about waiting, Veronica had begun to relax, but she still tortured and teased him at every turn by stealing kisses or touching him in places and ways that drove him a bit insane. Maybe there was some karma in that, given how he'd been holding out on her for so long. The waiting might have started out as a bet with Jared, but that hadn't mattered in a long while. He wanted their first time to be special, and this felt like the perfect place.

"The teacups!" Lyra dashed toward the teacup ride. For a four-year-old, she could move fast when she wanted to. Thad and Veronica chased after her. Lyra wore jeans and a little Princess Elsa sweatshirt to keep her warm, which meant she looked like nearly every other adorable girl there, so they had to keep a close eye on her.

"You want to ride with us?" Veronica asked him.

"Do you want me to?" he asked. He was doing his best to let Veronica decide his level of involvement with Lyra, but he was secretly glad to be asked.

"Pleeeease!" Lyra grasped his hand and dragged him toward the line. Veronica joined him and laced her fingers through his.

Joy filled him as he gazed at her and Lyra bouncing beside him. When they arrived at the front of the line, they were pointed toward a bright teal teacup. Thad lifted Lyra up and helped Veronica in before joining them. Lyra sat between them as the teacup began to move. Within seconds they were all gasping and laughing as they spun and twirled amid the other cups. For the first time in who knows how long, he felt a rush of pure, unadulterated joy surging through him. He felt like a kid.

By the early evening, they'd taken Lyra on at least

twenty other rides, even It's a Small World, where Veronica covered her ears with her hands the entire ride. Thad and Lyra had teased her by singing the song long after the ride was over.

Now laden with bags full of T-shirts, Mickey Mouse ears, Princess costumes, and other Disney gear that Thad had decided Lyra couldn't live without, he escorted his girls back to the castle.

Veronica checked the schedule on her cell phone. "We have half an hour before the kids and parents separate for dinner."

Thad nodded. "We can get comfortable in our rooms and rest for a bit."

He led the way, showing his castle VIP pass to the security team inside. A young woman in a Disney uniform of a blue polo shirt and khaki pants met them at the entrance to the suite.

"My name is Candace, and if you need anything during your stay, there's an old-fashioned looking phone in the parlor where Lyra will be sleeping. Just dial 9, and either myself or someone else will answer. You have unlimited private room service for twenty-four hours."

"What's room service?" Lyra asked in confusion.

"It means we can order food if we get hungry and they'll bring it straight to our rooms," Veronica explained.

The little girl's eyes lit up as she whispered "wow" to herself.

Candace grinned and turned to Thad and Veronica. "We're so excited you're here." She led them into the concierge office. "This is where one of us will be, whenever you need something. The desk is staffed twenty four hours a day."

Thad spied a pumpkin tapestry and mice carved onto the pillars at the corners of the room. A grandfather clock showed the time was almost midnight, but not quite. The hands of the clock weren't moving.

"Let me guess, that never strikes twelve?" he asked Candace.

"Nope. Because here the magic never ends."

Lyra gazed up at the clock. Veronica giggled and smiled at Thad, which made him feel like a king.

"If you'll come this way." Candace led them to an elevator.

The warm walnut wood panels that made up the base and the gold tufted velvet cushions on the upper walls of the elevator looked like the inside of Cinderella's coach. Gold shimmering vines were painted on the doors to remind those inside that Cinderella's coach had once been a pumpkin. A mosaic of Cinderella's crest with beautiful tiles covered the elevator floor. As they exited the elevator, they entered an antechamber with another large gold coach mosaic on the floor.

Lyra pointed at the glittering coach. "Mommy!"

"The tiles were all hand by laid, nearly 30,000 of them," Candace said.

"Mommy! Look!" Lyra rushed over to a display in one corner of the antechamber where several objects were on display inside a glass case.

A glass slipper rested on a purple velvet cushion. Below those, a glittering crown and a scepter sat. In the third case, a trio of golden-orange pumpkins sparkled in the light cast from the gilded diamond-encrusted chandeliers.

Candance put a hand on Lyra's shoulder. "Cinderella left these here. Will you watch over them while you stay with us?"

Lyra nodded solemnly, her eyes fixed on the princess objects in fascination.

Candace then waved them into the next room. "Here's the main bedroom."

Thad had seen dozens of the world's best hotels over the years, but nothing compared to the Cinderella suite. The details on display were so perfectly on theme, late 17th century France if he wasn't mistaken, that it transported you into a medieval fairytale.

Two large beds filled the space. Their shimmering blue and gold brocade bedding was enhanced by a carved wood crest of the letter "C" for Cinderella, which also secured draperies that swept down both sides of the headboard. The floors glittered with fairy dust, and a large white stone fireplace was already lit.

Candice pointed toward the walls. "If you'll notice the stained glass windows, they show Cinderella's story.

You can see her father's cottage, the invitation to the ball, the clock striking midnight, the glass slipper, her mice friends, and finally, the Prince's castle."

"We assume mom and dad might want their privacy. Miss Lyra, would you like to see the parlor? We've got it all set up as your bedroom."

"I get my own room?"

"Yes, you do!"

Lyra was bouncing so much Thad half expected her to rocket across the room. Candace winked at Thad and Veronica as they followed her and Lyra into the parlor. It was a cozy room with a large red velvet couch that had been turned into a bed. On top of the red coverlet was a pile of toys ranging from Winnie the Pooh stuffed animals to Princess costumes, as well as a set of Mickey Mouse ears along with dozens of brightly colored bags full of various sweets.

Candace pointed to a beautiful, gilded mirror hanging on the wall opposite Lyra's bed. "And this mirror is magical."

Suddenly the glass turned into a TV screen as the movie Frozen started to play. Lyra's little jaw dropped.

"Why don't you two look at the bathroom?" Candace nudged Thad and Veronica toward a gold curtained entrance that lead to a massive bathroom.

Twin brown granite sinks were accompanied by a large shower with its own gold brocade curtains on either side. Beyond that was the usual facilities and a massive Jacuzzi tub surrounded by a trio of wall mosaics depicting scenes from *Cinderella*.

Candace pointed to a series of buttons by the tub. "I suggest you explore this when you two have some private time. You won't be disappointed."

"Wow," Veronica whispered, almost as awestruck as her daughter. "Just wow."

"I'll have someone come get Miss Lyra for dinner and escort her to the night parade. She should be back around ten, if that's not too late?" Candace asked.

"That sounds fine," Veronica said.

"Just remember to dial nine if you need anything." Candace left the two of them alone.

Thad took Veronica's hips in his hands and pulled her to him. "So, do you like it?" He was strangely nervous and needed to hear her say it. Before, he'd always been so confident about impressing woman, but as with everything else, Veronica was different.

"*Like* is probably the biggest understatement of the century. You literally made this a magical trip."

"Good. Because I don't think I can pull this particular magic off again. This was a once-in-a-lifetime chance."

Veronica gripped the collar of his shirt and pulled him down to her. He gave a deep and slow kiss, teasing in all the best ways. He couldn't resist cupping her bottom and giving it a squeeze. Veronica let out a soft gasp against his lips that tortured him in the best way.

He deepened the kiss, flicking his tongue against hers, making her want to get closer. He could have kissed her for hours and never grown tired of it. She made every moment feel new and exciting.

"Mommy!" Lyra sprinted to the bathroom. Mickey Mouse ears were perched on her golden curls. Veronica jerked away from Thad, covered her mouth with one hand and blushed as she faced her child.

"Yes, baby?"

"I want to live here forever." Lyra hugged her mother and then hugged Thad.

"Well, other princesses have to stay here, but you get to be the Princess tonight."

"Oh, okay." Lyra sighed and walked back into her private room.

Thad pulled Veronica close again, chuckling as he kissed her temple. "She makes me want to build a castle just for her."

Veronica giggled. "If you do, we'll never hear the end of it."

AFTER LYRA LEFT FOR AN EVENING OF FUN AND wonder, Veronica was surprised to find a small dining table just big enough for two set up in the antechamber of the Cinderella suite. It was like magic elves had conjured it into existence when her back was turned.

Candles were lit. White china dishes covered with metal domes awaited her inspection. A bucket of ice with chilled champagne also sat on the table. Thad pulled out a chair for her and then seated himself. A waiter exited the concierge's office, removed the covers from the dishes, popped the champagne, and poured them each a glass. After that, the waiter left them alone.

Veronica stared at the chicken piccata in front of her. It was one of her favorite dishes. Thad had a ribeye steak with sweet potatoes and mango salsa, which she guessed was his favorite. The smell drifting off their plates made her mouth water and her stomach grumble. She'd done her best all afternoon to avoid eating park food. But she wasn't going to feel guilty about indulging in this dinner.

Soft music came from somewhere outside their suite. A string quartet played "This is the Night."

"They're playing—"

Thad smiled. "Our song."

"That's our song?" she asked.

"Why not?" he said, taking a sip of champagne. "It suits us, I think." He paused. "Unless you don't like it?"

"No, I love it. I really do. It's not a song that everyone expects. It makes me think of Angelo."

"Our song makes you think of *Angelo*?" Thad's comical outrage as his eyes flared and he tossed his napkin on the table made her laugh.

"You know what I mean." She covered her heated

cheeks with her palms. "I loved that night at the Italian Village. It was wonderful."

"I'm glad." Thad cleared his throat. "And I'm glad you're here with me. You and Lyra."

They ate dinner and drank quite a bit of the champagne while they discussed how fun it had been to see Lyra play and enjoy the rides at the park.

"Thad, you've been..." Veronica had to take a moment to calm her racing heart. "You've been like a father to her and that means everything to me. I know you didn't ask me out that day expecting to deal with Lyra, but you're amazing with her."

Thad's gaze remained focused as he listened to her. She loved that about him, that he truly listened to everything she said.

"Thank you," he said. "But honestly? You've been a gift to me. You and Lyra. I didn't realize what I was missing in life." His expression softened. "From the moment I saw the Chi-Bean from my car, I knew I wanted to live there, to exist in that cozy world. It only got better, a *thousand* times better when I met you." His voice grew rough. "This is probably too much to say too soon. Please don't say it back, just let me say this..."

Veronica could barely think. Blood rushed to her head so fast it nearly drowned out his next words.

"I've fallen in love with you. Don't feel like you have to say it back if you aren't ready, but I hope someday you might. I love you and Lyra." He looked away a moment, as if trying to control his emotions. "I didn't know that something was missing until you both came into my life. I thought I had everything I wanted and then... You were sick, and I saw that adorable little girl asking me if I was going to take care of you... Something clicked into place. I told her I would, not out of some sense of obligation, but because I think I was already falling in love with you."

Veronica's throat was so tight it hurt. She raised the back of her hand to cover her trembling lips.

I love you too. Those four small but powerful words were on the tip of her tongue. She was too afraid to say them just yet, but she had to show him how she felt. Veronica got up from her chair and closed the distance between them. He started to stand, but she pushed him back down into his chair and slid onto his lap. He wrapped his arms around her waist, holding her close as she curled her arms around his neck.

"I think we've waited long enough," she whispered against his lips.

His eyes darkened and his lashes fell to half-mast. "Are you trying to seduce me?" he asked.

"Trying?" she asked innocently as she began to unbutton his shirt. She kissed his neck and blew softly on his ear. His body stiffened beneath her as she felt his arousal under her bottom.

"Lyra will only be gone for another two hours," he reminded her.

"I think we can accomplish quite a lot in two hours... if you're game," she countered.

He didn't answer. Instead, he lifted her up and carried her into the master bedroom. She laughed in delight as he dropped her on the bed, then laid back and gazed up at him as he began to undress. She was really going to enjoy this private show.

Soon, he was down to his jeans and turned the tables, removing her boots and socks next. He knelt and kissed the arches of her feet, tickling her. She fell back on the bed as he reached for her jeans to unfastened them. He pulled away each bit of her clothes slowly until she was naked. Only then did he crawl on the bed with her and lay at her side so they faced each other.

Thad stroked a hand down her shoulder, then over the flare of her hip. His feathery caress both soothed and excited her. She grinned back at his infectious smile and touched his chest, feeling his heartbeat beneath her palm. She leaned into his side, and he fell onto his back, letting her climb on top of him.

She kissed softly, exploring this gorgeous, kind, sexy man who'd just confessed he loved her. The knowledge of that made her tremble with wonder. With every kiss, the darkness that formed after Parker's death began to fade; her shadows were now bathed in a bright, burning light. He gently pulled her underneath him before he kicked off his jeans and briefs. They lay tangled together like two teenagers, kissing and caressing each other. He brushed his fingers over her breasts, making her shiver and gasp.

Thad moved down her body, his lips leaving a trail of kisses until he reached her thighs. She writhed as his tongue licked the wet folds of her sex. She clawed at the bed and moaned as pleasure rocketed through her. He continued to tongue her as she came down from the orgasm, drawing out every glorious second of it. Muscles limp, she caught her breath only to gasp as he moved up her and slid between her thighs. Their gazes met as he braced his arms on either side of her head. God, she loved being caged between this man's arms...she felt safe and yet excited about what was still to come.

"You want this?" he asked.

She nodded. They had had the discussion the day before about protection. Thad had volunteered to bring condoms, but Veronica told him she had an IUD and didn't want anything between them. It made this moment so much sweeter. Thad sank into her, his body filling hers, joining them in a way that made her head spin.

"You okay?" he asked, holding still as she gripped his shoulders tight.

She leaned up to kiss his ear and nibble the lobe. "Oh God, don't stop."

"Christ," he hissed and thrust deeper into her.

She threw her head back as he sank into her again, their hips crashing together. He kissed her throat and captured her hands, pinning them onto the bed as he began to move. Each thrust ignited fresh waves of excitement and pleasure. It was the feeling of connecting to him, of removing the last few barriers in her heart that sent her shooting toward another peak.

Thad seemed to sense it and moved faster, rougher, claiming her in a way that left no question that she belonged to him. When the next climax hit her, the ripples of her muscles squeezed around him. The feel of him driving into her...she never wanted it to end, but she feared she might die from such intense pleasure. It was as though liquid fire surged through her veins. Her body was nearly boneless as oblivion threatened to carry her away.

Thad came a second later, his harsh cry in her ear sounding both sweet and love drunk. He collapsed on top of her, his quickened breaths soon slowed as he pressed tender kisses to her face. She wrapped her arms around him, holding him as dozens of emotions rippled through her. It'd been so long since she'd had this sort of intimacy, since she'd trusted herself to let go and let someone in. She knew she'd found love again at last.

"How do you feel?" he whispered against her ear. She kissed his cheek and closed her eyes.

"I feel alive."

She felt like she'd been trapped in a glass coffin for years, seeing the world go on around her. She'd been frozen somewhere between life and death after losing

Parker. She nuzzled Thad's neck and inhaled his scent, letting it surround her.

"You woke me up with a kiss."

Thad lifted his head to stare at her, and she saw the man's fierce love shine in his eyes.

"*You* were the one who woke *me* up."

THAD SAT BACK IN THE JACUZZI WITH VERONICA wrapped in his arms. The tub jets rumbled low, and the aroma of forest pine filled the air as the bath salts they'd added to the water soaked into their skin. Above them, the bathroom ceiling glittered with bright blue-green stars, making the mosaics of Cinderella's Castle glow as though bathed in starlight. The hot water came up to his chest and he settled Veronica on his lap. She feathered kisses on his neck, and he sighed at the heavenly feel of her just being near him.

Thad had always enjoyed sex but being with Veronica afterward was amazing in a completely different way. He felt as though he'd woken from the grayest of dreams. This new reality was everything he'd hoped for, all the colors he was missing, and he never wanted to go back to the dull world he'd lived in before he met Veronica.

"We should get out," Veronica said. "Lyra will be back soon."

Thad reluctantly agreed. He kissed her again as she

moved on top of him, straddling him. He groaned when she reached between their bodies and guided him into her.

"I thought you said we should get out."

"We still have time."

He gasped as she sank down, wrapping him in her wet, hot body. She was so tight; it made him almost come just being inside her. She raised her hips and came back down, a soft sound escaping her lips. He held her gaze as she rode him at her own pace.

He basked in the sweetness of watching pleasure capture her features and hold her in its thrall. When she came, she sagged against him and chuckled.

"I can't believe we..." she murmured in embarrassment.

"Oh, we're not finished yet," he promised.

Veronica slid off him and faced away with an impish grin, arching her back so her bottom was facing him. He moved in behind her in the spacious tub, able to put his knees on either side of hers as he sank into her from behind. They made love slowly, and Thad left her panting and begging for him to be harder and faster.

"You want it harder, honey?"

She couldn't even vocalize any more, she merely nodded, and he gave in to her demands. They were frantic in their passion now, as though this first night together might also be the last. He buried himself so deep within her that when he finally found his release, his eyes dotted with stars. They both collapsed against the comforting jets of the jacuzzi.

"Oh, God... How do you do that?" she asked with a sleepy grin.

"Do what?"

"Fuck me so hard I forget my own name." She turned and curled her arms around his neck as he held her waist, enjoying the feel of her body against his again.

"It's one of my *many* talents," he teased. He fisted a hand in her hair and held her captive for a kiss, demanding her mouth to open form him so he could thrust his tongue inside.

It was a while later before he dried her off and carried her to bed. They managed to pull their pajamas on minutes before Lyra returned. The adorable little girl was almost asleep on her feet as Candace led her to the entryway of the suite.

"Did you have fun?" Thad asked as he lifted Lyra into his arms.

"Uh huh." She rubbed her eyes as her head collapsed on his shoulders. Veronica mouthed a silent "thank you" to Candace as she closed the suite door.

"Wow, she's already out."

Veronica giggled as Thad carried the unconscious little girl to the parlor room. Veronica changed her into her pajamas, and they tucked her into bed together. Veronica came to stand beside Thad, hugging his waist as they gazed at the little girl before they turned out the light.

Thad's heart was so full part of him wondered if he was having a heart attack. This night had been everything he'd hoped it would be. Damn Jared, he'd been right. Dating a woman, falling in love first, made sex all the better. He couldn't imagine going back to the man he'd been before, the playboy with nothing but one-night stands to look forward to.

The thought of never seeing Veronica again made him feel anxious and hard to breathe. He'd never felt this way about anyone before.

He climbed into bed beside her, listening to the fire crackling on the logs. He noticed the stones in the back of the fireplace held tiny lights, which glowed in the shape of fireworks. He drifted to sleep with the thought that this really was the happiest place on earth, and that the magic truly didn't end. He vaguely heard his phone vibrate with a notification, but whatever it was could wait until tomorrow.

18

Veronica woke early, her body still attuned to waking for her work schedule. She rolled over in Thad's arms and gazed at his sleeping face. A warm tingle filled her belly as she studied his features, burning them into her memory. He moved in his sleep, pulling her closer to him and let out a soft, satisfied smile with his lips faintly curved up. Whatever he was thinking of must be wonderful. She wished she could get a glimpse into the land of his dreams.

She leaned in and pressed a kiss to his shoulder, soft enough not to wake him. His body was so warm she felt like she was curled up close to a fire. She wasn't sure how long she lay there as she enjoyed feeling content for the first time in ages.

A buzz drew her attention to her nightstand. One of their cell phones was emitting the noise. She carefully disentangled herself. Her watch on the nightstand told her it was 5:00 a.m. Chicago time, so 6:00 a.m. in Florida. She dropped her watch and moved back to Thad, but she saw his phone illuminate again and vibrate.

He'd mentioned yesterday he'd been expecting an urgent set of documents to be sent to him immediately from his assistant, Brandon. Worried that might be it, she picked up the phone and was about to give it to Thad in case it was something important. She wasn't *that* woman, the one who looked at her boyfriend's phone, but as the screen lit up again with a new text it was impossible not to read it.

Brandon: Annette Becker sent us the executed sale agreement and deed for the house. I put the deed in the paperwork on your desk for when you get back.

For a long second, Veronica stared at the name. Annette Becker. It couldn't be. But what were the odds of two Annette Beckers selling a house in Chicago?

The evil sea witch. This was *her* house. Why was Thad—?

The truth hit her so hard she couldn't find the strength to breathe. She stared at his phone, her lungs burning as the words "executed sales agreement" blurred before her eyes.

No... No... No...

She moved out of the bed, putting as much distance between her and Thad as she could. *He* was the one who'd bought her house? Why? No. How could he do this to her? That was her home. Hers and Lyra's. The betrayal knifed her so deep she clutched her chest, feeling an invisible wound with unspeakable pain.

Veronica rushed into the bathroom, closing the curtains as she wrapped her arms around herself. Shivers rippled through her. Beneath the shock and agony, a wave of anger began to build to a tsunami. She balled up her fists in a silent rage and pummeled the wall of the shower with the heel of her hand until it throbbed.

She had to get control, had to think, had to plan. She turned on the shower and got inside when mist covered the mirrors of the bathroom.

A plan began to form. She would play it cool, act normal, and then when she and Lyra were back in Chicago, they would move out and she would never look back. As the hot water ran down her body, she remembered Thad's words from last night. *"From the moment I saw the cozy world of the Chi-Bean, I knew I wanted to live there."*

He'd stopped his car that day because he liked the house. It had always been about her home and not her. He wanted into her life to see the piece of real estate he was interested in. What better way than to seduce her? She was just another challenge, another exciting adventure for him and this time he would walk away and take her home with him.

God, she wanted to hate him, she wanted to despise

him for betraying her and using her, but even as furious as she was, she couldn't. He'd broken her heart and let her down by what he'd done.

Veronica covered her face with her hands. Her body quaked with silent sobs. She was such an idiot. Men like Thad didn't change, not for her. Last night she thought she'd woken up from a dream, but she'd been wrong. If last night was the dream, today was the sad reality. She didn't know him, not like she thought. He just used his money to do what he pleased, but he couldn't buy his way out of this situation.

Thad's voice came from outside the shower. "Want company?"

She bit her lip hard enough to taste blood as she tried to suppress the surge of panic inside her. "No! I'm almost done."

"Oh, okay." She heard the disappointment in his tone, but she was too hurt to care. She was done being a toy.

She waited for the shadow of him to disappear before she emerged from the shower and snatched a towel off the rack. She exhaled, her shoulders drooping. She would have to face him, there was no avoiding that. She did her best to pretend everything was fine and stepped into the bedroom.

Thad sat on the end of the bed, still wearing his flannel pajama pants and nothing else. His hands rested on his knees as he stared at her. Even now, his beauty was so captivating, so alluring, but it only made her fury at him—at herself—that much stronger.

"Hey, we should talk about last night," Thad said. "If I said or did something to upset you that made you feel—"

"It's not that," she lied. "I'm just feeling shy... Last night was a big step and I might need a few days to process it." She couldn't believe she wasn't crying or flying into a rage. Somehow, she'd found a reserve of control and was clinging to it like a life raft.

"Oh, okay." His gorgeous hazel eyes were full of concern. She wanted to believe him, to believe he meant it, but how could she?

"You should shower," she said. "We have to leave for the airport in an hour. I'll go wake up Lyra."

"Sure." He stood, walked a few steps, and reached for her. .

She flinched and he froze in his tracks, hands half-raised. Her heart was pounding, and she forced herself to move toward him and brush her lips against his cheek before she moved past him to her suitcase. She didn't look back until she heard the shower turn on in the bathroom. When she was sure he was inside, she picked up her cell and went to Lyra's bedroom, dialing Michelle's number.

Michelle answered after a few rings. "Hello?"

"Hey, I don't have time to explain, but I need you and Steve to help me."

"What? Are you okay?" Her friend sounded more alert now.

"Lyra and I have to move out when we return. We need a place to stay. Can you find us a small apartment? We can put the furniture in a storage unit until I can find a more permanent place."

"Honey, you're scaring me. What's going on?"

"It's Thad. He's the one who bought my house. He made a deal with Annette. I just found out. He doesn't know I know. When I get back to Chicago today, I'm breaking things off with him and he'll probably request we leave since he owns the place now. So, we're going to need a backup plan."

"Oh my God..." Michelle gasped. "You're sure? You didn't even talk to him? He didn't strike as the type to throw someone out on the street."

"He said last night he wanted to live in my house ever since he first saw it. Remember the day I had to meet you at the park so Annette could show the house to someone? That had to have been him. I mean, how can he possibly explain that he just bought my house? Why would he do that? Either he always just wanted the house and I was nice bonus, or he is going to use the house so I'll owe him." As she said this, Veronica's stomach knotted and she drew a deep, pained breath.

"But that doesn't sound like him...he doesn't seem like a guy who would do that."

"I've seen him doing business, Michelle. He's tough

as steel. Maybe I've just gotten a glimpse of his rare soft side and now I'm going to find out who he really is."

"Honey...you know that sounds crazy, right? He's a nice guy."

"Then why buy my house and not talk to me about it?" Veronica demanded.

"I don't know, but just take a deep breath, okay? And don't overreact right now."

"I've got to go, Michelle. Text me when you find a place in case we need to move right away."

"Okay, sure. I'll wake Steve up right now. God, Ronnie, I'm so sorry. We both really liked him."

"I know. Me too." She'd fooled herself thinking she could find love again. But she was starting to realize that what she had with Parker, she would never have again.

Thad was yet another girlish dream that would fade as the clock hands moved past midnight. The magic would end, and this would all be over.

SOMETHING WAS OFF.

This morning should have been incredible. He'd had one of the best nights of his life. Spending all day at the park with Lyra, feeling like the father to her in the way he hoped someday to be, a romantic dinner with Veronica, and finally making love to that gorgeous woman. It had been worth the wait in a way he'd never imagined.

He'd never felt so connected to another person in his entire life, both physically and intimately. Afterward, just holding her in his arms had been the most wonderful and unexpected gift he ever could have dreamed of.

Now he'd heard from Brandon that Annette had signed off on all the papers. Veronica's home was safe. He'd stopped it from being sold out from under her and when the time was right, he'd transfer full ownership over to her. He just had to find the right time to tell her what he'd done. Yet after all of these perfect moments, something hadn't gone right. He just didn't know what it was. What mistake had he made to cast a shadow over this perfect vacation?

Thad tried to make conversation with Veronica on the flight back and the car ride home, but she'd been distracted and quiet. Lyra was still sleepy from the weekend.

"Let me carry her up." He reached to unbuckle Lyra's car seat.

"No, I'll take her." Veronica gently pushed him aside and got her out. "You should get home too. I can handle her." Lyra rubbed her eyes as they walked up the steps to the Chi-Bean.

Thad shoved his hands in his pockets and watched them to make sure they got inside safe with their luggage before he went back to the car.

Simons brows knit together in slight concern. "Did something go wrong?"

"I honestly don't know," Thad admitted.

He got into the car and Simon dropped him off at the Golden Circle. By that point, he couldn't wait to text Veronica any longer.

Thad: Everything okay? I'm worried I did something to upset you. Can I see you tomorrow?

It was nearly half an hour later before his phone pinged with a response. He was halfway through a second shower, trying to clear his head.

Veronica: I think I need some time alone for a while.

Thad stood in his bathroom as he stared at the message. He debated a thousand different ways to respond to this before settling on one.

Thad: I can give you all the time you need. I'm here for you and Lyra, whenever you want me.

She never responded.

It was an eerie, unsettling feeling having to wait for the woman he loved to decide whether she wanted him. He was genuinely worried. Having to wait for the woman he loved to decide whether she wanted him. He'd never been in this kind of purgatory before. At least with Victoria, he'd proposed and been immediately rejected.

He dressed slowly, his thoughts replaying events in his head as he pulled open the top drawer of his dresser that held his ties and watch collection. He ran his fingers over the bundled up silks of the various colorful ties before he reached a small blue box from Tiffany & Company.

Thad removed the box from his safe spot and opened it. A pear-shaped cut sapphire surrounded by diamonds sparkled at him. He'd bought it a few days before leaving for Disney World, ready for the right moment when they got back. Now he wondered if that moment would ever come.

He snapped the lid on the ring box closed, nestled it back between the silk ties, and shut the drawer. He picked up his phone again and checked his other messages, hoping work would distract him.

Brandon had texted him about getting the executed deed for Veronica's house. He started to type a reply when he froze. He noticed the timestamp on the message. It had been sent around the time Veronica had woken up. His phone had been on her side of the bed. If she'd heard it vibrate and picked it up... She might have seen Brandon's message mentioning Annette Becker and the house.

Shit... what if she'd seen the message? Could that explain her behavior? What would she make of it? Surely, she wouldn't think he'd used her to somehow get the building? No... but he was at a loss as to why this news would upset her. Maybe if he got a chance to speak to her, to explain what happened and actually give her the deed, maybe he could clear things up.

He dialed Simon.

"Yes, sir?"

Thad dragged a hand through his hair as he tried to fight off the panic that had taken root in his chest. "I need to get to the office as soon as possible."

"I'll be right there."

WHEN HE ARRIVED AT HIS OFFICE, HE SEARCHED HIS desk for the executed deed. Brandon had everything ready, even the transfer documents. All he had to do was sign them. He tracked down a notary on the first floor and executed the transfer that would give the house to Veronica. Then, he had Simon drive him back to the Chi-Bean.

He held the folder of documents tight between his fingers as he came into view of the coffee shop. Zelda saw him and waved as he stepped inside.

"Hey, Zelda, is Veronica upstairs?"

She jerked her head toward the private access door. "Yeah, go on up."

Thad held the papers tight as he climbed the stairs and knocked on the door to Veronica's home. The door cracked open. Veronica's face peered at him through the crack.

"Can we talk?" Thad asked.

"Now isn't a good time," Veronica said.

Thad could see she was pale and red eyed. Had she been crying? Fuck, this was all his fault. He should have told her about his interest in the apartment the first night he learned she lived there, but she'd been so sick it hadn't felt like the right time. Was there ever right time for a talk like that? If there had been, he'd been a fool and missed the opportunity. And later, he'd figured he could possibly surprise her with the deed if things continued to head where he'd hoped they would.

"Please," he begged.

Veronica sighed, her eyes downcast before she nodded. "Lyra, I'll be right back."

"Okay." He heard Lyra say. He wanted to go inside and hug the girl, to listen to her talk about Disney princesses all day. And he had a sinking feeling that might never happen again.

This was the end.

It was written all over her face. He broke her trust, and he was never going to get it back no matter what he said. But that didn't mean he wouldn't try. He'd been in bad positions before in business. Surely, if he could just make her see that he'd saved her house and wanted to give it to her...then she'd forgive him for hiding the truth.

She opened the door wide enough to step in the hall, but closed it behind her. They stood on the small landing at the top of the stairs, close but not touching. His hands ached to grab her shoulders and hold her tight until she listened to him, to understand the truth and let him back into her life.

"There are some things I need to say, and I need you to promise to listen to me." He waited and she finally nodded, still silent, her lovely blue eyes shadowed with sorrow, a sorrow *he'd* caused. He held out the folder of documents. "I want you to have these."

With some reluctance, she took the folder and opened it, scanning over the papers.

He cleared his throat. "This is the deed to your home. I purchased the townhouse from Annette Becker, and I deeded it to you. All you have to do is file the deed with the County Clerk's office."

He waited for a reaction, but she'd closed herself off to him. He could see it in her face; a stony reserve had replaced the usually animated looks he'd come to love. But he pressed on.

"Before I met you, I intended to buy this place and live in it." He stared at her, even though the words were hard to say. "When we went on that first date, I didn't even know you were the tenant here. I didn't know this was your childhood home." He tried to give her a reassuring smile, but it faltered. "I found all that out the weekend you got the flu. I rescinded my offer to buy this place—until Annette forced my hand."

"How could anyone force the great Thad

Worthington to do something he didn't want to do?" Veronica's tone dripped with bitterness tinged with a hint of despair. "When have you ever *not* had the power to just do as you please in life? You didn't have to buy my home!"

Something didn't add up. Maybe he wasn't explaining things correctly. Thad struggled to find the right words to explain.

"I'd found out Annette had been telling anyone who would listen about my interest in this place to use it as leverage to find other buyers. It didn't take long for her to find another interested party. So I bought it from under him so they wouldn't be able to throw you and Lyra out to plant a Starbucks." He didn't tell her he'd actually talked Roarke out of buying it, but he was growing desperate. He was certain she'd be happy to learn he'd saved her home, and yet the more he explained, the more disappointed she looked. What had he missed?

"I never meant to hurt you. I was going to tell you. I was just waiting for the right time." He reached for her hand. She flinched, just as she had in the Cinderella suite, and it cut his heart to shreds.

Veronica clutched the papers to her chest and seemed to almost wilt in on herself as she spoke.

"I can't pay you for the house. I can't get that kind of money together. Can you give me a week to move out?"

His lips parted in shock. Didn't she understand? He'd

never take the home from her, not even if they broke up. He was trying to help her. How could she not see that? He dragged a hand through his hair, pulling so hard on the strands it hurt.

"Veronica, I *don't* want you to pay me back. I'm *giving* this place to you. This is *your* home. Your stepmother should never have been allowed to sell it. It wasn't fair to you or Lyra. So I did what I had to do to stop her from hurting you."

He reached for one of her hands once again, but she stepped back. Despair twisted inside him, poisoning what last hope he had left.

"Do you expect me to repay you some *other* way?" she asked, a coldness filling her voice. She didn't want him to even touch her and yet she'd asked that?

Now he felt betrayed. "Is that who you think I am? After all the time we've spent together you just..." He curled his hands into fists, needing to expend the pained energy that made him want to rage at the idea that he would demand that of her. He drew in a deep breath to help calm himself.

Veronica slowly shook her head. "You really don't get it, do you? I *know* why you bought the place, even if you don't. You bought it for the same reason Annette wanted to sell it, because it gives you a hold over me."

Thad began to protest, but Veronica raised her hand. "I know you don't see it that way. You probably see yourself as the big damn hero in all this. And maybe I really should just be grateful. But here's the thing...it's not just about the house. Once I figured out what you were doing, I realized something. This is how you handle *all* your problems. You throw money at them until they go away. You get flustered if you pay too much, or pat yourself on the back if you manage to get a bargain, but at the end of the day, you always get what you want, don't you?"

Thad still didn't understand. "I thought you'd be happy."

"So did I. I was confused at first about why I was so upset by all this, but now I think I understand. I only know half of you, Thad. The half whose success made him *GQ*'s Gentleman of the Year. The half who has absolutely loved everything about spending time with me and Lyra. And I can admit it now, I love *that* man."

That gave Thad some hope, if it wasn't for the *but* waiting in the wings.

"But I don't know the other side of you. The side that is going to have to deal with the realities outside your bubble. You think you've seen family life at its worst because you've dealt with one flu and a fall down a slide, but that's nothing compared to what you'd be in for. And I'm not sure if you can deal with it."

"I'm worried...No, I'm *terrified* you'd try to treat those problems like you treat all the others, by buying your way out of them. I'm terrified you'll be the sort of man who soothes a child's tantrum by giving her whatever she wants or sends her off to boarding school if she becomes too much to handle. I'm terrified you'll think every argument can be fixed with something from Tiffany's. I'm terrified that you're so used to getting what you want you won't know how to handle it when you don't. I used to live in your world, Thad. Maybe not in the penthouse suite, but close enough to see it. Before I met Parker, I knew boys who thought that way, always so charming when things were going well, but as soon as someone said *no* to them, things got ugly."

"But I'm not like that." Thad instantly realized he'd said exactly what she'd expect him to say.

"How do I know? How *can* I? If I let myself go any deeper into your world, I'm afraid there will be no way out. And what happens if I don't see the other Thad until after that? Maybe if it was just me, I could risk it, but with Lyra?" She shook her head. "I just can't... It's too much to ask. I'm sorry."

There was silence between them for a while as Thad tried to process everything she'd said. The worst of it was that he could see her point. He'd never faced a problem he couldn't solve with money... until now.

Veronica tried to hand the folder back. "You should probably keep this. We're already looking for another place to live."

Thad took a deep breath and stood as straight as he could. "Please accept this from me. I promise I won't ask anything else of you ever again." God, he wanted so badly to touch her. If he could just hold her...

She lowered her gaze to the papers again. "No strings attached?"

"Not one," he promised, his voice rough with emotion. "You *know* me. You know I'd never ask anything for this."

Her teeth sank into her bottom lip as she nodded.

Thad stepped back. He had to clear his throat again. "I'm not a romantic, not when it comes to words, anyway." He chuckled dryly, hiding a deep well of pain. "I'm the fool, not you. I shouldn't have kept Annette's plotting and scheming from you. That was my fault. I know you want this to end, and I understand why. You're right. I'm used to getting what I want, which is what makes this so damn hard... because I want you. I love you." The words were stated calmly, sincerely, and with a bittersweet melancholy. "I will *always* love you. But you're right. This isn't a situation that can be fixed with a checkbook. Maybe it can't be fixed. But if you change your mind, you can call me, text me, or come over. Whatever you wish. I am yours, Veronica, no matter what."

He turned away and clenched his hands at his sides so he wouldn't be tempted to reach out to her one last time. It would only break his heart to see her pull away again.

He'd made a mess of everything. He'd been blind to

what Veronica was really worried about, and what that was, essentially, was *him*. At that moment, he hated Annette Becker and her selfish cruelty for forcing him into this situation, but truth be told, she'd simply made him reveal his true self.

Zelda saw his face as he left the stairwell and turned pale. "What happened?"

"It's over," was all he said as he walked toward the front door.

Zelda rushed after him, stopping him at the door. "Wait, *what*?"

"She ended it."

He was done. He'd never thought he'd had the strength to open his heart again after his first attempt at love, but Veronica had showed him what love could really be like. Now, all that strength was gone. There would be no trying again because there was a Veronica-shaped void where his heart used to be.

"But why? You guys were always so happy." Zelda blocked his path.

He gently gripped her shoulders and moved her aside. "I suppose that was part of the problem. She never learned to trust me, and I didn't prove her wrong." He opened the door and left Zelda staring after him.

Simon met him on the curb, his face grim. "Where to, sir?"

"The Klimpton hotel," he replied. He had every

intention of drinking himself into oblivion at the Vol. 39 bar.

VERONICA STARED AT THE BOTTOM OF THE STAIRS. Flashes of harsh chills swept through her over and over until suddenly she couldn't breathe. She sank to the ground, clutching the folder he'd given her, and tried to stop the panic from taking over.

She'd done the right thing hadn't she? She'd protected her daughter, protected herself. They couldn't tie their lives to a man who saw money as the solution to every problem and didn't talk to her about anything. There was no trust in a relationship like that. She'd done the only thing she could to handle this.

What she didn't know was how to handle what came next. The emptiness, the bleak hole left inside her chest. She wanted to go after him, to tell him she'd changed her mind, but she couldn't. The weight of the folder in her hands grew heavier as she realized she'd gotten what she'd always wanted: her home, now hers forever.

But at what cost...

The door at the bottom of the stairs opened again. Her heart gave a brief leap of hope.

"Thad?"

It wasn't Thad. Zelda came up the stairs, her face

strained. "Ronnie, breathe, okay?" She sat down beside Veronica and put an arm around her shoulders.

"I feel like I'm having a heart attack," Veronica whispered.

"It's an anxiety attack. Just breathe from deep within your belly. *Slowly.*"

Veronica got her breathing back under control and let her head hang between her knees.

"What did he do?" Zelda finally asked. "All he said was that you didn't trust him and that he didn't prove you wrong."

"He's the buyer." She could barely speak.

"What buyer?"

"The house. The coffee shop."

"*He's* the one?"

"Yes."

"Shit. But...what are these papers?" Zelda touched the folder Veroncia still clutched to her chest.

"The deed to the house. He gave it to me."

"Wait... that's good news, isn't it?"

She shook her head. She didn't want to talk about it anymore. She needed to think about what she was going to do now. Stay here and owe him for the house, even though he said she didn't, or leave as she'd planned and give him back the paperwork.

Zelda seemed to read her thoughts. "What do you plan to do?"

"I don't know. Lyra will be crushed," Veronica said.

She would be crushed too, but she didn't have to tell Zelda that; it was written all over her face.

Her friend hugged her. "Hey. Just give it a week. You don't have to think about it right now." Zelda's voice soothed her as she rubbed Veronica's back, but Veronica felt like she was sliding out of control down a hill, and she was terrified of where she'd land.

She wanted to chase after Thad and tell him she loved him, but the truth was she didn't know if she could trust him. What if he only *thought* he loved her? What if the feelings he thought he had were, in reality, guilt related?

He saw himself as the Prince Charming in her little story, as the hero who saves the damsel in distress. But that couldn't be the foundation of a relationship. She closed her eyes to fight off fresh tears.

Somewhere in that Cinderella suite in Disney World, that antique grandfather clock had struck midnight. The glittering coach had crumbled away while her ball gown turned back to rags. A silly metaphor, she knew, but she could feel every second of that beautiful dream of her life fade away as she sat with her friend in the quiet stairwell.

19

That first week following the breakup was hell. He'd thought after a few days, she would have been convinced of his sincerity and called him, but that hope had sunk into dread as the week went on. The more days that passed, the more he'd given up.

Now he hoped to get Veronica out of his head, to learn to love and let go. He'd gone to the office as though nothing had happened, buried himself in work, staying until past midnight most nights and barely venturing away from his desk or apartment except when necessary.

But that Saturday night his doorbell had rung, and all of his plans were torn to shreds again.

"Sir, I hate to disturb you," Winston said through the door. "But you've received an overnighted package."

Thad dragged himself to the door and accepted the package with a nod to the anxious butler. He took it into the kitchen, where he dug around in his utensil drawer for a box cutter.

The package revealed a blue box about the size of a shoebox with a cream-colored envelope taped to the top. He slid out the letter and found a note written on expensive card stock with a golden coach logo at the top.

Dear Mr. Worthington,

We hope you and your guests enjoyed your stay at Cinderella's Castle. As a part of being our special guest this week, we always provide a silver slipper for the princesses of the suite. Enclosed is one for Veronica and one for Lyra. Thank you for being a part of our magical world.

Remember, the clock never strikes midnight as long as you believe in magic.

Sincerely,

Candace

Thad opened the lid of the pale blue box. There, nestled within velvet blue cloth, were two glass slippers. One for Veronica and one for her daughter.

He didn't touch them, not at first. An hour later, he sat by the fire drinking scotch and holding Veronica's slipper in one hand. It was made of Swarovski crystal, but had a clear gel insert to bring comfort and the bottom of the slipper had a soft clear rubber sole. It could *actually* be worn. The firelight sparkled over the surface of the shoe, making it glitter so bright it cast flashes of rainbow light across the living room.

Everything came flooding back. The hours he'd spent at the brownstone with Veronica and Lyra, the Friday night boardgames, the Disney movies, the popcorn fights, and singing Lyra to bed before joining Veronica in hers. The dozens of small intimacies in a world he'd never imagined he'd become a part of.

All gone.

He put the glass slipper back in its box and closed the lid before tucking the package away at the topmost part of his closet, out of sight, and turned off the light.

"MOMMY, IS MR. THAD COMING OVER TONIGHT?"

Veronica froze at the stove where she'd been boiling macaroni and cheese noodles. She'd lost count of how many times Lyra had asked her that. It had been a hellish week since returning from Orlando.

"Honey, I don't think he's going to be able to come over for a while." Veronica didn't know how to tell her child she'd broken up with Thad.

Lyra came to the kitchen and stood beside Veronica,

her tiny hands reaching for the countertop edge. She looked up into Veronica's face.

"Mommy, are you mad at me?" She had such a soft wounded and worried look that it made Veronica put aside the large spoon she'd been using to stir the pasta cooking in the pot.

Veronica knelt and cupped her daughter's cheeks. "Mad at you, baby? I'm not mad. Why would you think that?"

Lyra gave a slight shrug. "I thought maybe you wouldn't let Mr. Thad come over, 'cuz I made you mad."

An awful tightness squeezed Veronica's chest. "You've done nothing wrong. Thad and I aren't dating anymore, honey. It's just...difficult. I know you liked Thad, and so did I, but he wasn't quite right for mommy. Do you understand?" She knew asking that of a four-year-old was impossible. There was no way for Lyra to really understand. How could she, when she barely understood it herself?

"Why don't you put on a movie for us while I get the mac and cheese finished?" she asked.

Lyra looked at her a long moment before she turned away and headed for the TV, allowing Veronica to refocus on cooking their dinner.

Later, as they watched *The Little Mermaid*, and the evil sea witch destroyed the mermaid's life when the prince nearly drowned in the sea, something bubbled up inside her. She couldn't hold it in anymore. Tears streamed down her face and she sniffed while wiping them away. Lyra cuddled against her and turned to look up at her.

"Mommy? Why are you crying?"

The question had a thousand answers, but they all came back to the same problem. She'd fallen in love... but she had to let him go.

"I've just had a long day, baby." She tried to dispel her tears and force a smile. Things would get better with time. They had to.

BY THE SECOND WEEK, THAD STOPPED SHAVING. HE didn't come into the office except to conduct meetings. He let his best deals lapse and he paid too much for properties on others even though his father and Jared did their best to help. But he just didn't care anymore. It was as though that part of his life along with everything else had lost its appeal.

He barely ate. He ran himself to exhaustion on his treadmill and stayed alone in the penthouse every night. He ignored most of the calls from his friends and parents. He just didn't want to face reality anymore. The beautiful luster that cast a glamour upon his life before this, was gone.

But Thad couldn't keep all his friends away. Angelo and Jared soon found a way to force their themselves into his penthouse, and he'd reluctantly let them stay and do their best to cheer him up.

"You can't keep doing this to yourself," Angelo said.

"Why not? I can do what a please. I have the power to do whatever the hell I want," Thad muttered. Veronica's accusations were still fresh in his mind.

"Oh, come on." Jared growled. "You're not an idiot. It was one girl. She was great, but it didn't work out. It happens. You get back out there. You don't hide in your room like a coward."

Thad, who'd been carrying a nearly empty whiskey bottle, spun and glowered at his friends. "Coward? You, of all people, call me a coward? This is *your* fault. You never should have bet me to ask her out."

"I wasn't trying to fix you up with Mrs. Right," said Jared. "She seemed like a nice girl and I thought you'd have a good time together. I *also* thought you'd end up dating other women after her, not latch onto her as your one true love. This feels like Victoria all over again."

"Shut the hell up," Thad snapped.

Angelo and Jared shared a look that only made Thad angrier. He slammed the bottle down on the counter and walked toward the tall windows of his living room overlooking the glittering Chicago skyline.

"Look, maybe it's not over," Angelo said more quietly as they joined Thad at the window.

"You didn't see her face, Angelo. It's over. A man can't come back from that. And the worst part is, she's not wrong. She's better off without me. They both are..." The anger at his friends had deflated almost instantly. He was just...empty. So damned empty. It was as though he had no will left to fight for anything.

Angelo put a hand on his shoulder. "Have a little faith in love...and yourself. It will get better."

Soon he was alone again in his penthouse. By the time he'd summoned the will to *really* talk to them, they were long gone. He walked into his darkened bedroom and reached for his e-reader on the nightstand.

When he turned it on, the first page of *The Golden Compass* greeted him in the dark. The first page few chapters were filled with the name Lyra. He eased down on his bed, stretching out before he started to read.

Perhaps it was foolish to bury himself in a book, but this series had meant everything to Veronica, so much so that she'd named her daughter after the main character.

He wanted to know what Veronica had seen, what she'd felt as she turned the pages of the story. That need to feel connected to Veronica somehow, to have at least one small tie to her, was too strong to ignore.

MICHELLE WAVED A HAND IN FRONT OF VERONICA'S face. "Okay, this has to stop."

"What?" Veronica briefly snapped out of the bleak spiral of her thoughts.

She, Michelle, Steve, and the kids were eating at one of their favorite pizza places, but Veronica had been poor company and she knew it. Thank God Lyra had Sam to play with. The boy was trying to teach Lyra how to play Tic-Tac-Toe.

"You're moping." Michelle fixed her with a non-nonsense sort of "mom" look that made Veronica smile.

"I know," Veronica agreed. "I shouldn't, but I am."

"You should be happy. You got your home back. Hell you got it out of the sea witche's control entirely, and the Chi-Bean is still open. Things are looking up, right?"

"I know. I know." Veronica sighed. She thought back to the transfer deed that gave her ownership of the house. She still hadn't filed it. Technically, that meant Thad was still the owner of the house. For some reason, that made it much harder for her to file the deed. Some part of her *wanted* Thad to still own the home, to still be connected to her life and Lyra's. It was totally messed up, but it was the truth.

Veronica looked toward the end of the table where Lyra and Sam had their heads bent together while they drew on the brown paper tablecloth.

"No, you should put an X here." Sam told Lyra with authority, though he was sweet about it.

"Okay!" The little girl chimed in and marked an 'X' where Sam had pointed. Most boys his age didn't seem to care about girls much, but Sam had always been so sweet with her, even when he wanted to run off and play with his other friends.

"Ronnie, seriously, there will be other men and other chances. It's not over," Steve said. "I liked the guy. He was great. But sometimes things don't work out. It doesn't mean that you won't get lucky again. I dated two girls seriously before I met Michelle, and both times I was convinced they were 'the one.'"

Michelle turned on her husband with a curious look. "*Excuse* me? What girls were these? I haven't heard about them. How serious are we talking?"

"Oh, it was college. I got stuck on one girl freshman year and one in senior year. You know what they say, when the lust fades you have to have something else to build a life on."

"Mister—" Michelle poked Steve in the chest "—our lust is *never* going to fade, you got that?"

Steve grinned. "Yes, ma'am."

Veronica watched the two of them. It was as though they could read each other's minds. She couldn't help but think of Thad and wondered how many of the moments they'd spent together had been driven by lust.They hadn't even had a chance for moments driven by something deeper.

She remembered all the nights she'd laid in his arms, listening to his deep, even breaths and the mornings where they'd whispered in the early light about things they planned to do that day. Those moments had been infinitely more important to her than sex.

But God, the sex... he'd gotten her addicted to him in just one night, only to lose him the next day. She didn't want to go on another long drought without sex, but she wasn't going to start jumping into men's beds, either. Nothing had changed, really. She was still the kind of girl who wanted to wait until she fell in love with a man before she gave that part of herself up to him.

"So, what's it going to be, Veronica?" Michelle asked. "Are you going to be brave and put yourself back out there?"

She wanted to say yes. She wanted to say she would be brave, but something deep inside her heart resisted.

"Someday. Just not now." A coward's answer.

If only there was a way to turn back time. To cast a spell upon the grandfather clock that had ticked past midnight and force the hands back just a few minutes. To beat back against the past until she was dancing once again in Thad's arms.

Two weeks, and he hadn't tried to shower her with expensive gifts trying to win her back. He hadn't tried calling her at all hours, trying to use his smooth negotiating tactics to work out a deal. He hadn't gotten angry at her rejection or blamed her for everything. There were a thousand things she'd expected the side of Thad she hadn't seen to do, and yet he hadn't done *any* of it.

He'd respected her position and had left her with a simple offer.

"But if you change your mind, you can call me, text me, or come over. Whatever you wish. I am yours, Veronica, no matter what."

Only that was impossible, wasn't it? Saying she was sorry, saying she trusted him now after everything that had happened. It wouldn't be enough. She'd said terrible things to him, even accused him of using her, when deep down, she'd known he hadn't done any of that. She'd let her anger speak for her and it had cost her everything.

20

By the third week following his breakup with Veronica, Thad had created a chilly distance between himself and his heart. It allowed him to function, at least.

He shaved, dressed, and went back to work. He made the deals he'd always made and negotiated with a new efficiency. But he purchased new properties with no enjoyment, merely as a means to an end. He gave up creative focus of the company to his father. He continued to avoid his friends and family, except in necessary situations. He didn't need or want to talk about what had happened, what he could have done differently, or how he should have seen it coming.

The anger he felt at himself faded, and there was just a bleak emptiness left where his heart should have been.

He sat in his office, staring out the skyline, but not actually seeing anything. The minutes, hours, and days blurred together.

"Thad."

Thad reluctantly turned to where his father stood at the doorway to his office. He looked resigned, and Thad steeled himself for a conversation he didn't want to have. "Dad..."

"I know you don't want to talk about what happened. But..." He held out a gift bag Thad hadn't noticed before. "Your mother found these for Veronica. Even after everything that's happened, I was hoping you would be able to deliver them to her."

Thad held still as his father put the gift bag gently on his desk. He smiled, a sad sort of smile, and then left without another word.

Thad didn't touch the gift bag right away, but eventually, with a slightly numb curiosity, he opened it. Three books with an *autographed by the author* sticker on the cover were inside. He read the titles: *The Golden Compass, The Subtle Knife, The Amber Spyglass,* all by Philip Pullman.

He'd devoured the series on his e-reader the week before, drowning his sorrows in the magical world Pullman had spun while Lyra's face floated in his mind as he pictured the young heroine fighting, quite literally, half the world to save her friends and, eventually, the universe itself.

Every night he'd fallen asleep dreaming of Veronica, glittering arctic snow, fierce armored polar bears, and a little girl holding a golden compass. His heart had broken as Lyra had grown up to fall in love with a young man named Will and at the end of the third book, they'd had to stay in their separate worlds, never to be together again. He felt that same searing pain in his own soul now.

He held the trio of books with the author's signature on the first page of each in his hands. The longer he held them, they seemed to almost vibrate with energy. He hastily put the books back into the gift bag and closed it up.

Veronica deserved to have the books, but that meant taking them to the Chi-Bean. He could mail them, he supposed, or have Simon drove over and deliver them. But something about that felt wrong. She deserved better.

Brandon poked his head into Thad's office. "Mail's here." He came to Thad's desk and set down the stack.

Thad reached for the pile of letters and envelopes. "Thanks." An unmarked one sat on top. He opened it first.

A bright blue papered flyer unfolded in his hands. "Open Mic Night—Sing Your Heart Out at the Chi-Bean—Thursday from 8pm to 10pm".

He stared at the flyer, then at the scrawled note at the bottom.

Find closure. -Angelo.

Maybe he could take the books himself tonight, see her one last time, and that would help him finally move on. He checked his watch. Open mic night was ending in half an hour. She would be working. He could swing by, drop the books off, and go.

Thad called Simon to pick him up. He got into the back and set his briefcase on his lap. He'd just shoved a bunch of papers inside and hadn't bothered sorting them out. He could work on that while Simon took him to the coffee house. He sifted through contracts, negotiation memorandums, and other documents, but paused as he found an odd-looking page that was slightly crinkled.

He turned the paper over, and his heart stilled. It was one of Lyra's drawings: a picture of him, Veronica, and herself in between them both, holding their hands.

Someone, most likely Lyra's preschool teacher, had put a tracing of words at the top of the drawing for Lyra to connect the dashes so she could practice her letters. It said: My family. Mom, Me, and Dad. She'd drawn hearts all around the three stick figures.

My family...

He swallowed hard and clenched his hand into a fist. As Simon stopped in front of the Chi-Bean, Thad folded the illustration and tucked it in the inside pocket of his coat. For a wild second, he thought about going after Veronica, winning her back, but he instantly backed away from it. He didn't want to prove her right.

"Wait for me. I won't be long," he told Simon. He picked up the package and headed for the coffee shop. From outside, he could the shop was full as aspiring musicians were taking turns on the stage. It was 9:45 and the shop would soon close.

His hand hesitated on the knob. A sudden cold wind tugged at his scarf, carrying a hint of snow in the air. With a strange sense of finality, he turned the handle and stepped into the warmth of the Chi-Bean.

He caught Zelda's eye as he came up to the side of the counter, trying to stay out of the way of customers. He pushed down a sudden flair of nerves, wondering what Veronica had told her, and if Zelda would hate him for what had happened.

"Thad, it's so good to see you." Her genuine honesty and delight at seeing him pulled at his heart in a different way. He'd come to love the coffee house almost as much as Veronica did, including the people who worked here.

"You, too. I wasn't sure if you'd kick me out once you saw me."

"I thought about it, but honestly I don't know what happened between you. I've seen you with her. You would *never* hurt her, no matter what she thinks." Zelda's gaze softened. "As far as I'm concerned, I'll let you come in anytime."

He scanned the room but didn't see Veronica. "Is... she here?"

She nodded her head at the half-opened door. "In the storage room. It's inventory day, so she's been organizing our new deliveries."

From his vantage point, he could see Veronica with her back to him in the storage room. She hadn't noticed him yet. For a moment, he was lost in watching her, lost in just taking in the sight of her and how it made his heart bleed. He'd convinced himself the last three weeks had forced him to get over her. He was so damn wrong. He would love her until he drew his last breath.

"I...uh... These are for Veronica. My parents got them for her before..." He set the gift package on the counter in front of Zelda and turned to leave.

"Hey, wait... Why don't you sing one last song?" Zelda caught his arm. "Please?"

"I don't think I should." He also wasn't sure if he could. He hadn't even touched his guitar in three weeks. Along with everything else, he'd lost the will to sing.

Zelda squeezed his arm gently. "Listen. Some things are best said in a song. You feel me?"

Veronica still had her back turned, still unaware he was there. He was relieved she hadn't turned to see him.

He stared at Veronica's back, then at the fireplace and the now empty stool with the microphone and the guitar. That strange urge filled his veins, making his blood hum as he thought back to how this had all started. Veronica had told him that night when she'd heard his voice that it had called to her and affected her deeply.

What if...what if he could reach her again somehow? At the very least, he could end things the same way they'd begun...with a song from his heart.

"Fuck," he muttered and moved toward the fireplace.

Maybe this would be the best way he could speak to her one last time. He walked up to the stool, retrieved the guitar, and drew in a deep breath.

VERONICA WAS EMPTYING SUGAR PACKETS INTO A storage container. It was almost closing time and she was looking forward to going upstairs to hug Lyra. It had become one of the most important things to her, holding Lyra at night and trying not to think of how much she wished Thad was there with his arms wrapped around her. What she'd done had been right it, hadn't it? She'd protected Lyra and herself. But it didn't erase the fact that she missed him so much it hurt.

Had it really been three weeks since she and Thad had parted ways? It had felt like centuries. So many times, she'd imagined herself walking into his office and telling him she was sorry, that she'd been wrong and she could see now he wasn't like the kind of men she'd accused him of being.

Sharing a life meant learning more about each other,

about coming to trust each other, and about seeing each other at highs and lows but riding the roller-coaster of it all together. And they'd barely begun before she'd called it off. She hadn't even given him a chance, because she'd convinced herself the risks for her and for Lyra were too great. It had been a mistake, the biggest one she'd ever made, and now she was too afraid to try to go after him.

Even now, the thought of him was never far from her mind. She'd tried to avoid open mic night by focusing on the inventory, because all she wanted was to hear Thad's voice again. And each time she didn't, it created a fresh stab of pain.

With a sigh, Veronica finished with the sugar packets and was ready to find another way to distract herself when she sensed a silence fill the room. Another singer must have taken to the stage. She looked deeper into the storage room. Napkins. There were napkins still to sort.

The fine hairs on her arms rose as the man began to sing. She *knew* that voice. There was no other voice like it. That voice still haunted her dreams. It had both broken her heart and made her whole. It was the one voice she'd wished to hear over and over again.

She moved out of the storage room to stare at Thad on the stool, guitar in hand, eyes closed, and singing from the depths of his soul.

He sang a song that spoke straight to her broken heart. *I will Always Love You* written by Dolly Parton but made famous by Whitney Houston. She'd never heard a man sing it before, but with Thad…it was spellbinding. The audience sat captivated. Thad's eyes stayed closed as he sang of always loving her but not being what she needed and how he hoped that life would treat her kind. He wished her joy and happiness and…love.

The last three horrible weeks played in her mind as his song moved through her with the force of a relentless river. She'd cried so much the first week that she wondered if she'd ever run out of tears. It had scared Lyra enough that Lyra's preschool teacher had called, worried about what was going on at home because Lyra had told her teacher that her mother cried a lot.

She thought of how empty the house felt. She missed watching Thad stand in the bathroom and shave, how the razor slipped over his chin in clean strokes. How Lyra always wanted a bedtime story and a song, and he never said no to her, even on the nights he wasn't staying over. She missed seeing his beautiful silk ties draped over the bed at night as she undressed. She missed how cherished he'd made her feel and how she'd loved *loving* him.

Veronica stared at Thad now and all those memories, all those feelings were as raw in this moment as they'd been that day she hadn't stopped him from leaving. She'd been so afraid of the side of Thad she hadn't seen, and yet here it was now, right in front of her. She'd let a possibly happy future walk away because she wasn't sure how things would turn out. But wasn't that how love worked? You had to trust someone with your heart in order to love. You had to take risks. You had to hand them your very soul and hope they wouldn't hurt you.

She'd been brave enough at eighteen to trust her heart to Parker. She's been so afraid to try again that she'd looked for reasons to deny what they had together... and now that fear seemed so silly.

Here he was, the charming prince straight from every fairytale she'd ever loved, singing from the heart that he would always love her.

Veronica covered her trembling lips She struggled to breathe as he ended the song.

He held the guitar, his own breath slightly harsh against the microphone, and finally opened his eyes to look straight at her. Then, as the room burst into wild applause, he put down the guitar and gave her just the slightest nod and a bittersweet smile before he walked away from her, just as his lyrics had promised.

Panic seized her as she saw Thad's private car parked outside. Simon was waiting on the curb. If she didn't act now, she'd lose him forever...

Thad had opened the door by the time she finally got control of herself and dashed after him.

"Thad!" she called out, causing everyone to turn their heads. He paused, his hand on the doorknob.

"You are what I need," she said, echoing against the lyrics where he'd said he wasn't what she needed. He couldn't have been more wrong.

They were a dozen feet apart. She saw his shoulders

relax as he turned. The pain mirrored her own. They had both been hurt but he'd done all he could to prove to her who he really was.

It was up to her now. She didn't need to stand in front of the microphone to tell him how she felt. As stupid and cliché as it was, she did the only thing she thought she could do that wouldn't make her cry.

Sing.

She chose the song that had touched her heart the first time he'd ever come into her life like a shooting star in the dark abyss of her night sky: Calum Scott's *You Are The Reason* came from her lips.

She sang about how she'd been losing sleep and wanted him back, how she always thought about him. By the time she reached the first chorus, Zelda had rushed over with the microphone, and the song now filled the entire room.

Her heart pounded and her hands shook. She stepped closer to him as she sang of how she would climb every mountain and swim every ocean just to be with him, of how she wanted to fix what she'd broken. Her heart pounded with every word and her hands shook as he took a step closer to her with every verse she sang.

When they were only a foot apart, he cupped her face in his palms and the last of the words tumbled from her lips.

When the chorus ended, he leaned down and kissed

her. Her racing heart went blissfully, peacefully, still for a moment as the pain bled away and that encroaching darkness was bathed in a fiery beacon of pure, powerful light. It took her a moment to realize all the cheers she heard were coming from everyone in the coffee shop, and not just inside her head.

This was love. This sweet ache in her chest and burning hope left her dizzy with euphoria. This was explosive passion mixed with quiet mornings in each other's arms. It was shared smiles in the dark as they both tucked Lyra into bed.

Thad's lips moved slowly over hers, a sweet hesitancy to his kiss that made her want to cry again. She curled her arms around his neck, holding him tight to her. A moment later, he wound his arms around her back, gripping her tight as though he feared she would vanish. When at last their mouths broke apart, he was breathing hard and so was she.

"Hey..." he whispered.

"Hey..." she breathed back.

She bit her lip as she peeked at the crowd staring at them, some still applauding. More than one person had their cell phone out and had been recording them, Zelda among them.

Veronica's face heated and she buried her cheek against Thad's chest, completely mortified. His arms tightened around her protectively.

Zelda started toward them. "You guys should go upstairs. I'll close things down with Zach."

Veronica reached out and squeezed her friend's arm. "Thank you."

She took Thad's hand and led him to the private stairwell, her heart still beating way too fast.

21

The second they were alone, Veronica looked at him with her heart on her sleeve and a silent prayer on her lips.

"I'm sorry," Veronica whispered. "I'm sorry I didn't trust you. I sorry I didn't believe you. Can you forgive me?" She wanted to be in his arms again, to feel safe and loved, but she needed to feel certain that he wouldn't push her away, even after that life-altering kiss they'd just shared.

Thad pulled her back into his arms. "You never had to ask," he said. "I am and always will be yours."

It was as though the weight of a century of pain had been lifted off her at that moment. She wasn't sure how long they stood there in the stairwell, simply holding one another. Eventually she felt him chuckle.

"What?" she asked.

"I have a present for you, from my parents. That's why I came here. I didn't intend to talk to you, but then I saw the guitar and I just had to say what was still in my heart. My father will never let me live this down."

"What? Why?"

"Because my parents will have been the cause of bringing us back together. Believe me, they will *never* let me forget that." He brushed a lock of her hair behind her ears. His smile was both seductive and sweet at the same time. He held her a long moment before he stepped back. "Don't move."

He left her in the stairwell, more than a little nervous that he might not come back. Part of her was wondering if she'd been dreaming. When he returned, he held a gift bag out to her. She opened the beautifully decorated bag and pulled out the tissue paper. A trio of Philip Pullman books sat inside.

"They're autographed," said Thad.

"Oh my God," she said, opening the cover of the last one to see.

To Veronica, Thank you for believing in the power of my stories so much that you named your child Lyra. I know she will grow up to do great and wonderous things. -Phillip Pullman

She looked up at Thad, who'd suddenly gone pale, no doubt he was terrified about how this looked.

"I swear it wasn't my idea. It was my father. I thought he just—"

She hugged him. "They're wonderful." He didn't

need to explain. Not about this. "Let's go upstairs. Lyra's been missing you, and so have I."

She was still ready to cry, but this time from joy. The tightness that had built in her chest the last three weeks was beginning to ease and she knew that the longer she had him back in her life, the better she would feel.

They walked up the stairs hand in hand, fingers laced tight. How had she thought she could survive without him? When she opened the door and let him inside, she felt something change inside her, a shifting of tectonic plates beneath the surface. It was a massive change, and one she knew she wouldn't regret. She had a few moments to speak before Lyra would realize Thad was there. She nodded to the folder on the table.

"I didn't file the paperwork you gave me."

"What?" He picked up the papers and studied them before turning puzzled eyes to her. "Why not?"

"Because removing you as the owner would have been removing the last thing connecting us. I guess, deep down, I couldn't lose that last small tie to you."

Thad set the papers down and wrapped her in his arms. "God, honey, you are killing me." He nuzzled his face in her hair and she swore she could feel him trembling.

Lyra's door opened and her sleepy face peered up at them. "Mommy, I had a bad dream..."

Lyra's lip quivered as her gaze fell on Thad.

"Mr. Thad!" She dropped her large teddy bear and

rushed toward him, tears in her eyes. Thad released Veronica just in time to catch the child in his arms and hug her as she started to cry.

"Hey, I'm here," Thad murmured, stroking Lyra's hair. "It's okay now."

"You won't leave again?" Lyra asked, her tiny fingers curling against the collar of his coat.

"No, honey. I'm here to stay." Thad's eyes closed as he smiled, his expression full of love and relief.

Lyra buried her face in his neck and sniffled. Veronica had to fight to hold back her own tears. Thad truly loved her daughter; it was written all over his face.

Veronica held her breath as she saw that bright, beautiful future with Thad unfurling once more in her mind. This man who had *saved* her home, though no doubt he'd argue she was the one who'd saved him. But it didn't matter who saved who, she would never turn her back on him again. He really was her prince.

"Why don't I sing to you?" Thad said as he carried her back to bed. Veronica followed them and watched from the doorway as he sang to Lyra, and she drifted back to sleep.

Thad came over and turned off the bedroom light. They both simply stared at one another in the hall.

"You'll stay the night?" She wanted to ask him to stay forever, and she would, soon.

"If you want me to."

She put her hand on his chest, feeling his heartbeat through his shirt. "I do."

"I need to tell Simon to go home for the night." He slipped his phone out of his pocket and called his driver. "Simon, it's me. I'll be staying the night... Yeah..." His gaze met hers as he spoke again. "You're right about that. Have a good night." He hung up.

"What did he say?" Veronica asked.

"He said, 'I guess sometimes miracles do happen.'"

Veronica smiled and motioned for him to follow her to her bedroom. "I guess they do."

Veronica dashed about, picking up clothes scattered on the floor and a few of Lyra's stuffed animals, which had wandered in here with the little girl when Lyra had needed to share her bed. It felt strangely like the first night she'd met him. Her heart beat nervously as she tried to give herself something to do by cleaning up. Thad came over and gently grasped her wrist, taking away the shirt she'd picked up from the floor. He let it drop back down and then clasped her hands in his, holding them as she trembled.

"Are you okay with this?" he asked.

She nodded, afraid she'd burst into tears if she tried to speak. He pulled her once more into his arms, sensing what she needed.

"I want to fight to keep you, you understand?" he asked. "I'll do whatever it takes to make this work. If you're still angry with me, we can talk about it. Tell me what I need to do to be a better man for you."

The tears came then, but she kept herself from falling completely apart. "You don't have to do anything," she said. "It just took me a while to realize what sort of man you are deep down. The flash and sparkle of the dream of you, I was so afraid that wasn't real...but it *is* real and you're so much more. You aren't just a man who lives from sunny day to sunny day. You'll be here for me when it rains. I know that now."

Thad smiled. "Storms could never keep me away." A shiver swept through her as she felt the gravity of that promise. "Just don't hold it against me if I buy an umbrella now and then?"

Veronica laughed despite herself. "Deal."

Thad pulled her into him with a kiss. Neither of them spoke as they took turns undressing each other. Her fingers searched for the buttons of his shirt, taking her time slipping them through the slits while he unfasted the knot of her Chi-Bean Apron and let it fall to the floor. She pushed his jacket off his shoulders and it slid to his feet before she started pulling off his shirt.

Thad's lips made love to hers, devouring her, proving to her that she was his. He cupped the back of her head, tilting her face so he could kiss her as he pleased. She adored that gentle physical command of his when they came together like this. She felt desired, and she surrendered to it, feeling safe with letting him set the pace.

She gasped as he pulled back to remove her sweater. His hands cupped and gently squeezed the mounds of her breasts, still concealed by her sensible bra. She felt a little embarrassed she'd didn't have on any fancy lingerie when she was with him, but he never seemed to mind.

His lips covered her skin, teasing her in the most sensitive places, like the curve of her neck, which made her body flare to life with heat. He removed her bra, jeans, and panties with agonizing slowness. She, in turn, explored him just as slowly, softly kissing his chest, his throat, his shoulder. She reveled in knowing that this beautiful noble man was *hers*, now and forever.

"This is punishment, isn't it?" he moaned. "You are trying to drive me crazy."

"*I* call it a reward."

She whimpered as he turned the tables on her, sucking one of her nipples between his lips. She hissed as he gently nipped the tip before sucking on it again. That slight hint of pain sent bolts of need shooting through her. She was going to lose control if he didn't make love her soon.

"I've spent three weeks torturing myself with dreams of how I'd take you, Veronica," said Thad. "Thinking about how I'd show you that you'd never want another man after being with me." He shot her a dark, hungry look that held a hint of teasing to it. "Consider this a necessary torment for the both of us. Next, I think I'll—"

That was it. She'd had enough. "Enough thinking. Just shut up and kiss me." She dragged his head to hers and claimed his mouth.

This loss of doubt left her aware of him on a whole new hard to explain level. It was as though some divine being had dragged its hands through the cosmos, yanking her and Thad's private stars together in alignment.

She pulled him down on top of her. The weight and heat of his body were so welcome.

"Love me," she begged him, her voice almost breaking. It was a plea not just for sex but something infinitely more.

"For the rest of our lives," he promised, and she shivered with the flood of emotions. She parted her thighs and he slid between them, his muscled body settling perfectly against hers. Thad kissed away Veronica's quiet tears of joy as their bodies united. He filled her completely, and she clenched herself around him. He groaned and began to move within her. She gripped his hips with her knees, rocking against him as he joined himself to her.

"I love you," he whispered between slow deep kisses. She came apart in his arms, pleasure sweeping through her like a tidal wave. She held on to him as he gasped her name, his breathing a harsh contrast to the softness of his eyes.

Long afterward, as they lay entwined beneath the sheets, she pressed a kiss to his chest and met his gaze.

"I love you. All of you." Those words were so full of power and filled her with a surge of hope for where life would take them. Whatever happened, they were together and they loved each other—the only things that mattered. Perhaps that old grandfather clock had held onto some magic after midnight had passed.

EPILOGUE

C*hristmas Eve — 1 month later — Orlando, Florida*

"Are you ready?" Thad called through the door to Veronica.

"Just a second." Veronica called back.

Thad looked down at Lyra who stood by his side. Lyra wore her Princess Elsa gown, all blue and glittering. She twisted her body slightly, so the filmy see-through top layer of her gown decorated with snowflakes glittered in the light over her dark blue underskirt.

"You remember what we planned?" Thad asked in a low whisper.

Lyra covered her mouth to stifle a giggle so Veronica wouldn't overhear their plotting. "Yep!"

Today was the most important day of his life. He'd planned everything down to the last detail, but it didn't change the fact that he was still nervous as hell. He shoved his hands into the pockets of his costume's trousers, hoping to keep his hands still while they waited.

At last, Veronica opened the door. She looked incredible. Her dark hair was pulled up into a lovely hairstyle off her neck and a frosty pale blue ball gown hugged her body at the bodice and spilled out into voluminous skirts of iridescent blues and purples. She looked like Cinderella.

"Mommy!" Lyra gasped. "You're *so* pretty."

Veronica's cheeks reddened. "You think so? I feel a little silly to be wearing a Cinderella costume."

"Well, we are at Disney World and I think it's perfect. If you're ready should go, I don't want to miss our photo shoot." Thad offered his arm to Veronica and she obliged before she touched the gold braiding on his shoulder.

"Your prince costume turned out nice," she said.

Thad grinned. He'd spent top dollar on having a seamstress from Hollywood create costumes for Veronica, Lyra, and himself when they'd decided to celebrate Christmas at Disney. They'd even planned a photoshoot on the steps of Cinderella's Castle. Candace had given them access to a private room near the front of the park to change into their costumes.

Now came the big surprise. Thad hoped Veronica wouldn't think it was too silly, but that was the advantage of having a little kid around all the time… you learned to appreciate the silly things in life.

They left the small office building and stepped into the park. Veronica halted suddenly as she saw what awaited them.

Six white horses pulled a glittering white carriage. It resembled a pumpkin turned into a coach with leaves and vines carved into the white wheels.

Veronica was momentarily stunned. "Oh my God."

Lyra was already running for the coach. A footman in a white and silver uniform with a white powdered wig lifted the little girl onto one of the seats.

"You ready?" Thad asked Veronica.

She nodded, her eyes still wide as he escorted her to the coach and helped her inside.

"I'm afraid to even ask how much this costs…"

Thad waggled a finger. "Uh uh. This is for Christmas; I'm allowed to be a bit excessive. Besides, in case you haven't figured it out by now, I'd give you the world."

Veronica cupped his face and pressed her forehead to his. "We only need you."

He smiled and kissed the tip of her nose. "Well, you get me and all of this too."

Lyra sat facing them on the opposite cushion, kicking her feet as the coach started to move.

Everyone in the park stopped to stare and some waved as the coach rolled along the cobbled streets of the park. The coach stopped in front of the path that led to the castle. The footman lifted Lyra down and Thad helped Veronica. Their photographer, Hazel, started taking pictures as Thad pulled Veronica close and kissed her in front of the coach.

"Is it too much?" he whispered into her ear. "Too cliché?"

"No, this is wonderful. Just look at Lyra." Her child was clearly in princess heaven.

For several minutes, they paused for shots both with and without Lyra as well as poses of Lyra alone. After a short time, Lyra caught Thad's attention and gave him a big thumbs up when Veronica wasn't looking. It was their signal, the secret one that said she was ready for what was about to happen next. Thad gave the photographer a subtle nod and Hazel nodded back.

"Veronica, I have one more idea. Come over to me." Hazel called out.

Thad turned to the footman, who had retrieved the blue box, and then started toward where Veronica faced away from him. He was going to put it all on the line again, and he could think of no better way to do it than this.

VERONICA LISTENED AS HAZEL EXPLAINED WHAT SHE wanted.

"Just start walking away. Then let one of your shoes

slip off when I tell you to look over your shoulder at me."

"Okay, I think I can do that."

She wore two white blockade slippers that fit perfectly, but she was confident she could coax one off for the photo.

"Okay, I'm ready when you are. When I tell you to, look back at me," Hazel reminded.

Veronica raised her skirts and began to trot down the path, not quite running, but fast enough to make her skirts billow behind her.

"Look back!" Hazel called out. Veronica let one shoe fall off as she ran.

Veronica looked over her shoulder. Thad was a half dozen feet behind her, with Cinderella's Castle behind him. He reached for her as though to catch her with one hand, and in his other was a sparkling glass slipper. The sight was so unexpected, so captivating, she stopped dead in her tracks.

The world faded away as she turned fully to face him. He walked slowly toward her, dreamlike, and she reached out to grasp his outstretched hand.

Thad's hair fell into his eyes as he knelt at her feet. She lifted her skirts as he held out the slipper and slipped it onto her foot. She winced as something pricked her.

"Oh, I forgot." Thad took the slipper back removed a tiny object from inside it. It was a ring, a pear cut sapphire nestled in a bed of diamonds. He put the slipper back on and then held the ring up to her, still on one knee.

"Veronica Hannigan, there are no words to express the joy you make me feel and the love you give me. I am offering you all that I am to be the man you want to spend the rest of your life with. Will you do me the honor of marrying me?"

There was no stopping the tears welling up in her eyes. She let them come as she nodded and said yes. He slipped the ring over her finger and his gaze met hers as he stood and held her hands in his.

"You are my everything. Even when I die, I will find a way to be with you again, my atoms drifting until they find yours, until we live in the petals of flowers, on the wings of hummingbirds, in the shining droplets of light within the largest rainbows, or the quiet space between sunbeams. Whenever new lives are made from you and me, they will not be able to take just one but the pair."

Veronica heard a familiar tone to his words, a promise of love forever, one that reminded her of the books which had given Lyra her name. Thad understood that those words above all others were love in its most powerful form to her. She pulled his face to hers, kissing him as he held her tight, as if to prove that nothing would tear them apart ever again.

When she opened her eyes, she saw the crowd at the end of the path to the castle. People were cheering, so she waved at them. But one face stood out in the crowd, a face she hadn't seen in four years except in dreams... His warm smile was brighter than any memory, purer than any song. He nodded at her, then faded into the crowd and the bright winter sunlight. She waved at the vanishing shimmer of light.

"Who are you waving to?" Thad asked.

"Just someone who is glad I found you," she said. *Someone who is glad I found you.*

Lyra hopped with youthful energy toward them. "Mommy? Did you say yes?"

"I did, sweetie." Veronica bent to face her daughter. "Are you okay with this? With me marrying Thad?"

Her daughter stared up at her, suddenly wise beyond her years.

"Okay with it? Mommy..." she sighed dramatically. "It was *my* idea."

"Oh, that's right. I forgot." Veronica chuckled and stood, taking one of Thad's hands in hers as Lyra ran over to Hazel to see the pictures on her camera.

"You know, I have to confess something," Thad said sheepishly.

"Okay..."

"How I met you? Jared dared me to ask you out. He even turned it into a bet." Thad's cheeks turned a slightly reddish hue.

Veronica wasn't sure she liked the sound of that. "A bet?"

"Yeah. I had to go on fifteen dates with you before we could sleep together."

"Wait, what? You bet that you had to *wait*? Isn't that like the opposite of what guys usually bet on?"

He laughed. "Well, the point of it was that Jared wanted me to spend time with you and get to know you before we *made* love. He thought it would change how I looked at relationships. He was right."

She tried to count the dates in her head but lost count of whether some were considered real dates or not.

"Well, how far did we make it?" she asked.

Thad cupped her cheek, his eyes soft and yet mischievous. "Twenty-three, give or take." He brushed his lips over hers in a teasing kiss. "But by the time we reached two I wanted to wait until the moment was right. I have no regrets. What about you?"

"I don't either," she said. It had been torture to wait, sure, but the Cinderella Suite had been a kind of magic she'd never forget, despite the detour that came next. "I was just worried you didn't want me in that way," she confessed. It was a relief to know how wrong she'd been.

He traced her lips to the pad of his thumb.

"Not want you?" he echoed. "You couldn't be more wrong. You didn't just tempt me. You became the very reason for my being. I can't live without you."

Veronica closed her eyes as her very own prince

swept her into his arms for one more kiss, the first of many, the first of *forever.*

We will be together in a thousand petals and part of an endless sea. We will move in the blowing breeze and shimmer in the morning dew, beneath the stars, under the light of the moon.

Christmas Eve — Chicago

Angelo Vertucci entered the corner soup kitchen on North Clifton Avenue. Snow swirled around him as he passed through the doorway. The bell jingled a welcome when he stepped inside.

The room was crowded, the smells of sweat and unwashed bodies and clothes were masked by the evergreen shaped air fresheners someone had hung from the ceiling throughout the large room.

The soup kitchen was more full than usual tonight, given the holidays. Hundreds of people had been lining up all day to get inside for the Christmas Eve meal. It was why Angelo always took this shift.

Once a month, he donated his time and his restaurant's food to the kitchen. Christmas Eve and Christmas Day were especially important to him. Tonight, his family would celebrate in the usual Italian-American tradition of the Feast of Seven Fishes. They'd fast all day and then dine on a grand feast of seven different seafoods that night. He would miss taking part in that, but his family knew this was his way of paying back his gratitude for a happy, healthy family and a blessed life.

"Angelo!" Paul Hill, the director of the soup kitchen, waved him over to where the trays of food had been set up.

He shook the man's hand before he removed his coat and hung it up behind on. "Paul, how are you?" He then put on a white apron and serving gloves.

"Good, good. It's a full night tonight. We'll likely see most of them tomorrow, too." Paul's eyes filled with sympathy at the sight of all the hungry and the homeless that stood before them.

"Then we'll give them full bellies."

"That's the spirit."

Angelo noticed a young woman further down the food line preparing to serve Christmas cookies, one of his non-Italian specialties. He could easily have prepared something fancy, but the kids at the shelters that came here seemed to love the cookies. And every kid deserved a Christmas cookie.

"Who's that?" he asked Paul. He took in the young woman's tired face, but the smile she gave the people lining up before her was warm and genuine.

"That's Kara. She's new in town. She's worked the last three weeks, just after you came by last month."

The girl had long red wavy hair, a color he rarely saw, and he wondered if she was real. It paired well with her over-sized dark green cable knit sweater. She glanced his way at one point, her big blue eyes framed by dark lashes, and something inside him stirred with curiosity. But now wasn't the time. He focused back on the task at hand.

For the next two hours, he, Paul, Kara, and the other volunteers served food until the very last person in line had a full plate and a place to eat. Then, Paul and some of the other volunteers sang a few Christmas carols while their hungry charges ate their meals. Angelo stood at the back of the room, watching it all with quiet joy.

Kara came to stand beside him. "It's beautiful, isn't it?"

"There's nothing more beautiful than Christmas carols," he agreed.

She blushed. "Oh. I meant...I meant the way these people have a home here, at least for a few hours. A place with joy and food and companionship. That's beautiful."

Angelo stared at the young woman. She was so petite, not more than a few inches above five foot, and she looked both fragile and beautifully strong. Her heart-shaped face was enhanced by an adorable, upturned nose that gave her an impish look.

"Yes, that's beautiful too." His gaze ran down the length of her body as he took in the worn look of her clothes, the scuffed boots and faded coat. Whoever Kara was, she'd seen better days and something about that moved his heart.

"Could you tell Paul I'm leaving?" she asked him.

"Sure," he turned to speak to Paul, but then he realized he forgot to ask what her last name was. She was already heading out the door.

"Wait!"

Dashing for the coat rack, he slung on his own coat and chased after her. Something had urged him to not let this woman go without at least knowing her last name.

She was already across the street, snow dancing around her as she ducked her head into the wind and moved quickly on the path. He ran after her but was too late to stop what came next. A man lunged out of an alleyway and grabbed Kara, throwing her to the ground as he grabbed her purse.

"Stop! Help!" She screamed, but the sound was swallowed in the snow and wind, and the darkness of the alley hid the struggle.

Angelo sprinted toward the man and grabbed him at the waist, throwing him him to the ground. They rolled, trading punches, grunting, and cursing until their bodies slid apart. Angelo jumped onto the balls of his feet, fists raised, but the other man, also on his feet again, held up a small knife.

The man snarled and turned to run out of the alley,

back toward Kara, who'd retrieved her purse and was getting to her feet.

"Kara!" Angelo reached her at the same time as as the armed man. The mugger made another grab for her purse. Angelo threw a haymaker that caught the bastard off guard. The man held his chin with one hand and slashed his knife at Angelo.

"Get out of here!" Angelo advanced on the man. All six-foot-two of him was ready to tear the man to pieces if he tried anything.

The man turned and ran, vanishing into the snowy night. Angelo caught his breath, a stitch in his side making it hard to breathe. He put a hand to his side and faced Kara.

"You okay?" he asked.

She nodded, her blue eyes wide. "Are you?"

"Yeah, of course—"

She pointed a shaky hand at his side where he'd been holding himself. "But you're bleeding..."

He looked down as he pulled his hand away. It was coated in red. He groaned as a wave of dizziness swamped over him.

"Oh my God," Kara gasped as she rushed to put an arm under his to keep him standing when his legs buckled.

"Call...911..." he gasped as he dropped down into the snow.

"I don't have a phone..." she said, her beautiful blue eyes filling with tears.

"Left pocket..." he nodded down at his jeans and thankfully she understood.

She pulled out his phone and as she spoke to the dispatcher, Angelo started to feel tired. He must have really exerted him in the fight. But he couldn't be that badly hurt... he wasn't in that much pain. Just tired. Really tired.

He could hear church bells ringing in the distance and the beautiful sound of carolers. He couldn't even feel the cold anymore. Part of him knew that was a very bad sign.

But if this was the end, this wasn't so bad. He only wished he'd had a chance to steal a kiss from this mysterious Kara, to see if he could make her laugh and chase those haunted shadows from her eyes. He could see the flashing red of emergency lights reflect off her face now as she tried to talk to him, tried to keep awake. Yes, he definitely would have liked to get to know her better.

Maybe in the next life...

DON'T WORRY ANGELO WILL GET HIS STORY NEXT IN *Finding Prince Charming*! Be sure to sign up for my newsletter HERE or follow me on BOOK BUB HERE so you won't miss when his story is out!

. . .

If you haven't read Jared and Felicity's story, *Legally Charming*, please turn the page to read the first chapter or just go ahead and grab the book HERE!

She objects.
But he's about to
overrule the laws
of attraction...
LEGALLY
Charming
LAUREN
SMITH

LEGALLY CHARMING

CHAPTER 1

A man wearing only the bottom half of a *Star Wars* stormtrooper outfit streaked past Felicity Hart. She ducked out of the way as the half-naked frat boy whooped and bounced to the music, heading straight for a group of girls wearing white bunny ears who were gathered by the kitchen bar.

So this is what grad student parties are like.

Drinking, dancing, and insanity. Felicity shook her head, trying not to laugh. After growing up in a small town in Nebraska, she hadn't been prepared for college life in Chicago. Talk about culture shock. She was used to everyone in town knowing not just her name, but far too much about her personal life. Even after six years of living here, being surrounded by thousands of strangers who knew absolutely nothing about her, it was still both completely unsettling and oddly liberating.

For the first four years of college and the past two years of her master's, she'd hidden in her little shell. But a few months ago she'd met Layla Russo, a graduate student just like her, and they'd hit it off. Layla was the only reason Felicity had pulled a Cinderella and come to the ball. She would have laughed at the thought, but she was dead tired and stifled a yawn instead. At this rate, she'd turn into a pumpkin before midnight.

Happy Birthday to me, she thought and fisted her hands in the voluminous skirts of her Tudor gown. She stood out too much at this party—which happened when you skipped over the sexy cat costumes and zeroed in on the classy Anne Boleyn Tudor ball gown. Felicity should have worn some cheap costume, but she just couldn't do it. Halloween was her favorite holiday. She'd scrimped and saved to buy a good costume, one that meant something to her. She'd been lucky enough to find this gown on a deep-discount rack at a costume warehouse. Hence the beautiful, elegant, yet still sexy gown she wore at that moment. At least it had been sexy in the sixteenth century.

I am such a nerd.

She had gotten her share of raised eyebrows and smothered laughs when she'd entered the apartment with her friends, but she didn't care. She was ready to celebrate her entrance into adulthood at a normal party. Even if it had taken her until graduate school to be brave enough to attend a social gathering like this.

And why shouldn't she? She'd worked hard—late-night study sessions, endless art exhibit submissions—all in the hope of attaining grades that would be good enough to take her from a small Nebraska town to the hip art communities of Chicago. She *deserved* a party. And going to one at Layla's boyfriend's fancy apartment was safe enough since it was close to the school and the gallery where she worked.

Several laughing girls bumped into her, plastic cups brimming with alcohol. She danced back a step, narrowly avoiding drenching her gown in cheap beer as one of the girls stumbled in her heels, sending her cup flying through the air.

"Shit!" the girl hissed, then started giggling with her friends as she bent over to clean up the mess.

The entire night had been one near miss after another. The last thing Felicity needed was her costume smelling like beer.

She glanced at the group of pretty girls in the bunny ears and the gathering of boys around them.

Why didn't I think of wearing something like that? She glanced at the girls with their perfect bikini bodies, and she blushed. There was no way she could run around in something skimpy like that and feel confident. She just didn't look good in tight clothes...or revealing clothes. She was a size twelve, which was just a little too plump to look good in a skintight costume. She shuddered at the thought of being so exposed.

The crowd of people thinned out as she headed toward the room she sought. She took a moment to pause, one hand resting on the wall as she tried to suck in a breath. Maybe the corset was a bad idea.

"Hey!" A familiar feminine voice cut through the noise, and Felicity looked over her shoulder.

Layla was the official hostess of the party even though the apartment belonged to her boyfriend, Tanner, and she certainly acted like it as she strode toward her. She was a sight—five foot, curvy, and completely rocking her zombie stripper costume. Amazingly, Layla managed to look both scary and cute as she crossed the room in her four-inch stilettos. Felicity knew without a doubt that she'd break her neck in shoes like that, which was why she'd opted for red silk slippers that matched her gown.

"Hey, you okay?" Layla reached her and linked her arm through Felicity's. "I saw you yawning from across the room."

Felicity wrinkled her nose. "Just tired. Been up since dawn, have a midterm paper due tomorrow, and I feel every minute of a year older." Felicity wrinkled her nose. "Is it still all right to crash in Tanner's brother's bedroom?"

"Of course! I don't want you having to travel across half the city tonight to get back to that little hole in the wall you live in." Layla linked her arm through Felicity's. "I really wish you'd just move in with me." Her friend pouted dramatically, but Felicity stiffened her spine in an attempt resist Layla's begging.

"As much as I love your apartment, Layla, it's out my budget at the moment." It was double what her tiny place was, and Felicity's budget was already stretched thin. "You sure Tanner's brother won't mind?" It still felt weird to be sleeping in a guy's bed whether he was there or not.

"Yeah. Jared won't be back till Sunday night, so you're welcome to stay the whole weekend," Layla said. "Besides, even if he wasn't spending the entire weekend working, he'd never be caught dead anywhere near a party like this. That workaholic wouldn't know fun if it bit him in the ass." She snorted as though picturing just that. "Are you sure you're just tired, birthday girl?"

With her classes and her part-time job, Felicity was grateful for early nights where she could find them—and the prospect of staying up into the wee hours and endangering her beloved dress didn't hold much appeal. No, the sweet song of a comfy bed and a few hours of oblivion was calling to her.

"I'm good!" she insisted. "Go have more fun and don't worry about me. Go find Tanner before he realizes you've ditched him." Felicity pointed to Layla's boyfriend, who was politely escaping the group of bunnies and searching about for Layla.

Tanner Redmond and Layla had hooked up the first day of classes five years ago and had been together ever since. He was hot, smart, and totally nice, not at all like some of the entitled jerks she had to deal with when she handled rich clients at the gallery where she worked, which was a shocker given that he was a rich kid. He and his older brother, Jared, shared this beautiful apartment. She'd never met Jared. Even though she'd spent the last three months around Tanner and Layla, the mysterious older brother had never once shown up.

Layla's dark eyes ran up and down Felicity with concern. "You sure you don't want to stay out here? You don't have to crash now. Unless you're not feeling well?" Layla cocked one hip, her hand perched there as she continued to study Felicity. Felicity swallowed down the flutter of nerves that always came whenever her friend tried to make her participate more in the student culture, but she shook her head. She wasn't good at being fun and spontaneous or wild. Graduate student life seemed to be built on those three things when one wasn't studying or writing papers. It was just her luck that she was too shy to be bold in life like Layla.

It never ceased to amaze Felicity how much of a mother hen her friend could be.

"I'm good," she answered Layla, her voice firm. Sometimes she had to use a "parent voice" in order to get Layla to stop mothering her. "Go and have fun. You said the bedroom is the last on the left?"

"Yup. And seriously, stay the weekend. Just come back here after your midterm, and we can hang out."

Layla's offer was tempting, and Felicity found herself more than considering it. It sure would be nice to crash here for a few days. "I still can't believe you have a term paper due on the Saturday after Halloween," Layla muttered. "Ugh." Layla wrinkled her nose. "Some teachers are jerks. I'd be happy to make a voodoo doll of him, and we can shove pins in him." Her friend was grinning wickedly as she suggested this.

Felicity bit back a laugh. "If I didn't like Professor Willoughby as much as I do, I might take you up on that."

Layla escorted her all the way to the door and then curved her arms around Felicity in a hug. Her throat tightened as she fought off the fierce happiness that came over her whenever her friend hugged her.

Layla didn't hug by halves—she gripped you hard, squeezed the air out of your lungs, and made you feel loved.

Felicity just wasn't used to that—unlike Layla with her sprawling and loud family that found it natural to hug and kiss constantly, Felicity's parents were not overtly affectionate. They were sweet, and she knew they loved her, but they didn't put their affection on display like Layla—unbridled and consuming.

"Just do me a favor. Get some rest and kick butt on your research tomorrow."

"Yes, *Mom*." Felicity stuck her tongue out, and they both giggled.

As Layla turned back to the party, Felicity slipped into the sanctuary and relative quiet of the dark bedroom. Her breath caught as she took in the view of the city through the tall windows. The skyline of downtown Chicago was a man-made mountain range of lights twinkling in a sea of black. The sky behind the buildings was a soft purple, cutting a contrast against the silhouettes of the buildings. It was one amazing view, and it always made her breathless when she caught a glimpse of the monolithic buildings. Her hands ached to sketch the sight, but she hadn't brought her pad with her.

Fifteen stories up, none of the city sounds that kept her up at night could be heard from Jared's bedroom. She liked that. She wandered over to the window, wanting to sate herself on the sight of glittering lights and an endless glowing horizon. When she'd had her fill of the view, she turned back to investigate just what sort of room she would be spending the night in.

A massive bed against one wall with a cherrywood headboard and a deep crimson comforter looked soft and inviting. The scent of aftershave and an enticing masculine aroma made her all too aware again that this was a man's domain. She scanned the rest of the room. A large desk was laden with files and paperwork. If he was such a workaholic, why didn't he spend more time at this desk and enjoy the view? If she had this to look at all day, she could see the appeal of working from home. But as a lawyer, maybe he didn't get that option, and had to be in the office all day.

It suddenly bothered her that she had no idea what Jared looked like. Being in his personal space like this was oddly intimate, and it felt strange seeing so much of the man without ever having seen his face. As an artist, all she did was think about what things and people looked like. Not being able to see the features or the build of the man who lived here was unsettling.

Layla had said he was thirty and panty-melting hot—but not as hot as Tanner, of course. Layla wasn't the type of girl to really eye another man when she was happily in love, but she did appreciate beauty of the masculine variety. Felicity had laughed at the thought. She'd never seen any guy worth calling panty-melting hot, at least none outside of the movies. Layla said that Jared could give Jamie Dornan a run for his money on hotness and intensity.

Layla's words came back to her, and she smiled as she could hear her friend's voice so clearly in her head. "You know what I'm talking about. Tanner is all sorts of brooding and intense. He can just look at you and you go all wet and melty, you know? Like he'd fuck you so good you'd break the bed and ask for more. Jared's like that, too." Felicity hadn't been able to get that out of her mind. Layla had said Tanner was just like Jared, only younger. It explained everything. Tanner's intensity was tempered by his youth and sweetness, but his older brother had that jaded, hot bad-boy thing going on, according to Layla.

Now she stood in said panty-melter's room and couldn't help but picture a gorgeous, sexy man walking through the room, putting on a suit, critically eyeing his appearance in the mirror over the dresser.

Unable to resist and knowing it was completely inappropriate, she opened the top drawer of the beautiful dark dresser. Neatly rolled ties of a dozen different colors and patterns decorated the drawer, and a set of different styles of watches with leather and metal bands sat next to a box filled with cufflinks that glinted like jewels beneath the glass lid.

"Wow." She trailed her fingertips over the watches. A man with refined, expensive tastes.

Felicity watched the shadows play across the room, accenting the bed where Jared slept. What would it be like to share a bed with a man like him? To be the focus of all that raw masculinity and sexual energy? Her body hummed at the fantasy her mind seemed determined to play out. Her skin burned at the thought of what could happen if he came here tonight and found her in his bedroom. What if he just stood there, blocking the door, staring down at her? What if he told her to strip off her clothes and get into bed?

God, I need to get laid. Felicity shook her head. Even though she was a virgin, her fantasies could get wild. She struggled to get her libido under control.

Felicity sighed as she leaned against the bed, relishing the moment to bask in such luxury. She smoothed a hand over the red comforter. Satin? No, silk. She was tempted to lie down, just for a bit, but she knew she should change into her PJ's before getting in. She tried the nearest door, only to discover a large walk-in-closet with dozens of suits and a tall rack of expensive leather shoes. Not the bathroom. Her bag was supposed to be in the bathroom where Layla had said she'd put it. She approached the last door she hadn't opened. Felicity flicked on the light, found her bag sitting on the marble floor, and then searched through her clothes. When she didn't immediately find them, she dumped her gym bag over, muttering as she dug through the contents on the bed.

"Damn!" No pajamas. She'd left them at home.

All she had was her change of clothes for tomorrow. She wouldn't sleep in those. Returning to the bed, she put a hand to her stomach. The corset dug deep into her. How the heck did women live like this back in the day? Sure, it was fun to wear for a couple of hours, but spend her life in one of these? No way.

Gathering her skirts, she tucked her legs up on the bed and rested her head on the pillow.

So soft. Her mind started to drift in that hazy place between being awake and being asleep. What would it be like to live in a place like this? Surrounded by beauty, success, wealth? She'd likely never know. Her dream was to be an artist and a curator of a museum. Not much money in either of those dreams, but they were her passions.

Passion.

The word made her smile. The man who slept in this room definitely had passion, workaholic or not. He appreciated the finer things, and his taste was impeccable. Her fingers tapped along the bedding. It really was a pity she'd never meet the owner. A yawn escaped her, and she stuck a balled fist against her mouth. Her thoughts drifted, and she let them wander into dreams of the sexy man whose bed she was currently in and what would happen if he returned.

JARED REDMOND STUMBLED FROM THE TAXICAB, HIS brown leather briefcase smacking his back as he struggled to stay on his feet. He swallowed a growl of frustration. This was the last time he let the senior partners of his firm keep him out late to celebrate. He'd only had one drink, since he was dead tired from the last few months of overtime at the office. Having to smile, laugh, and socialize all night with the partners left him edgy and desperate to get home and crawl into bed.

God forbid he just do his job and do it well enough to earn respect. No, he had to spend hours at one of the most expensive restaurants with them, watching them pat each other on the back when he'd done all the heavy lifting in their multi-million-dollar transaction.

Big fucking mistake.

Now he was completely drained, and his body was determined to go to sleep on him right there on the street. His vision was fine, but his motor skills seemed to have abandoned him. He reached the glass doors of his apartment building lobby, leaning a little too heavily against the glass. Fishing around in his pocket for his keycard, he muttered a string of curses when his hand came up empty. He glanced up and rapped his knuckles. Thank God, the guard recognized him and buzzed him inside.

"Mr. Redmond." The security guard nodded, a knowing smile on the older man's lips.

"Hey, Randy," he greeted, wincing at the slur of his words.

A few more steps and he reached the elevator. After much effort focusing on the series of floor buttons on the panel, he pressed the button to the fifteenth floor and it lit up. He leaned his head back on the mirrored walls, resting. Jesus, it was like he was drunk, but he knew it was sheer exhaustion.

It had been a hell of a day. After two months of negotiations, sleepless nights, long hours, and no chance of reviving his obsolete social life, he'd closed the massive real estate deal, and closed it earlier than he'd anticipated. Everyone demanded they go out and celebrate.

He just wanted to crash and sleep off all of the stress pent up inside him.

He was going to walk into his bedroom and face-plant on his bed and not move all weekend from that spot.

Tanner would be out with his girlfriend, Layla, celebrating. It was Halloween, wasn't it? A little grin tugged at his lips. The apartment would be empty and *quiet*. The perfect benefit of arriving home early. He'd told Tanner he wouldn't be back until Sunday, and it was only Friday now. He expected his little brother and girlfriend would be out partying the night away, giving him total silence and a soft bed to crash on without any disturbances.

The second the elevator doors slid open with a soft hiss, he heard the music and the erratic noises of a party. Laughter, voices, all coming from their apartment.

Fucking hell.

"Tanner," he growled, fists clenched.

So the partying tonight was *in*, not *out*.

Jared contemplated turning around and finding a hotel, or worse, calling Shana. No, bad idea. They'd dated on and off during law school and after, but they'd never been exclusive. Currently he and Shana were off. *Definitely off.*

Lousy timing for Tanner to throw a damn party.

That was the main problem with letting his twenty-four-year-old brother live with him. He'd thought it would be nice to spend some time with his little brother, but with his work schedule he barely saw Tanner. The one night they might have hung out, he was too tired to care. He was not in the mood to dodge drunken graduate students all night and try to drown out all the racket they were making. Luck wasn't with him tonight. Fuck, he was turning into a crotchety old man if he was going to let a party piss him off.

The door to their place was unlocked, and when he swung the door open, a wave of fresh sound engulfed him. His eardrums throbbed, and he winced at the explosion of the music that drilled into his skull like nails. Scantily-dressed girls bounced about to the pounding rhythm of the music along with guys who were watching with giddy-schoolboy expressions. Some of them cheered and smiled, drunkenly overjoyed that a new person had shown up to the party. Several familiar faces, Tanner's friends, waved at him or nodded as he walked past them.

"Jared! I thought you weren't coming home till tomorrow?" A zombie stripper stepped in front of him, hands on her hips. Through the gory makeup he thought he recognized her.

"Layla?"

Tanner's girlfriend was dressed as a zombie stripper. Only Layla could manage to pull off that look.

"Layla, what the hell is going on?" he demanded, gesturing to the insanity. A girl in a sexy *Lara Croft* costume was singing a bad karaoke cover of "Somebody's Watching Me." Holy fuck. He was going to need some noise-cancelling headphones to survive this shit. For a brief second he considered tossing everyone out on their damn asses, but this place was half Tanner's and he'd told Tanner he wouldn't be here tonight. Brother code demanded he suffer through this bullshit.

Layla didn't look chagrined in the least. "It's Halloween. Oh, and Felicity's birthday, obviously."

"Who is Felicity?" He'd never met anyone named Felicity. Not that it was surprising, because he was never around when his brother was hanging out with Layla and their friends. He didn't really remember what it was like to be that carefree. Law school and work had a way of consuming a person's good memories.

"Scratch that, I don't care. Is this thing"—he waved a hand around—"ending anytime soon?" He shifted his briefcase strap over his shoulder. His suit was starting to suffocate him, and as much as he liked the particular steel-gray tie he wore at the moment, he was desperate enough to cut it right off his neck if he couldn't get to his room fast enough.

"Uh..." She licked her lips. "Don't know. But you said you weren't coming back until Sunday."

"Well, here I am and tired as fuck. So I'm going to bed. Try to keep it down," he growled.

"Uh, Jared." She dodged around him, trying to prevent him from getting past her.

"What did you do?" He arched a brow, sensing by the way her eyes widened and she shifted in her stilettos that something was wrong.

"I might have given your bed away." Layla bit her lip, yet she was brave enough to still meet his eyes.

"What do you mean you gave my bed away?"

She attempted to smile. "You were *supposed* to be gone until Sunday, and Felicity needed a place to stay tonight. It's late, and I didn't want her to go home alone. She lives in a sketchy part of town—so I told her she could crash in your bed since *you* weren't going to be here." She glared at him, accusing him of something he wasn't entirely sure was his fault. "So she's in your room tonight." She ended with a finality that did not entirely make sense to his tired brain.

"Let me get this straight. Some girl is in my bed... right now?"

Layla swallowed, her eyes darting away before coming back to him. "Um...yeah?"

"No," he stated and stalked toward his room, Layla at his heels. Whoever this Felicity person was, she was in his bed, and since it was *his* bed, whatever Layla and this girl had seemed to think otherwise, he'd have her out of it.

Reaching his bedroom door, he crashed it open and strode in, prepared for all the hell and fury that came with drunk, twenty-something females—and instead, as his eyes adjusted, he found a princess in his bed.

Layla clattered behind on her too-tall stilettos. “Jared, wait—”

He pushed the door open, and a yellow beam of light from the hallway cut across the dark room, revealing a figure lying across his bed.

A princess. There was a princess in his bed.

The burgundy-and-gold gown was draped over his comforter with pearls glowing like tiny moons on the bodice of her gown.

What the fuck?

“Please don’t wake her,” Layla begged.

Wake her? Jared shook his head. *What nonsense.* He wasn’t a romantic. Even though she was certainly a fantasy. All luscious curves and mystery. Her dark auburn hair cascading over the pillow looked soft. His hands ached to reach out and fist in the strands. She looked like the kind of woman a young man dreamed about and ruined his sheets over, the kind of woman he’d stopped dreaming about a long time ago because he was convinced they didn’t exist.

He didn’t turn to look at Layla as he spoke. “Who is that?”

“Felicity Hart. Birthday girl and, more importantly, my best friend.” The threat was heavily implied. Don’t screw with Layla or her friends. Her loyalty in that respect was one of the things he admired most about his brother’s girlfriend.

Layla's fingers curled around his biceps and squeezed, getting his attention.

"I told her she could sleep in your room since you weren't supposed to be here. It's the only place available for her to sleep."

"I'm not giving up *my* bed. I worked seventy hours this week. I'm going to sleep." He got one step inside his room before Layla practically tackled him, climbing up his back like a spider monkey.

"You. Will. Not. Wake. Her. Up," Layla growled, nails digging into his arms. "She has a really important research paper due tomorrow, and she needs to sleep."

"She can stay, but I'm sharing my bed with her. End of discussion. Go back to your party." With a little shove, he made sure Layla couldn't get back in before he shut the door in her face.

When he turned back around, he studied the girl in his bed. Without the hallway light he could barely make out her features. Just a silhouette, really, of a princess. Arousal slammed into him. He felt like an idiot. He never dated anyone who was still in school. They were too young. A year ago he'd tried to date a girl who was twenty-four, but she'd gotten pissed every time he'd had to work late. She didn't get the pressures of his job. None of the girls younger than him seemed to understand that. Layla was all right, but she was still a kid. He needed someone mature who was at the same point in her life as him, an adult.

The hot little princess was the last thing he needed to be thinking about.

Don't think about her or how much fun it would be to wake her up and kiss her. Just be a gentleman and go to bed.

His inner voice was a goddamn control freak, but he was thankful someone was still responsible.

Turning away, he started to strip out of his work clothes. He kicked his shoes off and then slipped a pair of pajama bottoms on. He didn't bother with a shirt. He always got a little hot at night anyway. As he moved deeper into the room, he caught his foot on a chair. It screeched as it slid across the wood, and he winced, catching himself against the back of it. He glanced at the bed, but the girl hadn't woken. A few quick steps and then he hit the bed, landing on his stomach and bouncing a little. The princess next to him didn't stir. He shifted a couple of inches and slid one arm beneath his pillow to puff it up as he laid his head down. The toll of the night's celebrations dragged him to the edge of the abyss of sleep. He was so close...

A little gasp and a half-strangled whimper pulled him to the surface again. "Whah?" He groaned and rolled onto his side facing the girl.

She was thrashing and whimpering beside him. Her hands clawed at the bodice of her dress, as though trying to escape it.

"Damn it!" He sat up and flicked on the lamp by his side of the bed. The wash of color in the room showed how flushed the girl was. She still shifted and kicked, moaning as if in pain. Jared leaned over and gently jostled her shoulder.

"Hey, kid, wake up."

She jolted awake. Bright gray eyes like liquid mercury flashed in shock and fear as her gaze fell on him.

"Hi," he said.

The princess blinked, her eyes darting around the room, then back to him, focusing on his bare chest. Her pupils dilated.

"Did we...um...who—" She shook her head as though to clear it. "Who are you, and what are you doing here?"

Jared let out a raspy chuckle. "I'm the one who should be asking questions. But it's been a long day and I'm beat. I'm Jared, and you are in *my* bed."

He stood and walked back to his cherrywood dresser. His fingers curled around the brass handle, and he opened the top drawer.

"You're Tanner's brother?" Her voice was soft, husky. It rolled over him, soothing his irritation.

He selected a silk striped button-down nightshirt and a pair of boxers from his drawer and then returned to the bed. "Here." He held the clothes out to her.

"What are those for?" she asked. One elegant brow rose.

"You. You woke up clawing at your dress. Looks like it's too tight around your chest and it's restricting your breathing. Unless you have clothes of your own, you're changing into these so we can both get some sleep. Layla said you had some paper due tomorrow."

When she opened her mouth, he could see the protest in her eyes and it amused him. *Feisty little thing.* And damned if he didn't picture all the things he'd like to do to that little mouth.

"Take the clothes and change in the bathroom. *Now.*" He deepened his voice, and she hopped out of bed, snatching the clothes as she darted into the bathroom. She froze, then slowly looked over her shoulder at him.

"What?"

"My dress...it's the laces in the back. I can't reach them."

A sigh escaped him. "Come here." He crooked a finger and sat farther back on his bed. She sidled up to him, bashfulness in her every movement.

There was something sinful and suggestive about the way she nibbled her bottom lip. He twirled a finger, indicating for her to spin around. She offered her back to him. The silk ribbons on the back of her gown came undone easily enough, but he was surprised to see the second set of laces beneath, which belonged to a corset. It was black with embroidered red roses that set off the color of the loose tangles of her hair. The strands teased the back of his hands as he unlaced the corset. The creamy skin of her lower back made his mouth go dry. The princess was trying to kill him with these temptations.

All too soon the view disappeared as she rushed into the adjoining bathroom to change.

He fell back onto the bed, staring up at the ceiling. His fingers tapped a rhythm on his stomach as he waited. This was not at all how he'd predicted his night would go. He wasn't complaining—not exactly.

The princess emerged, gown gone. She looked so young, standing there dwarfed in his button-down shirt and a hint of his boxers beneath the hem at her mid-thighs. Her gorgeous hair was wild and long, and it looked like she'd been well loved in bed. He didn't miss the swell of her full breasts against the thin, expensive silk. The top button was low down her chest, exposing a wealth of creamy skin. Damn.

He was about to say something bad, something that his exhausted mind would probably get him slapped for, when his bedroom door burst open and light from the hallway illuminated them both.

"Dude...found a bed." A man wearing the bottom half of a stormtrooper costume stumbled toward Jared's bed. Behind him trailed a girl in a Playboy Bunny outfit.

Jared glanced at Felicity, who'd frozen in shock, her hands pulling the button-up shirt closed against her throat, her cheeks a bright pink in the dim light.

"Oh...hey..." The stormtrooper finally noticed Jared as Jared got to his feet, scowling. "Do you mind if we—"

"Get the fucking hell out of my room," Jared growled. "*Now.*" He may have been almost half-dead with fatigue, but he could still throw a punch if he needed to.

"But come on, man, I want to get laid..." the boy whispered too loudly, and the bunny behind him giggled.

"I'll lay you flat on your goddamn ass if you don't get lost." Jared took a menacing step toward the inebriated pair, and they stumbled back into the hall. Jared didn't hesitate. He slammed his bedroom door in the wooden frame and clicked the lock into place before he turned back to face Felicity. Her hand was covering her mouth, and her eyes were wide.

"Sorry about that, princess. I locked the door. No one else will stumble in—I promise."

She blinked, dropped her hand, and then her eyes drifted from the door to his face as though debating whether she was safe with him in a locked room.

"Come on. I don't bite." *Hard,* he silently added, and flashed what he knew was a wolfish grin.

"I could sleep elsewhere," she hedged, playing with the collar of the button-down shirt. "Layla said you'd be gone all weekend."

"It's fine. This thing is a California king. Plenty of room for both of us. It's just one night."

He waited for her to pad on little bare feet to her side of the bed. It dipped slightly as she got in under the covers. She tensed when he crawled beneath the blankets, but after a moment, when he didn't move toward her, she blew out a breath. He rolled away to turn off the lamp by his bedside, then settled back, puffing his pillow again as he lay on his back and closed his eyes. A sweet, subtle scent filled his nose, like vanilla and fresh rain. When the princess shifted, trying to get comfortable, the scent grew stronger. Her scent.

"Thanks for letting me stay. I'm Felicity, by the way."

He could hear the yawn in her voice, and it made him grin.

"Good night, princess," he murmured.

She didn't respond. The soft little sound of her faint breaths did something funny to his chest. It tightened, and he sucked in a deep breath, hoping to ease the tension.

Now was not the time to be having a soft spot for a woman. He had so much to worry about at work, especially with Shana and her father. There wasn't time to seduce a sweet little princess, even if he wanted to. She really was a cute little thing, though.

Not for me. He sighed and let his body crash.

Want to know what happens next to Felicity and Jared? Get there story HERE!

OTHER TITLES BY LAUREN SMITH

Historical

The League of Rogues Series

Wicked Designs

His Wicked Seduction

Her Wicked Proposal

Wicked Rivals

Her Wicked Longing

His Wicked Embrace

The Earl of Pembroke

His Wicked Secret

The Last Wicked Rogue

Never Kiss a Scot

The Earl of Kent

Never Tempt a Scot

The Earl of Morrey

The Seduction Series

The Duelist's Seduction

The Rakehell's Seduction

The Rogue's Seduction

The Gentleman's Seduction

Standalone Stories

Tempted by A Rogue

Bewitching the Earl

Boudreaux's Lady

No Rest for the Wicked

Devil at the Gates

Seducing an Heiress on a Train

Sins and Scandals

An Earl By Any Other Name

A Gentleman Never Surrenders

A Scottish Lord for Christmas

Contemporary

The Surrender Series

The Gilded Cuff

The Gilded Cage

The Gilded Chain

The Darkest Hour

Love in London

Forbidden

Seduction

Climax

Forever Be Mine

Paranormal

Dark Seductions Series

The Shadows of Stormclyffe Hall

The Love Bites Series

The Bite of Winter

His Little Vixen

Brotherhood of the Blood Moon Series

Blood Moon on the Rise (coming soon)

Brothers of Ash and Fire

Grigori: A Royal Dragon Romance

Mikhail: A Royal Dragon Romance

Rurik: A Royal Dragon Romance

The Lost Barinov Dragon: A Royal Dragon Romance

Sci-Fi Romance

Cyborg Genesis Series

Across the Stars

The Krinar Chronicles

The Krinar Eclipse

The Krinar Code by Lauren Smith writing as Emma Castle

Lauren
SMITH
TIMELESS ROMANCE

ABOUT THE AUTHOR

Lauren Smith is an Oklahoma attorney by day, author by night who pens adventurous and edgy romance stories by the light of her smart phone flashlight app. She knew she was destined to be a romance writer when she attempted to re-write the entire *Titanic* movie just to save Jack from drowning. Connecting with readers by writing emotionally moving, realistic and sexy romances no matter what time period is her passion. She's won multiple awards in several romance subgenres including: New England Reader's Choice Awards, Greater Detroit BookSeller's

Best Awards, and a Semi-Finalist award for the Mary Wollstonecraft Shelley Award.

To Connect with Lauren, visit her at:
www.laurensmithbooks.com
lauren@laurensmithbooks.com

facebook.com/LaurenDianaSmith
twitter.com/LSmithAuthor
instagram.com/Laurensmithbooks